GOOD CRIME

A Kat Makris Greek Mafia Mystery

ALEX A. KING

For my Uncle George, who felt like it was in his best interests to die while I was writing this book.

His timing sucked.

But he was pretty awesome.

Chapter 1

MY FATHER WAS STANDING in the kitchen of my childhood home with a Microplane zester in one hand and a packet of red chili peppers in the other. The hot peppers had arrived on the arm of a pizza delivery boy. Nobody in the family liked their pizza spicy, so Dad was using it as a prop in his one-man play.

"How about I grate my skin off and shove these hot peppers up my nose, eh? How is that for an idea?"

"Jesus, Mike," Mom said. "Could you be more dramatic?"

He shook the packet of peppers. "To be Greek is to be dramatic. Theater is in our blood."

She raised an eyebrow in his direction. "I thought dodging taxes and fighting over politics and sports was in Greeks' blood."

"There are a lot of things in the blood of Greeks."

"All Kat did was ask for a puppy," Mom said. She unfurled Dad's fingers from the zester and stuck it back in the kitchen drawer where it would be safe and clean. "A puppy would be nice. I wouldn't mind having something around that barks when the neighbors walk by, minding their own business."

"Or a cat," I said. "It can live in my room. You wouldn't even have to know it's there."

My childhood was a pet-free zone. Eight-year-old me wanted, in no particular order, a cat, a hamster, a dog, a pony, goldfish, neon fish, any fish, or a parakeet. But Dad wanted to breathe through his nose and avoid hives, so I made do with friends' pets.

"Pets are good for children," Mom said. "They help foster empathy. If we get a pet there's a good chance Kat won't grow up to be a serial killer."

"Empathy. Serial killers." Dad made a face. "Do you know how many pets I had when I was a child?" He made a zero with his fingers. "Do you know why?"

Mom and I looked at each other and shrugged.

"I will tell you." He leaned against the kitchen counter, arms folded. That didn't last; Greeks can't talk without using their hands. "Because Baboulas would sneaky sneak in during the night and eat pets. Baboulas did not care if it was a cat or a dog or a hamster." He mimed dropping a rodent into his open mouth.

I started to cry.

Mom gathered me up in her arms. "Way to go, Mike. You're kind of a monster sometimes."

He looked surprised. "Me? It was Baboulas who ate pets, not me."

The next day Dad went on one of his road trips, delivering paper goods. When he arrived home, he presented me with a Tamagotchi.

"You want a pet? Here is a pet for you. Baboulas will not eat this one. Computer parts and plastic make Baboulas do this."

"Do what?"

2

Dad farted.

I had walked right into the trap.

———

A lifetime later, I hunkered down on a chair in Grandma's dingy kitchen, in the crappy hovel that was her house, and got ready to explain why I'd come home without my canary yellow VW Beetle. I reeked of smoke and I was in dire need of a *Silkwood* shower.

Grandma eyed me as she pulled ingredients out of the pantry and lined them up on the kitchen counter. Flour. Sugar. Nuts. Honey. Baking was Grandma's therapy, and it seemed to me like she had needed a lot of it since I arrived in Greece, drugged by my cousins and carried into the country like cargo.

"Start from the beginning," Grandma said in a low, dangerous voice.

I took a deep breath. Where to start? "Laki blew up my car."

Laki is a human (I think) relic from a generation where gold teeth passed as decent dentistry and a woman's place was in the kitchen, fixing him a souvlaki sandwich. Laki works for a mobster named Baby Dimitri, a slightly younger curio who doesn't realize this isn't Florida circa the 1960s. Laki has a hobby: Laki likes to make things go BOOM. And this time the thing that went BOOM was my car.

But according to the old man he did it for a good cause, so that made it all okay.

Right?

Grandma waited silently. It was a silence without much patience in it and a lot of expectation. While she did her silent waiting, she whipped up a batch of *finikia*, lumpy brown cookies that resemble turds drowning in honey syrup. Finally, when she realized I was done telling the story, she spoke.

"Hmm … I thought it would be a longer story."

"It doesn't take much time at all to blow up a car."

My name is Katerina—Kat—Makris, and in my old pre-Greece life my cars never exploded. A few months ago my father vanished, my cousins abducted me, and I discovered a whole family I never knew existed until after my twenty-eighth birthday. Dad kept them a secret for decades because they had actual skeletons in their closets, and also probably buried in the ground all over the family compound. Grandma runs the most notorious crime family in Greece. She's also a closeted Interpol agent, which basically means she's embroiled in Greece's law enforcement somehow, seeing as how Interpol is basically a message board where cops post their Who's Bad wish-lists. My paternal grandmother is a complicated woman, and for a woman who doesn't own any hats, she sure wears a lot of them.

This time last year I was a college dropout, working as a bill collector. My mother's death made me turn my back on formal education, although occasionally I made noises about going back to college and completing my degree. Those noises sounded a lot like "Do I have to?" and "Whhhhhy?" But it wasn't all doom and gloom—except the part about Mom being dead.

But on the good, slightly less than awful side, as of this week I was a receptionist at the Volos Hospital's morgue. Mostly I yelled at people when they wheeled bodies out of the elevator and then scurried back inside and tried to hastily leave without their human cargo. Greece's financial problems were having an unexpected side effect. People couldn't afford to bury their dead or move them out of the more crowded cemeteries when their three years of occupation were up. So they went the cheap route and accidentally-on-purpose forget to collect them from the morgue. The Volos Hospital morgue was currently wall-to-wall bodies. I was working on a plan to fix that. It involved Grandma's money and the nearby village of Makria's graveyard.

"What did Laki have to say for himself?"

"He said he had a gift for me."

"Is it a new car to replace the one he destroyed?"

"Not exactly."

Not even a little bit like exactly.

Grandma bored a hole through my head, using her eyes. They were obsidian hard and a flinty black. "What did he give you?"

I pushed away from the table, preparing for the inevitable. "It's outside."

My only living grandparent sighed and wiped her hands on her black apron. Like all Greek widows who weren't disloyal *putanas*, peeing on their dead husbands' memories, Grandma had dumped her entire wardrobe in a vat of black dye the day my grandfather dropped dead. Every day she buttoned a billowing black dress over her short, lumpy body, shoved her feet into black slippers, and finished off the outfit with a black apron that she fastened around the part of her figure where her waist used to be before it became the final resting ground for her breasts.

"Okay, show me this new car that is not exactly a new car."

"Grandma," I said on the way out. "Did you ever eat anyone's beloved family pet?"

"No."

"No kitten nuggets or canine schnitzel?"

Her gaze stabbed me. "Katerina, what did I tell you about listening to your father's stories?"

"Don't do it?"

"Your father is my son, but sometimes he is a *booboona*."

Dad isn't really a dummy, but those stories he told me were definitely steeped in hyperbole and fried in melodrama.

The good news is that Greece is only accountable for half of my DNA.

———

My new car was Greek.

Like the Beetle, I could have the roof down. Unlike the Beetle, there was no roof waiting to pop up at the press of a button. There was no roof. Or windows. No doors either.

The new car had four legs, a volatile temperament, and it looked like a donkey. Probably because it was a donkey.

"That is a donkey," Grandma said. We were near the family compound's entrance, outside the massive garage where Grandma kept the family's fleet of vehicles. The main building is a giant square, filled with apartments for the family. Grandma's shack crouches in the middle of the courtyard, begging for sweet condemnation and demolition. Apparently it's an heirloom that passes from eldest child to eldest child, and it's coming right for me, with a detour through Dad. My plan is—who am I kidding? There's no salvation plan.

Normally I parked my car right here outside the garage and let the garage attendant deal with it. Today I'd parked my donkey because where else was I supposed to park it? The compound was seriously lacking in posts where a moseying cowgirl could tether her faithful beast when she came to town, looking for a stiff glass of ouzo and a chunk of baklava.

My face buried itself in my hands. "I was afraid of that. Now that you've said it, it's real. Before I could lie to myself that it was a really hairy bicycle."

Grandma rolled her eyes so far back in her head that I thought she was going to keel over. At her age anything was possible.

As previously mentioned, Baby Dimitri's sidekick and henchman Laki got his kicks making things go BOOM. Recently he had inherited an airplane from his father's estate, and he had used the plane to blow up several abandoned buildings in the Volos and Mount Pelion area, for funsies. Along the way, he'd managed to get himself kidnapped by Baby Dimitri's crazy half-sister, whose whereabouts were currently unknown but probably not anyplace good. I rescued Laki by accident and won his undying gratitude. To thank me, he set my car on fire and gave me a prize-winning donkey. What prize, he didn't say. The beast was knock-kneed and looked like it wanted to kick everyone when they were down.

"How did you get it back here?" Grandma asked. "Did you ride it?"

"Have you seen the size of this thing?" Okay, it wasn't like she could miss it. "We're not talking horse-sized here. It's not even pony-sized. It would be cruel to ride this donkey."

Grandma shrugged. She made a face to go with it. "I see a normal-sized donkey."

"Exactly! It's a donkey-sized donkey. Do you really want me to crush the poor thing?"

For the record, I weigh a hundred and twenty-something pounds (that last digit is always in flux, its upward or downward trajectory determined by how many hours I've spent that week with my beloved Netflix and chips), so probably I wouldn't crush the poor beast like an empty soda can. But the guilt would eat me alive anyway.

"In the old days, everybody rode donkeys. Greek people still ride donkeys—people much bigger than you."

Something twinkled in her eyes--probably evil.

My hand went to roost on my hip. "Are you messing with me, Grandma?"

She held up her finger and thumb, a fraction of an inch apart. "Maybe a little bit."

No car—no real car; the donkey didn't count—left me with a getting-to-work problem.

"I hate to ask this …"

"Ask," Grandma said.

"Could I please borrow a car?"

"It would be rude not to ride the donkey. It was a gift."

"Are you still messing with me?"

"No. Gifts are serious business. Do you want to bring shame on our family by refusing to ride it? I do not think so."

The raucous, jeering laughter of rabies-inflicted monkeys cut off my smart-ass reply before I'd had a chance to formulate one. Mankind's cousins—and unfortunately mine—were coming, and they had metaphorical buckets of poop to fling.

Takis, my cousin's cousin's cousin, was the first to emerge from the archway that separated the courtyard from the ostentatious front, cackling his head off. Takis is a short boneless weasel from the neck down and an asshole from his feet up. He has a face like a ferret and a personality like the fatberg in London's sewers. The man has no redeeming qualities, except that he occasionally shows up at the right time to save my bacon. He also, like now, shows up at the wrong time to mock me and whine about various grievances. Takis has a YouTube channel that always manages to capture my worst moments on camera and put them on display for the whole planet to Like and comment on. Apparently his subscribers love watching me screw up. Behind him today was a handful of the other cousins, including Stavros and Elias, my bodyguard. The latter wasn't my cousin but would be if Greece were cool with same-sex marriage. Nobody else knew that Stavros and Elias were an item except the five-year-old boy who had revealed their secret love to me.

"Hey, Katerina, a *poulaki* told me you got a donkey. Which is the donkey and which is Katerina?" Takis glanced from me to the donkey and back again. "I cannot tell the difference. You both smell the same."

A *poulaki* is a little bird. It's also a small penis. I was confused about which of those two things had delivered the news.

His barrel of monkeys hooted and hollered. Elias rolled his eyes at Takis; he was there when Laki presented me with the donkey.

"Is this going on your YouTube channel?" I asked Takis.

He cupped a hand to his ear. "What is that? All I hear is 'hee-haw, hee-haw.' "

I moved around to the back of the donkey and bent down, carefully avoiding the kick zone. "You'll have to speak up, Takis. You're talking through your *kolos* again."

Takis shook his head. "Your jokes are not funny … or jokes."

"Takis," Grandma barked. Takis jerked upright as though someone had shoved three-feet of rebar up his pancake butt. "Tomorrow morning you will take Stavros and some of the other cousins to the morgue."

Takis nodded. He was all business now. "You want me

to kill them first or do it there? Now that I think about it, there would be easier."

Protests broke out. Various cousins begged Takis not to kill them.

My only grandparent rolled her eyes. "Nobody is killing anyone. Tomorrow you will go to the morgue as I said and wait for Katerina's instructions. You do what she tells you or you will answer to me."

"I am going to need a donkey-to-Greek dictionary," Takis said. He elbowed the cousin next to him. "Hee-haw."

"Keep it up," I said, "I'll call your wife and tell her to spit on your *tiganites*." Tiganites are fried potatoes, also known as fries. Takis has an addiction to the crispy, thinly sliced carb sticks. Marika, his wife, is his enabler. Cooking is her insurance policy against him running away.

"Call her. I am not scared of Marika." His eyes darted left and right. He was totally scared of Marika.

Grandma's phone rang. In the same moment, the guard shot out of the guardhouse and jogged over to where we were standing.

"We have a problem," he said.

Grandma held up one finger. She was already on the phone.

"Tank," she said.

The guard, who was also one of my cousins, nodded. He had a big, scary gun in his hands and he knew how to use it. "One tank, and it is rolling this way. What do you want me to do?"

"Wait a minute," I said. My head ping-ponged left then right. "A tank? There's a tank rolling toward the compound? Are you talking about a fish tank, an oxygen tank, or one of those humungous metal machines with the caterpillar treads? Because you can't be talking about one of those. It's not 1940. Not in some parts of the world, anyway."

Grandma thrust her phone under my nose. Sure enough, a big metal war machine was trundling along the compound's long, dirt road, headed straight for us.

Another day, another bizarre moment in Greece. "Huh. That's a real tank."

"That's a real tank," Takis said in a girly singsong voice.

Grandma turned around, her face tilted upward. She aimed a cutting motion at the compound's roof.

I looked up. Normally at least one sniper was on duty on the rooftop. Today there were five, and they had what appeared to be rocket launchers aimed at the road. At Grandma's command, they lowered their weapons but their shoulders stayed high and tight.

The tank was moving closer. I could hear the hum and the *snap, crackle, pop* of stones as all that weight rolled over them.

Old me would have hurled myself in the bushes, hands wrapped around my head. The new me, the one that had shot an Italian gangster in the toe and fired a few rounds with Dad's old slingshot was tough enough to stand in place, shivering. New me had a thicker coating but diminished survival instincts.

"Relax," Grandma said.

Impossible. I pointed at the road. "There's a tank. How can I relax? I know what tanks can do. Television is pretty clear about that. Did you know that big pointy thing at the front isn't a nose like it is on an elephant? It shoots stuff. Bad stuff."

She ignored long enough to aim a command at the guard. "Open the gates."

"What?" I squeaked.

Was she high? Because Grandma got high. She had a thing for edibles, choosing to bake her weed into *koulourakia* —hard Greek cookies—instead of toking up. She didn't look stoned but her actions said she wasn't playing with a full deck.

The guard jogged back to the guardhouse to press his little button. There was a metallic groan, and then the gates slowly swung open just as the tank emerged from between the trees, huffing and shuddering.

This was bonkers. Fleeing en masse was the smart thing to do, but Grandma was standing her ground. Wait, no, she was hobbling through the gates. Takis and the other cousins were swaggering along behind her, hands on their weapons, just in case things went Wild West.

A light went on in my head. I hoofed it to where she was standing, hands on her hips. "Grandma, did you buy a tank?"

"No …"

At least she hadn't lost all her marbles—just some of them.

"… I already have one."

Another marble rolled away, never to be seen again.

The tank trundled closer, until it was almost level with the guardhouse. Grandma held up her hand, palm out, fingers spread.

"*Parta*," she called out. *Take it.*

Whoever was in that tank, she was giving them a serious *moutsa*. The *moutsa* is one of Greece's favorite insults. The open palm means you're rubbing poop in the recipient's face. It can also mean you think they have a chronic masturbation problem. Greeks are liberal when it comes to dishing out the *moutsa*. They'll do it to friends, enemies, and their coffee tables when they catch their little toes on the corner.

Like magic, the tank stopped. The rumbling ended with an exhausted sigh.

Clanking happened. Metallic groaning.

Then the tank flipped its round hatch. A greasy, graying head popped up.

"I need a place to hide," Baby Dimitri called out. "What do you say? Have you got a bed for an old man, preferably in a secure location?"

Chapter 2

TEN MINUTES later we were crowded in Grandma's kitchen. Baby Dimitri wasn't allowed to sit, on account of how Grandma didn't trust him as far as she could kick his skinny corpse.

"All you do is sit in front of your shop all day," she said when he complained about the lack of seating. "The change will be good for you."

The Godfather of the Night, Shoes, and Cheating Tourists glanced at me. "You are nicer than your grandmother. Remember I said that."

Grandma pinned her eyebrows to her forehead wrinkles. "Your henchman gave my granddaughter a donkey."

Two palms up. "What? It is a very good donkey."

Not even half an hour ago, Grandma had finished whipping up a batch of Greek cookies. That didn't stop her reaching for her baking ingredients again. She lined them up and got to work, creaming sugar and butter by hand. Grandma looked doughy and delicate but she was made of steel. I suspected she might be a Terminator.

"Why are you here?" she asked as she beat the sugar

and butter until the mixture was creamy white. The urge to stick my finger in the bowl was overwhelming. Too bad it was an excellent way to lose a finger.

"I told you," Baby Dimitri said. "I need a place to hide."

"Why?"

"I like to play Hide and Seek. Why else would I come here, eh?"

Outside, Grandma's gate squeaked. A voice punched its way through the door. "Where is that greasy old *malakas*?"

The beating went on. "Just what we need," Grandma muttered.

A moment later the door squeaked open and Papou rolled in, an eagle perched on each shoulder. He kicked Stavros's shin until my cousin moved, and wheeled up to the kitchen table.

One of the eagles is real and its name is Yiorgos. The other one used to be real before it got a butt full of cotton and a pair of glass eyes. *Papou* is the Greek word for *grandfather*, but as far as I know this Papou doesn't have grandchildren. He's been around since the Big Bang and he's got the complexion to prove it. If his face was a roadmap you'd wind up in Yellowstone. Papou is Grandma's advisor, what the American Mafia calls a consigliere. Mostly he complains and whines like it's his Olympic sport, and before he inherited the eagle he spent his days trying to find a fast exit out of life and his wheelchair with the shotgun mount and colostomy bag holder.

"Get that bird out of my kitchen," Grandma said.

Papou scoffed at her serving suggestion. "An eagle is not a bird. It is a majestic and noble creature that can also eat your face if you look at it funny." He turned his jaundiced gaze on the shoe salesman. "Careful, Dimitri, my

Yiorgos might peck your nose. He loves rats." For the record, Yiorgos didn't love rats. Either the eagle didn't know how to eagle, or he didn't want to. Personally, I wondered if the bird was grieving for his owner, a psycho who had tried to strangle the life out of me after I turned down his proposal. That same whack-a-doodle was also Papou's nephew, but nobody talked about that—not to his face, anyway.

Baby Dimitri's eye twitched.

Grandma reached below the counter and pulled out a shotgun. Everybody hit the deck. Duck and cover time. She aimed it at the eagle that wasn't stuffed. "One … two … three … *Re*, why are you on all on the floor?"

Slowly, we all went back our places. Takis was muttering under his breath. Not me: I did my muttering out loud. It wasn't every day Grandma waved a gun around. Every other day … yes.

Papou raised his hands. "Okay, okay." He grabbed a ball out of his pocket, thick red rubber, dotted with holes. It was oozing vicious red liquid that looked suspiciously like blood. He pitched the ball outside. Yiorgos zeroed in on the ball and flitted after it, flicking poop at Baby Dimitri on the way. The godfather didn't notice the gray slimy oyster of doo-doo on his head. Papou winked at me, held a finger up to his lips.

Grandma looked at us both and shook her head, mouth pursed into a tight colorless line.

"That was a Kongk," Papou said. "I fill it with treats for Yiorgos."

Kong. He meant Kong. Greeks have a hard time with some incarnations of the letter G. This was one of those times.

"What kind of treats?" I asked him.

He looked at me. "What kind of treats do you think an eagle likes?"

Yikes. I really didn't want to know. "Aren't Kongs for dogs?"

"Eagle, dog, same thing. I ordered a box of them from England."

"*Gamo tin panayia mou*," Baby Dimitri muttered, verbally making not-so-sweet love to the Virgin Mary. Greeks do that a lot. Probably because she's unhelpful when it comes to solving Greece's financial problems.

Grandma stopped beating long enough to point the spoon at him. "Do not use that kind of language in my kitchen. Now talk."

Before Baby Dimitri could get a word in, the gate opened again. "Is there a *malakas* in the house?"

Aunt Rita.

Aunt Rita started life as my uncle, but that was long before I met her. Now she's my aunt and she's fabulous. Today she was glamorous in a hot pink miniskirt suit with boots that looked like she had skinned a pink yeti. Aunt Rita did the family's accounting, which meant probably she knew where the actual bodies were hidden as well as the financial ones.

"Kyrios Dimitri," she said. "I heard you were here."

Baby Dimitri nodded. "Rita, you look interesting today."

"I am interesting every day," she said. I scooted over so we could share the chair. She slung her arm around me and dropped a perfumed kiss on my cheek. If I had a million aunts Aunt Rita would still be my favorite. "Why are you here?" she asked the aging mobster.

Baby Dimitri opened his mouth, then closed it again when the gate telltale squeaked a third time.

"Who is it this time?" Takis griped. "I need to *kaka*."

"Thanks for sharing," I said.

The door opened and Dad peered in. He'd recovered well from his fake kidnapping, although he was still maintaining a low profile. There is no doubt Dad is my biological parent. We have the same nose, although mine is—thankfully—the smaller version. He has my dark hair and much smaller boobs. Back home he was always looking over his shoulder and formulating conspiracy theories. In Greece he does the same paranoid thing with a National Intelligence Service (the NIS is Greece's CIA) badge in his pocket and a better wardrobe. And for some inexplicable reason, whenever I see him these days he's always eating. Today he was nibbling on a *tiropita*—cheese pie—in a white paper sandwich bag. He was wearing a gray suit with a pale purple tie. This Greek version of Dad was stylish. At home he was jeans and polo shirts.

"I followed the smell of *skata*," Dad said. "What are you doing here?"

Baby Dimitri shook his hands at the ceiling. "That is what I am trying to tell you, but you Makris people keep coming and coming. You are like rabbits, screwing and breeding and making more of yourselves."

Papou had something to say about that. "I am not a Makris."

"You are the same *skata*," Baby Dimitri said.

Dad swallowed a mouth of *tiropita*. "That is my saying."

He was right: *They're the same shit* was his signature quote.

The tension thickened. I was curious, yeah, but I didn't want to be here where things were liable to get bullet-ridden fast. Time to defuse the situation.

I raised my hand, careful not to aim the open palm at anybody. "I just want to hear the story."

"Katerina is right. Tell the story, Dimitri," Grandma said. "Everyone else, *skasmos*."

Baby Dimitri helped himself to one of Grandma's apples in the fruit bowl. He whipped out a knife and began peeling the fruit. Grandma raised an eyebrow but she said nothing.

"Someone wants to kill me."

Grandma snorted. "Trust me, a lot of people want to kill you. That is the business. We do not always do it but we fantasize about it late at night when we cannot sleep."

All righty then.

"This one is an old enemy," Baby Dimitri said mildly. The apple's skin unraveled in one long, coiled strip. "Very old."

"How old?" Grandma asked him.

The godfather made a so-so gesture with his hand. "Thirty years."

Grandma dumped flour into the bowl, one spoon at a time. "Impossible."

"That is what I thought, but if I was wrong, then you are, too."

"I am never wrong, except when I am. And this time I do not believe I was wrong."

"Katerina, I am not asking you to believe me. All I need is a safe place to hide."

"You are a resourceful man," Grandma said. "What is wrong with your own hiding places? You can afford to go anywhere, be anyone."

Baby Dimitri chuckled. "Katerina … Katerina … you and I both know you are a woman beyond compare. There is nowhere safer in Greece than here."

Grandma wasn't impressed. "Flattery will get you nowhere."

"Unless you are me." My aunt waved her hand in the air. "Then flattery will get you a lot of places."

"We know," Dad said. Aunt Rita winked at him.

"Enough," Grandma said. "You can stay here while I make some inquiries. I do not like to be wrong, and if I made a mistake I intend to fix it."

Her words were heavy, like me walking out of the State Fair with several corndogs, funnel cakes, and whatever new deep-fried thing was popular that year.

"Great." Baby Dimitri cut a slice of naked apple. "What is my room number?"

Grandma grinned a toothy grin.

Oh boy.

———

Baby Dimitri's expression shifted from surprise to horror. "What is this?"

"Katerina?" Grandma said to me.

I was only too happy to help. "Looks like a dungeon to me, but I could be wrong."

We were poised at the entrance to Grandma's dungeon, or rather the outer chamber, which to be fair looked like something from another century; one of the early ones, before things like indoor plumbing, beds, and flea powder. Each cell had a pile of straw and a wooden bucket—toilet or drinking water, prisoner's choice. Like all good dungeons, it was underground. This particular one was buried in the rocky dirt beneath the family compound.

The Godfather of the Night and Postcards looked horrified. "You expect me to stay here?"

Grandma shrugged. "Why not? It is the safest place in Greece. That is what you said, yes?"

"I was hoping the safest place in Greece would have a bed and maybe a television so I do not miss my shows."

"You have shows?" I asked him.

"Sure, I have shows. All the best things are on the Playboy channel."

"I can't believe you pay for cable." Baby Dimitri was tighter than three feet shoved into a sock for one. The idea of him springing for cable was unthinkable.

"Of course not. I borrow it from my neighbor. He does not care."

More like he didn't know, I was willing to bet.

"Today is your lucky day," Grandma said. "This is a little something I built for fun. Okay, sometimes I leave people in here, but only if they have been extra bad."

The old mobster rubbed his palms together, grin freshly reapplied to his face. "Lead me to the good place. What is your security like?"

He and Grandma spent the next couple of minutes discussing the dungeon's security. If everything I'd heard was true she wasn't telling him half of it. Still, it was fun to hear about some of the measures she'd had installed. Like that metal door between this section of the dungeon and the real one. In an attempt to penetrate the door without the proper security protocols, it could electrocute a rhinoceros on PCP.

The real dungeon was empty at the moment, not counting its one permanent resident. If the man in the last cell had a name, I didn't know it. In my head I had dubbed him Monobrow because of the caterpillar of black hair that ran from one side of his face to the other. The man who had reached AARP age at least twenty years ago called himself "Makria's only homeless person", and he had a serious addiction to *loukoumia*. Chances were good he'd beg me for a box of the powdered sugar smothered jelly squares, also known as Turkish delight, the moment he realized I was in the house.

Baby Dimitri held his hands down low, fingers splayed, that wide grin oozing across his face. "This is more like it."

As far as dungeons go, Grandma's is somewhere in the vicinity of Marriott suites, on a smaller scale. The beds are comfortable, bathrooms are included, and each "cell" comes with a desk and chair. Some even come with televisions and bookshelves crammed with books. Monobrow's cell contained a door that lead to Grandma's underground bunker. To get through it had to be unlocked from both sides, so it wasn't like the man with one jumbo eyebrow could go wandering. Whoever he really was, he seemed to embrace his comfortable captivity.

Monobrow had a booming voice that blasted through the slot in his door. "Do I hear the biggest *malakas* on the planet?"

Baby Dimitri laughed himself sick. Whatever the joke was, I didn't get it. There was a lot today that I wasn't getting.

"Is that who I think that is?" the godfather asked.

"*Po-po*, I am nobody," Monobrow answered. "A figment of your imagination."

"I wondered where she had been hiding you."

"Katerina," Monobrow said, "tell me you are not going to leave this *malakas* down here with me."

"I am not leaving this *malakas* down here with you," Grandma said.

Monobrow laughed. "Do not lie to me, old woman. I know you."

The cat hair in my DNA twitched. "How exactly do you know each other?"

"He is my prisoner," Grandma said casually.

Makria's only homeless person roared with laughter.

"You have no idea how true that is."

Grandma pursed her lips, but if I had to guess I'd say it was more she was suppressing a smile than a frown. She shoved a key into one of the cell doors. Gears clicked. The latch opened. Baby Dimitri stuck his head in to take a look.

"Not bad. Not bad at all. You even have television."

"Barbarian," Monobrow said. "Civilized men read."

"Civilized men do not hide underground with their books because they are too busy living. You would not believe the things I see on my beach. Did you know *vizia* come with extra stuffing now? They take plastic bags of salty water and shove them…" From the dance he was doing I assumed he was either stuffing a chicken or inserting breast implants.

Grandma grunted like a pig.

There was a noise behind us. Xander appeared, carrying two enormous suitcases. For a moment I stood and gawked at him. Xander is big and bad and also good, which, at times, confuses me. My brain doesn't know which compartment to store him in. My body is less conflicted. It knows what it wants and it wants Xander. The trouble is, my body also wants Detective Melas, who currently wasn't speaking to me. Both men want me back, and neither keeps their interest a secret. Xander is just quieter about it, that's all. He's tall, built like he knows how to start and finish a fistfight with one punch, with dark discerning eyes, a chiseled jaw, and bronze skin. He moves through the world like a panther, one soft, dangerous footstep at a time. Although he works for Grandma as a multitasking henchman he's also a super-secret NIS agent. And though Xander never talks, I'm one of the few people who knows he can.

Xander set the suitcases down in Baby Dimitri's room. His eyes found mine and held them for a moment too long.

He brushed past me, and I caught the unmistakable smell of clean man and warm skin. My hormones surged forward to whisper terrible, wonderful ideas in my ear. My hormones are idiots with exceptional taste.

"If living is so good, why are you hiding underground?" Monobrow said through his door's slot.

For a moment, Baby Dimitri didn't say anything. It looked to me like he was weighing the cost of confession.

"It turns out an old, dead enemy is not as dead as I thought he was, although he is probably as old as the rest of us now."

Monobrow didn't look worried. Monobrow looked amused at Baby Dimitri's discomfort. "So you are hiding here, like a scared child? Who is this enemy?"

Baby Dimitri hummed a few bars of a song I vaguely recognized but couldn't pin an artist to. Didn't help that he had the musical skills of someone who had no musical skills whatsoever.

Monobrow lost his color. That was saying something for a man who lived like a mole. I guess he really hated people humming.

I replayed the song in my head. A chorus presented itself. A hit from the 1980s. A-Ha's *Take On Me*. But how was the trio's biggest hit tied to Baby Dimitri's old foe?

"How do you know he is alive?" Monobrow said.

Baby Dimitri went digging in his pocket. He presented Monobrow with a small plastic box. "This was delivered this morning."

"You do not have security?"

"It was taped to the *kolos* of a Care Bear—the angry one. He will come for me," Baby Dimitri said. "You know he will."

The man with one solid eyebrow let out a sigh like Baby Dimitri was busting his hump. "You are a fool, you old *malakas*, if you think you are the only one he will be coming for."

"You think I do not know that?"

"Oh, I think you know. But do you care? Who can say? Only you and God."

This was getting interesting. Where was the popcorn when I needed it?

"Katerina," Grandma said, zeroing in on my burgeoning interest. "You can go now."

Aww, man. My only grandparent could be a real buzz kill.

I let myself out. Xander was waiting on the other side of the door, looking all casually secretive, with his folded arms and his sexy lean.

I nudged him with my elbow. "Are you eavesdropping? Because it looks to me like you're eavesdropping."

He said nothing. Silence was what he did best. Although he did make a mean cup of hot chocolate and he was great at tying a ponytail.

"Can I eavesdrop with you? Let's rustle up some glasses and listen through the wall."

Xander put his hands on my waist, turned me around so that I was facing the exit. Gave me a little push.

So that was a "no" then. Spoilsport.

Cutting across the courtyard, I headed for my small apartment. I waved to family members, yelled out greetings, and petted dogs. My mind wasn't on any of them, except maybe the dogs because dogs are awesome. Before today, Baby Dimitri had always struck me as unflappable. Nothing bothered the godfather. He had power, money, and gave zero damns about things like other people's feelings and world peace. Then today he had rocked up to Grandma's gate in a tank, for crying out loud. Who was he so afraid of that he couldn't boost a car or put on a disguise and board a bus like a regular criminal on the lam? Not only that, but his revelation had rattled Grandma's chain. Grandma was unshakeable, like a mountain.

What was this enemy of his, a zombie?

———

Shower time. I reeked of smoke and engine oil and it took two generous doses of shampoo to restore me to human status. After, I dressed in a fresh black outfit: black jeans, black shirt, black boots, and then I bounded out the door. Siesta time was almost over, which meant I had to scramble to get back to work in time.

Halfway across the courtyard, Dad pounced. The *tiropita* was long gone; now he was stuffing his mouth with *spanakopita*. The same pie, now with spinach.

"I am going home next week," he announced. "You want to come with me?"

"Going home? Why?"

His eyebrows rose. He stopped chewing. "I thought you wanted to go home?"

"I did. I mean, I do."

Home. What a word. It wasn't a place; it was an idea, a feeling. Home is where the heart is, not necessarily the address the pizza delivery guy could find without GPS. Was Portland home? The longer I was in Greece, the hazier my old stomping grounds felt. Greece wasn't a vacation; for me it was a life makeover.

Dad couldn't hear my mental gymnastics, so he dropped the next bomb on me.

"I was thinking we could fix the house up and sell it."

My jaw dropped. Blood rushed to my face. My indignation saddled up and rode into town, prepared for a fight.

"Sell it? Are you high?"

Two palms up. One was holding the remnants of pie in a white paper sleeve. "Katerina …"

"I grew up in that house! Mom lived in that house! We were a family in that house!"

A red light blinked in my head; I had used my daily quota of exclamation points, and then some. But given that I was half Greek, wasn't I entitled to extra? Greeks sprinkled the punctuation mark liberally over all their conversations the way they did salt on food.

"It is a good house, yes, but things change. You and I, we can be a family anywhere." He put his arm around me, hugged me to his chest. "If we hold on to that house forever, where will we have to go except nowhere? We cannot move forward, not really. I do not want to stay stuck in the past, no matter that it was the happiest time of my life. What about you, eh? Do you not want a normal life? A husband? Children? Your own home?"

"If the house goes then Mom goes, too."

"We take her everywhere we go, house or no house."

He was right and I knew it. Who had two thumbs and had taken out a lease on her own apartment before Grandma burned it down?

Me. *Moi*, if you wanted to be French about it.

At least Dad was warning me that he wanted to move forward with his life. What had I done? Snuck around like a renter in the night.

"This had better not be about Dina," I said, trying to inject some humor into the morbid situation.

It was like watching an oil spill, the way horror spread about his face. "My God, what is wrong with you? I thought you loved me. I am not a perfect father but I am not a monster either."

I laughed and hugged him around the waist. "Relax, Dad. I'm kidding."

"Maybe you are the monster, eh?" His mouth smiled. His eyes, not so much. "Everybody is looking to you to become the next Baboulas."

Speaking of horrifying thoughts ... the last thing I wanted was to stagger around carrying all of Grandma's hats. She was too many things to too many people and organizations. I only wanted to be a few. Mob boss and law enforcement weren't on the list. Morgue receptionist wasn't either.

But what was on the list? These days I had no idea.

"Not me," I said. "All the genes that make Grandma Grandma are switched off in my DNA. I can't even master her basic recipes."

"I bet she cannot bake chocolate chip cookies as good as yours."

"She'd probably screw them up by putting weed in them."

He almost choked on his spinach and feta pie. "Mama takes drugs?"

Someone had to jump to Grandma's defense. Given that it was just Dad and me in this conversation, it had to be me. "It's not like she's sucking down meth. She's only a pothead, except she gets her high from *koulourakia*. Don't eat the green ones. Trust me on that."

He shook his head. "What a world we live in." He looked me up and down. "You need a ride someplace?"

Come to think of it, I did. "That would be great. Are you going somewhere? Dina's house maybe? She has a cool shrine that I think you'd just adore."

He sighed. "You remind me of your mother."

Could be worse.

"And sometimes you remind me of your grandmother."

Like that.

Chapter 3

GUS ZENTEFIS IS the morgue's only other employee. Originally there were others, Gus told me, but they insisted on things like money and benefits; and the hospital didn't have benefits to give, unless free enemas counted. The Mediterranean diet is high in fiber and swimming in olive oil, so constipation isn't really a Greek problem. Gus gave me the job against my will when he realized I had a pulse and access to bed sheets.

Up until a few days ago he was a human Chihuahua: small, shaky, stressed. Now that he knew I had enlisted Grandma's help with the space issue in the morgue, he was one of the more chilled out breeds of little dogs--maybe an underfed corgi. He whistled while he worked, cutting up the newest arrivals.

"I love this part," he said. "I am the one who gets to the tell the story about how they died. When I write the report I try to make it like poetry. So far nobody has appreciated my work, but one day they will say Gus Zentefis was one of Greece's finest poets."

I left him to his charting and went back to the reception desk, careful not to make too much eye contact with the dead. They were covered in sheets but I knew they had faces underneath. I tried not to think about Mom and her death, which meant my mind inevitably went there to wallow in those final days, where everything was gray and sad and steeped in tears. Dad was going to sell the house; the house we hid in after Mom's funeral; the house where we ate delivery pizza for the longest time because neither of us had the heart to putter around in Mom's kitchen. Soon some other, less broken family would be making memories in our house.

Where would we go? What would we do?

Who would we be?

Uh oh. I was looking pensive, wasn't I?

Elias zeroed in. "You okay, boss?"

"Great. Perfect. Wonderful." Big plastic smile. "What do you want to do with your life?"

My bodyguard shrugged. "I already have everything a man needs, except a family."

I measured my words twice before cutting them. "You and Stavros could get a surrogate."

He buried his face in his hands for a moment, then he peeked at me. "You know?"

"Tomas told me."

"The little one?"

"He saw you kissing."

"Baboulas will fire me—maybe even kill me."

"Grandma?" I gave him what I hoped was a reassuring smile. "Have you met Aunt Rita? If Grandma is cool with Aunt Rita, and she is, then she won't care about you and Stavros. But Takis might never let you live it down."

"He can never find out."

"He won't from me."

That didn't cheer him up. "We cannot get a surrogate in Greece because we are two men."

I made him a cup of coffee, handed it to him with a *koulouraki*. "Never say never. Grandma's reach is long. Maybe she can steal a baby for you or buy one on the black market."

Elias's gaze slid sideways, landing on the reception desk.

"What is that?"

He was looking right at a small plastic box, the size of a cassette tape case. Probably because it was a cassette tape case.

"A cassette tape case?" I said.

"I know what it is. That was not there earlier."

"Somebody probably left it down here while we were all at lunch."

I reached for it. Elias's hand snapped out and stopped me.

"I do not like it," he said.

"Cassettes? The sound quality was okay but the tape was a real pain, especially when it got caught in the heads."

"You remember cassettes?" he said, amazed.

Elias wasn't much older than me. "You remember them?"

"This is Greece. New technology takes longer to catch on."

That checked out. Dad was the reason we didn't get a CD player until MP3s appeared on the horizon. To this day he's suspicious of music that doesn't exist in a form he can see and touch. The Cloud is a complete mystery to my male parental unit.

"Maybe it belongs to Gus."

Gus appeared. "Are you talking about me? My ears feel hot."

It's rude to point but I did it anyway. "Is that yours?"

"Is that what I think it is?"

"If you think it's a cassette tape case, then yes, it is."

"Do not touch it," Elias said. "I have not decided if it is safe or not."

"What?" Gus wasn't used to the family's paranoia. He picked up the plastic case.

Elias pounced, throwing me to the ground. He landed on top of me like a heavy plank.

Nothing went boom. Nothing caught fire. The only sound was a plastic snick as Gus opened the case and peered inside.

"This is a mix tape," he said. "Look, somebody wrote the track list on the inside, and they decorated the cover."

"Are you sure it is a tape?" Elias said.

"What else would it be?" Gus sounded bewildered. The man worked with the dead but he still lived in a world where a cassette was a cassette and nothing more sinister. "These are good songs, too. I like this one." He hummed a few bars of A-Ha's Take On Me.

Now there was a coincidence. Baby Dimitri had massacred the same song in his attempt to whistle the chorus. Greece had made me suspicious of coincidences.

"I don't suppose there's a name on the tape so we know who left the thing?" I asked. There was no point in asking hospital security to roll today's footage. The morgue's security cameras weren't connected to anything except the wall.

"No. No name. Just the track listing and the artwork, all of it in glitter pen."

Elias peeled himself off me and then helped me up. I took a look at the track listing. They were all before my time but I recognized most of them. Some of them, like *Take On Me*, were favorites.

"Sandra, Modern Talking, who are they?"

"Germans," Gus said. "They were famous in the 1980s." He shook the tape. "Is it okay if I keep this?"

A spider crawled up my spine. Not a real one, thankfully, otherwise I'd be screaming for a flamethrower. "It was in your morgue," I said.

———

Morning came. Not my idea. Grandma had her fingers in a lot of pies; was one of them the passage of time? If so, maybe she could pull some strings, make some threats, and increase the ratio of night to day.

I eased out of bed, taking care not to dislodge the five-year-old who was hogging most of the queen-sized space. He was five. Tiny. How the heck did something so small take up so much room?

Now that I had my own room in the compound instead of living in Grandma's shack, I could use every item in the bathroom without having to do the walk of shame to her outhouse, which, as its name implied, was outside. I washed the last of my sleep away, wriggled into slacks, pulled on a button-down shirt, and shoved my feet into the boots I'd bought from Baby Dimitri before someone dropped a body through his shop's roof. That body had belonged to the five-year-old's mother, so my wardrobe was black until Greek mourning conventions let me off the hook. Forty days for a family member who isn't a sibling, parent, or grandparents. A year or two for a parent. For widows it's a life sentence. For widowers, I wasn't sure because Greece cherishes its double standards.

There was a knock on the door. Tomas's father had

come to collect him for school. He scooped up his sleepy son, flashed me a wan smile, and left me wondering if Grandma's heart had softened overnight. I needed a vehicle that didn't have four legs and a serious hay habit. Worst case I could catch a ride with Elias, even though Grandma didn't like us riding together for security reasons. Or there was the bus, although boarding a Greek bus is both war and masochism.

With the fingers of one hand crossed, I grabbed my bag and hoofed it to the garage.

Grandma employed at least one cousin full-time to maintain her fleet of vehicles. Today the cousin on duty was slumming it with Takis. The two men were laughing, and the joke was on me. Someone had saddled up the donkey and parked it out front, alongside the black compact Elias usually drove.

"Very funny," I said, wearing my definitely-not-amused face.

"Who is laughing? Nobody, that is who," Takis said. I'd say he was laughing his butt off but the guy had a pancake where most people had padding. "What are you waiting for? Get on your donkey."

"I can't ride a donkey!"

"Sure you can. You get on the donkey and sit sideways. Then you try not to fall off."

I called Grandma.

"We already had this conversation. It would be rude not to ride the donkey," she told me.

"Thanks for nothing."

"*Parakalo*," she said not at all sarcastically, using the Greek word for *please* and *you're welcome*.

More laughter broke out. This time it was from my last remaining parent, the dirty, rotten traitor in a very nice suit. This morning Dad was eating a *kourabiethe*. Somehow he wasn't wearing the powdered sugar all over his face. Me, I looked at the Greek shortbread and wound up looking like Al Pacino in *Scarface*. I guess eating *kourabiethes* was an acquired skill, which meant I needed to practice more. Challenge accepted.

"What did I tell you?" Dad said. "Greek cars are the best."

I put on a smile with only a hint of murder in it. "Did you go on that date with Dina yet?"

Dad's grin fell off his face. "Not yet. I was hoping she would forget."

Impossible. Dina was Dad's ex-girlfriend, the one he dumped by moving to America without telling her. On a scale of one to ten, not bothering to tell someone you're changing continents was the biggest dick move ever. Dina didn't care. She transformed her home into a shrine to Dad and truly believed that someday they would be together again and raise rainbow-farting unicorns, or whatever it was obsessive nutcases did when they attained their heart's desire.

"Keep laughing and I'll play matchmaker," I said. On that note, I grabbed the donkey's reins and led her toward the gate.

"You are supposed to ride it," Takis called out.

I waved goodbye with my middle finger.

An hour later I reached the hospital. Elias paced me the whole way, winning scores of insults and raised middle fingers for his trouble—most of them from Takis, who was following in a black van with Stavros and a couple of other cousins. There was no doubt in my mind that Takis was recording the whole thing and possibly even streaming it live on social media. The Volos hospital is a modern facility with no parking for donkeys and other traditional Greek cars. I looked left. I looked right.

The clusters of Romany folks who normally loitered outside the hospital avoided eye contact. Widows glared at me. They had no business being here except show business; and me and my donkey ... today we were the show.

"What are you going to do, boss?" Elias wanted to know.

I eyed my donkey. She was cute and fuzzy, with a furry cross on her back. I couldn't leave her out here. Grandma had told me to take the donkey, hadn't she? So what if my interpretation of her proclamation was more flexible than rubber.

The hospital doors wheezed open.

"Check your calendar," I told my bodyguard. "I do believe it's 'Take Your Donkey to Work' Day."

"Is that a thing?"

"It is now."

He bit back a laugh.

The security guard jumped up, hand on gun. "You cannot bring that in here."

"Service animal," I said.

"What service?"

"She helps me cope with stupid questions."

He gave me a dubious look, settling back down behind the counter with a grumble. His mustache twitched as I led my donkey into the elevator. Elias got on behind me. Not Takis and the cousins. They took the stairs, bundled up in their winter clothes. Thanks to the overload of bodies, the morgue kept its thermostat hovering just above freezing, because if there's one thing a corpse can't handle it's an ambient temperature warmer than a refrigerator.

The elevator pinged. I led the donkey out. Takis and the others were waiting, jiggling and jumping in place. I parked my donkey in the corner near a fake potted plant.

A ficus, I thought, although I hoped there wouldn't be a botany exam in my near future.

"Somebody want to tell me why are we here?" Takis asked.

My hand shot up. "Oooh me. Pick me."

He rolled his eyes. "*Re*, just tell me."

I gave him the happy news: he and the other cousins were tasked with loading up the abandoned and forgotten dead folks and taking them to the next phase of their existence.

"I cannot believe Baboulas is making us do this," Takis grumbled.

"If you like, I can pass on your complaints," I said.

Fear flitted across his ferret face. "Heh. Never mind."

"Anyway, this was my idea."

"Charity and kindness … bah." He shook his head in disgust and got to work.

I went to find Gus. He was picking through a pile of intestines, hunting for medical clues or possibly looking to divine the future. To my credit, I swallowed my vomit without flinching. It was a recently cultivated skill.

My boss's face lit up when I told him the good news. "It is like a dream I once had," he said, "except with cake and more henchmen." I presented him with one of Stavros's muffins. "Now it is even more like that dream. Do you know what this means? I will be able to walk from here to there without hitting my hipbones—and I am a very skinny man with almost no hipbones. But do you know what is more exciting? No more sleeping here. I can go to my own home—well, my mama's home. I cannot remember the last time I slept in my own bed that I rent from her."

"Who is going and who is staying?" I asked him. He followed me back to the lobby.

"Everyone in the lobby, the waiting room, and the bathroom have to go."

"What happens if their families come looking for them?"

"They will never do that." His gaze flitted to the donkey standing by the ficus. "What is that?"

"My imaginary friend."

"Then how can I see it?"

"Maybe you're as crazy as me."

His attention slid back to my face. He put on a smile because Gus really didn't want me to quit. "I have good news. The police say I can release Litsa's remains to your family."

That was good news—as good as sad news can get. Litsa was married to one of my cousins, until she was abducted by Baby Dimitri's half sister, chopped into little pieces, and pitched out of Laki's plane and onto Baby Dimitri's shoe and souvenir shop. Physics being what it was, her remains had put a hole in the roof. Litsa and my cousin George had three boys. The youngest boy, Tomas, was George's son in name only. Biologically he'd climbed out of a different gene pool because Litsa believed everyone wanted a piece of that and had devoted her life to proving her point. Now that the police had given their two thumbs up, the family could bury Litsa. Maybe then her small family could begin to heal. Litsa wasn't much of a mother but she had three boys who had loved her anyway.

"I think your imaginary friend is doing an imaginary *kaka* on my floor," Gus said.

I closed my eyes, counted to ten. When I turned around, my donkey was done using the floor as a toilet. Takis and the cousins burst out laughing, because puberty is a life sentence for boys.

"Just get these poor dead people out of here," I said.

Takis was a tool but he was an efficient tool. Within minutes he had the operation moving like a Swiss watch. I got to work contemplating the filing cabinets that covered the back wall. I hadn't opened them yet but there was a strange smell emanating from the bottom row. One of these days I'd be forced to tackle them, seeing as how filing cabinets are usually the receptionist's bailiwick.

A female voice cut into the cold air—a voice with a frigid smirk in it. "Now this is interesting. What exactly is this? Because it looks to me like your family is stealing corpses. Just as I suspected, there is no bottom to your depravity."

Hera. Ugh. Of all the people I never wanted to see again, she was definitely near the top of the list, directly below people who had recently tried to kill me, and Todd Burns, my cheating ex-fiancé. Hera is an NIS agent and Detective Melas's ex-girlfriend, and her goals are making my life difficult and aiming for another shot at the wife position. To comfort herself, in the meantime, she has been using Melas's house as a pay-by-the-hour motel, where she bangs guys who resemble the yummy cop. Hera excels at everything she does, including being sad and pathetic. She's tall, thin, a blonde (possibly even a real one), with a face peeled off the cover of a fashion magazine. I don't hate her because she's beautiful; I hate her because she sucks.

"We're not stealing them," I said.

"A renowned criminal's henchmen loading bodies into a van? I would call that theft."

"Do not listen to her, Katerina," Takis said. He and Stavros lowered a man into a body bag. Elias was the designated label guy, cross-checking the information on the toe tags and the list Gus had given him, that way he could keep an eye out for danger and be useful at the same time. Something told me he didn't want Takis flitting around here any longer than I did.

"That would be a whole lot easier if she'd get on her broom and fly back to her coven," I said.

Hera's eyes narrowed. "I am not going anywhere."

Grinning, Takis hoisted his end of the bag. "Because you have nowhere to go, that is what I heard."

My ears pricked. "You heard something? I want to hear it, too." Did I sound excited? Most definitely.

"You missed nothing," Hera said in a low, dangerous tone that was aimed at Takis.

The asshole gene was strong in Takis. Most of the time that notch in his DNA was a bug, not a feature. But sometimes, like now, it made me happy. A grin broke out on his face like a sexually transmitted rash. "Hera lost her job. Hera lost her job," he sang.

His grin was infectious. It spread across my face faster than zombie flu. "The NIS fired you?"

Hera took her sweet time inspecting her manicure before answering. "They did not fire me." She sniffed. "They called it a suspension without pay. Big difference."

"That's what you get for using taxpayer and Germany's money to be creepy and weird," I said.

"Just because I am suspended, does not mean I cannot still do my job."

"Funny, because that's exactly what it means." I pointed to the stairs behind her. "Do what you did before, but in reverse. Moonwalk, if you have to. And don't let the sliding doors upstairs hit you on the way out. Or do. I don't care."

She finally noticed my donkey. "What is that?"

"The only car you'll be able to afford without a job,"

Takis said. I wanted to cheer but that would only encourage him.

Hera didn't flinch. "I have other income streams."

"Like what?" I asked her.

She said nothing. Instead, she helped herself to one of the lobby's walls and leaned, arms folded, face haughty. "How about some of that coffee I can smell?"

"No," I said. "You want coffee, go buy some somewhere far, far away from here."

"I think I will stay."

"Because you have nowhere to be, no place to go, and no friends," Takis said on the way past.

————

Takis and the cousins loaded the last bodies before noon. All morning they trudged back and forth, ferrying the formerly living cargo to a local funeral home Grandma trusted. Since the Family was responsible for producing an overabundance of corpses it made sense that she would have a good relationship with at least one mortuary. The funeral home agreed to provide caskets before transporting them to their final resting places, in Makria's small cemetery.

"The newspapers are going to love this," Hera said.

"You mean this act of charity?" Gus materialized at my elbow. He looked impressed but not with Hera. All his admiration was for the men freeing up space in his morgue.

She fluffed her hair and put on what I assumed was suppose to be a sexy smile. Gus was appealing if you were into small dogs, which I suspected Hera might be. Now that she was out of fancy weapons she needed something to carry about in her roomy handbags. Gus looked like he would almost fit.

"I do not think we have been introduced yet," she purred.

I rolled my eyes. "Hera, Gus. Gus, Hera. Hera is a recently fired—"

"Suspended."

"—NIS agent—"

"Allegedly."

"—Who enjoys zapping unsuspecting citizens and banging men who look like her ex-boyfriend."

"The way you say it makes me sound pathetic."

"Newsflash," I said, "you are pathetic."

In movies demons and devils have red flashing eyes, or glossy black orbs where humans have whites and colors. Hera must have been one of the low ranking imps, because her eyes were blue and gloating.

"I heard a good story, too. Want to hear it?"

"Trying to work here."

"They say Nikos is angry with you and that he is not speaking to you. Interesting, yes?"

I made eye contact with the wall of filing cabinets. I really needed to tackle that thing, and soon. Was it part of my job? Probably I should ask Gus about that.

"Bored now," I said.

My peripheral vision caught her satisfied grin.

———

"Could you walk slower?" Takis yelled.

My feet intentionally mistook his sarcasm for an order.

He honked. He wasn't alone. Everyone honked—every last vehicle in the half-mile long line of traffic behind me. Some of them shouted encouraging words involving my dead mother's private parts, a watermelon, and several Romany men. The joke was on them; watermelon was my mother's least favorite melon.

"You wanted me to take the donkey, I'm taking the donkey," I muttered.

Dinner was on the table at Grandma's when I got back to the compound. Well, not dinner exactly because lunch is the main meal of the Greek day. But there was a plastic tub of assorted Greek cookies open on the plastic tablecloth.

"You make the best dinners," I told Grandma, who was sitting in her usual seat with a crochet hook, yarn, and my dead grandfather's tomb perched close by. After my grandfather died Grandma had him cremated and put to rest in a large olive oil tin that included a post-mortem picture of him all done up in a suit and wig.

"The best thing about being a widow with grown children is that I can eat anything I like, whenever I like. And tonight I want sweets."

Not that I was religious, but amen to that. I grabbed a small plate and loaded up.

"Gus got permission from the police to release Litsa's remains."

"So I heard."

"Do you have the morgue bugged?" Nothing would surprise me less if that were true. Grandma loved bugging things.

"Who needs bugs when there is a greater force at work?"

"Video surveillance?"

"Gossip."

That was Greece: leakier than a glass with no bottom.

"When is the funeral?"

"The day after tomorrow. Tomorrow we will have the

wake. Everything is organized. We had to get a custom casket, so I ordered it the day her body was identified."

I gave her a curious look. "Custom?"

"Shaped like a Y."

Cookie crumbs flew out my nose. "Grandma!"

My grandmother chuckled before her face turned grim again. The second expression was just her regular face. "You will be my emissary tomorrow."

"What? Who? Me? Why?"

"Because I said so."

That wasn't nearly enough answer to cover all my questions. "Could we renegotiate your answer and maybe put some facts in it?"

She plopped her foot down on my lap, slipper and all. "*Po-po*, my feet hurt. Do you want your poor old *yiayia* to stand on her feet all day?"

Grandma was good, I had to give her that. "Not buying it," I said.

Her foot left my lap. "Okay. I do not want to spend my day answering stupid questions and pretending Litsa was a good mother and wife."

"So you want me to do it?"

"Yes."

I eyed the container of assorted Greek cookies. "I'm going to need a bigger plate."

Chapter 4

IF YOU HAVE to pick a time to die in Greece, the most considerate season is fall or winter. That's because everyone in your family will have to wear black for at least forty days, and no one wants to commit to daily black in the middle of July. Litsa's main act of kindness in this world was getting murdered in September, when daytime temperatures were plummeting to tolerable levels.

In life, Litsa had spread herself around more than an oil spill in the Gulf of Mexico, but she was still a Makris, so Grandma set up her casket in the compound's conservatory and put on a dog and pony show so pretty that nobody would be able to deny Litsa walked on water. All day long, people traipsed up to the guardhouse, where they were patted down before they passed through metal detectors. Finally, they had to pass the bomb-sniffing test, courtesy of two hounds who had been borrowed from Greece's bomb squad for the occasion. We'd had one suicide bomber this year; Grandma didn't want another.

Papou watched mourners and lookie-loos come and go from outside the conservatory. I stood beside him, dishing out blessings and greetings, mostly because that's what Grandma had ordered me to do.

"You should have had that boss of yours flip her pieces over in the box. No one will recognize her the right way up. I hear she was Greek in every way." Papou winked at me. "And if you do not know, I can explain it to you. Here, turn around."

Suddenly, he yelped. Aunt Rita had Papou's fleshy earlobe trapped between her blood red fingernails.

"You cannot do that to me," he wailed. "I have known you since you were a boy."

Aunt Rita was the haute couture Grim Reaper in a black velvet dress with no back from her tailbone on up. Instead, her back had been painted with what looked like screaming souls. Her high heels were normal until you got a load of the stiletto heels, which were Virgin Marys carved in ebony.

She let go of his ear.

"I know, I know, do not disrespect the dead," Papou said.

"Wrong," Aunt Rita said. "Do not disrespect my niece."

"So you do not care if I disrespect Litsa? Good." He wolf-whistled at an older couple hobbling through the conservatory door. They were north of eighty and barely south of dust. "Did you have sex with the corpse? Do not feel bad because most people did. I just want to know if she was good."

The pair scurried away without looking backwards.

Papou looked pleased with himself. "I think they both did her, probably at the same time."

Aunt Rita inched closer to me. "Do not look now, but here comes the Melas family."

I looked because that's what you do when someone tells

you not to look. My stomach flip-flopped, then it plain flopped. Constable Nikos Melas and I hadn't spoken in days. After I heroically rescued him—Laki's plane was involved—he discovered I'd forgotten to tell him that Grandma has surveillance inside the Volos police station where he works. Apparently he didn't like the idea of Grandma keeping tabs on the police—even though she was the police—and he liked the idea of me keeping it a secret from him even less. We exchanged chilly words, and then afterwards he walked away without looking back to see if I was weeping prettily into a lace handkerchief.

Sure enough, the Melas family was coming right for us.

It was too late to run. That didn't mean I couldn't cast longing glances at Grandma's bushes.

Kyrios Melas, the detective's father and the village of Makria's baker, is a mountain with a hair on top. He has his son's looks and his wife's hand squeezing his balls; possibly literally, because Kyria Mela used to work for Grandma. In those days she got her kicks and paycheck torturing anyone who was feeling less than informative. To this day, Kyria Mela keeps a box of tools in a hole in her parlor room floor. She has chin-length helmet hair and she's built like a violent sneeze could blow her off Mount Pelion. Whether she likes me or not, I can't say; and frankly, I don't think she knows either. Today the Melas family was all in black. The men were in suits. Kyria Mela was wearing a no-nonsense skirt suit with low heels that were too sturdy to be kittens. The detective's mother didn't perform acts of whimsy or fashion. As someone who hated kitten heels, I grudgingly approved of her choice.

Detective Melas's eyes were on me, hard and discerning. Not normal for us. I felt like a bug. Not even a cool bug like a butterfly or a scarab beetle. Something icky, like a cockroach. I didn't like it. I was not one of life's roaches.

Okay, yes, back at home I had been a bill collector, but that was a job, a means to a financial end, not a personality trait.

In contrast, Kyrios Melas, the baker, beamed at me. He came at me with a warm, genuine hug. The comforting aroma of bread soothed me and made me wish I had a smoked salmon and cream cheese sandwich, with a few caramelized onions thrown in. His wife elbowed him out of the way so she could drop two stiff, socially correct kisses on my cheeks. Greeks don't air kiss; they make full contact. The smell of crushed and dying flowers overpowered the bread.

"Raise your hand if you stuck your *poutsa* or any other body part in the corpse," Papou said brightly. "Before she was dead. Or after. Who cares? From what I hear, she had no standards, that one."

We gawked at him in horror—all of us except one. The starched edges of Kyria Mela's lips twitched. Her son was a notch on the dead woman's glittery thong, and she did not approve. For years, Melas privately believed he was the biological father of little Tomas, Litsa and George's youngest son. Kyria Mela never believed it. She was right. Tomas's birth father was Baby Dimitri, although the list of people privy to that information could be counted on a single hand.

Somebody had to defend Litsa.

Grandma wasn't around, so that unfortunate somebody was me.

"She didn't have sex with Turks," I said, hoping that was an adequate character reference. Greeks of a certain age—old—hate Turks, and Turks hate Greeks. Back in the olden days, Turkey licked Greece, calling dibs on the country and its people. Greeks didn't mind the licking so much but the occupation and mass murders made them want to do some killing of their own. The rivalry is ongoing.

Papou threw his hands in the air. "Okay, okay, she had one standard, and now that I think about it that is a good one." He gestured for me to open the conservatory doors, then he and his eagles rolled inside.

Kyria Mela opened her handbag and flashed a compact at me. "Insurance."

The Melas family didn't stay long. They went into the conservatory to pay their respects—and in Kyria Mela's case, make sure Litsa was really dead—then they left. Melas glanced back.

I waved.

He didn't.

———

Aunt Rita raised her perfectly sardonic eyebrows. "I saw that."

The afternoon was warm but my face was suddenly cold. "You saw nothing."

"Exactly."

"Saw what?" Marika appeared between us. "What did we see? Or did we not see it? I am already confused."

Marika is my age or thereabouts. She's married to Takis and together they have a gang of boys and another child on the way. Marika is a big comfortable woman with a cheerful face, even when she's threatening to cut a witch. For a while, she fancied herself as my bodyguard, but now that she's expecting she's thinking of taking up the spy mantle. Somehow, in her head, that's safer and more glamorous.

"Nikos ignored Katerina's wave," Aunt Rita said.

Stupid ground; why wouldn't it open up and swallow

me whole?

Marika gasped and crossed herself. "He did not!"

"He did!" My aunt shifted into girly gossip mode. "Can you believe it? What was he thinking?"

That I betrayed him, that's what he was thinking.

"Can we not talk about Detective Melas?" I said. "It was never going to happen anyway."

"How can you say that?" my aunt asked. "It was already happening."

"It was a couple of dates and a few kisses," I said.

"People in Greece used to get married after less," Aunt Rita said.

Marika nodded. "They still do. I never kissed Takis until our wedding night, and we had a chaperone on all our dates."

"Same thing with my first wife," Aunt Rita said.

Before she came out as a woman, my aunt was married three times. She has a trio of sons she almost never sees, thanks to a dud custody agreement and an ex with an over-abundance of something the woman probably considers morality--although she is only too happy to cash my aunt's checks.

"Nikos Melas and I aren't getting married or anything else," I said, feeling distinctively huffy. My love life—or its continued non-existence—wasn't anyone's business but mine. Except this was Greece where everything was every-one's business, especially if it was gossip-worthy. And Melas and me? We were gossip-worthy. The mobster's granddaughter and the cop. People wrote made-for-TV movies and romance novels about this kind of stuff.

"I know lots of single men," Marika said brightly.

"Am I related to all of them?"

Her face fell. "Yes."

"That is a problem these days," Aunt Rita said. "Forty

or fifty years ago, people were not so picky. Now you marry a cousin and everybody checks your children for extra fingers."

The crowd was thinning out. Everyone who wanted to make sure Litsa was really dead had already been and gone.

Papou rolled out of the conservatory. "*Vre*, did you see Litsa's body? They did a good job stitching her back together. You can hardly tell she was woman souvlaki."

He said it big. He said it loud. People turned around.

I put on a smile and waved. Nothing to see here, folks. Nothing at all.

"Smaller," Aunt Rita said.

My smile dimmed. I kept on waving.

"You are good at this," she said. "Better than Mama, but do not tell her I said that."

Where was Grandma, anyway?

When I asked my aunt she said, "Mama went to Athens for a thing."

"She went to Athens?"

"That is what she said."

Nobody told me anything around here. Grandma ditching Litsa's wake to go to Athens might have been useful information, say, last night.

"For a thing? What kind of thing?"

"With Mama, who can say? A very important thing, I am guessing. She never goes to Athens unless it is very important."

Whatever it was, it had to be a big deal to pull Grandma away from a family funeral, even one for a peripheral family member with a lousy reputation and a sketchy past. Come to think of it, that was everyone in the family.

I sent her a text message and received a reply almost

immediately. She was in Athens and Dad was with her. If I had any problems handling Litsa's funeral tomorrow, Aunt Rita could help.

Aunt Rita peered over my shoulder. "Do you have problems?"

"I can think of at least five."

"Come back to my place when this is over. I have medicine."

"What kind of medicine?"

"Ice cream and champagne."

My favorite kind of pharmaceuticals.

———

The average human stomach is the size of a fist. My stomach was stuffed with two fists of ice cream and topped up with bubbles. The bubbles made me want to do unspeakable things with bad-for-me men, but the ice cream kept me grounded. What I needed was my bed and ten hours of uninterrupted sleep. The clock on my phone said I could have five hours—take it or leave it—before the funeral shenanigans commenced for the day.

High heels in hand, I wobbled out into the courtyard, headed for my apartment.

A voice slashed through the night—a voice I knew, although in my semi-inebriated state it took me a moment. "You need shoes? I know where you can get some."

I jumped. "Baby Dimitri, is that you?"

The old gangster materialized from behind a trellis. The courtyard has dozens of the climbing frames, smothered in vines. In late summer it's like slinking through Macy's perfume department but without the watering eyes and the saleswomen shoving testers up your nose. Baby Dimitri's hair was running out of grease. His normally sharp creases were limp. This was a man in need of an iron and bottle of white shoe polish to restore his faux Floridian glow.

"I need a favor."

"You're supposed to be hiding." I made little furtive glances around the courtyard in case anyone was watching. A National Geographic moment; I was some kind of small deer. "How did you get out?"

"Your grandmother gave me the key to my room."

"Really?"

"No. That old woman treats me like a prisoner not a guest."

"You know you're on the lam, right? She's trying to keep you safe—at your request. So what's the favor?" I wasn't the designated favor-giver in the family but maybe I could help. If not, maybe I could kick his request up the ladder.

"Tomorrow I need to pay my respects to Litsa."

Respects from the man who had spent more time inside my cousin's dead wife—before she died, of course—than inside his own shoe shop. "You already paid your respects. A lot, and for years."

"Okay, without my poutsa this time."

"You came to us for protection. If I let you come to the funeral you'll be compromising yourself. Or at least I assume you will. Who are you hiding from, exactly? Nobody tells me anything."

"A ghost. A memory. A nightmare with terrible taste in clothing, bad hair, and ugly shoes."

Specificity wasn't his strong suit. "Can you give me a name, at least?"

"For what?" He imitated a typing monkey. "So you can put that name into the internet and dig up old bones? No. Your grandmother wants to keep you safe, and I do, too.

You are a very good customer. You like shoes and you pay for them in cash."

"I do like shoes," I admitted.

"Katerina Makris-with-an-s, let me come to the funeral."

"Can't. Too many strangers."

Strangers. George. George and Litsa's children, including the one who, biologically at least, belonged to the man currently hiding behind a trellis.

"I could wear a disguise. Nobody would have to know."

My eyebrows took a hike. Now he had my attention. "What kind of disguise?"

"Who knows? I was hoping you would have something. You are a woman, yes?"

I eyed the older man. Not one of life's giants. Wiry. There was potential here … for someone who could work magic with disguises.

A yawn wracked my body. The sandman was standing over me with his sack, flicking sand in my face.

"Go back to your room," I said. "Right now I need to sleep."

"What about the funeral?"

"I'll see you in the morning."

————

The next morning, Aunt Rita and I met outside the dungeon.

"Ready?" I asked her.

My aunt had arrived with several garment bags and a rolling suitcase. She was in a black suit with a pencil skirt and yesterday's viciously religious heels. Her lipstick was the red of a violent crime scene and the rest of her makeup said she could take an army of Kardashian-

Jenners in a contour fight. My outfit was black, too, but I was dressed to bury not kill. The day promised to be long. I had things to do and people to provide with comfort and snacks, so I had dressed the part in a black sheath dress and cute flats that wouldn't put me in a wheelchair.

"I live for this," Aunt Rita said dramatically.

As often as she had wanted to dress me up, I believed her.

Baby Dimitri was waiting. He sat up and flicked off his television, took in the garment bags and suitcase. Two eyebrows rose. "What is this?"

"One disguise, coming right up," I said cheerfully.

"Are you going to make me look like a sister?"

Sister is one of many colorful Greek slurs against gay men.

Aunt Rita patted his cheek. "When I am done with you everybody will wish you were their sister."

Baby Dimitri paled. "*Re, gamisou.*"

"Not even on my worst day would I touch your *poutsa* with anything except a knife, or maybe an axe." Aunt Rita got to work, unzipping bags. The suitcase contained a dizzying array of cosmetics and floppy prosthetics. All the ingredients to create a whole new person.

The Godfather of Shoes and Eternal Soles was down in the mouth. "I do not want to be a woman."

"Well, I cannot make you a man …" Aunt Rita started.

Ouch.

"… or people might recognize you."

Baby Dimitri stood his ground. "No women's clothes."

My aunt selected a couple of skin-colored slabs of rubber and held them up to the mobster's face. "Do you know what I have noticed? Men who scream the loudest about these things are the ones who secretly want it the most. I think maybe you like to wear woman's clothes when the door is closed. And who could blame you?" She winked at me. "Women's clothing is wonderful. So many colors. So many styles. We can be anything we want. Men get to be maybe five." She unzipped one of the garment bags and pulled out a black skirt suit. Slim cut. Peplum. Perfect for hiding the fact that Baby Dimitri had hips like an eel.

Aunt Rita primped and powdered until the godfather was the prettiest princess in Makria. She topped off his new look with a smooth ash blond wig, which she styled in a French twist.

"It makes my head itch," he said.

"Pretend it's a hat," I told him.

He grunted into the mirror. "Not too bad."

"Not bad, he says." Aunt Rita rolled her eyes at me. "That is like saying the Parthenon is a nice pile of stones."

"He's beautiful," I reassured her, "all thanks to you."

She turned a thoughtful eye on me. "Hmm …"

"Don't even think about it," I said. "I'm comfortable and it's going to be a long day."

"Just a little—"

"No!"

Monobrow was waiting for us outside Baby Dimitri's room. He wolf-whistled at the old guy in drag. "Congratulations, this is the closest you have ever come to being a man."

"Are you coming to the funeral?" I asked Monobrow.

"No, but if you happen to come across some stray *loukoumia*, I would not say no if you made the trip down here to bring it to me."

Litsa's funeral took place at 10:00 A.M at Ayios Ekaterini—Saint Katherine's (K or C, take your pick). Her boys stood like four little statues at the front, between their father and me. Tomas held my hand. Every so often he squeezed it like he was telling me everything would be okay. In life, Litsa had been nothing to me; I hadn't been here long enough for her to be more than a name and a jumbo pair of implants. But her smallest son was the brightest star in my world.

They carried Litsa to Makria's cemetery after that, six of the family's men. Family, friends, and the entire village followed along slowly behind on foot. Not too many weeks ago the family had staged a funeral for me, all part of one of Grandma's elaborate crime-fighting schemes. Today was the real—heartbreaking— deal.

Makria's cemetery is a peaceful, sheltered place. An abundance of leafy trees protects the dead from the elements and spying drones. Headstones are white, over-sized, and most of the graves are decorated with statues. Some of those statues don't feature naked genitals or boobs. Today, on the far edge there was a rash of new graves where the hospital's abandoned dead had come to rest. Here they were no longer forgotten. Someone had left flowers resting against each new headstone. Knowing Grandma, the groundskeeper was paid well to make sure the graveyard remained a small patch of paradise.

After Father Harry read his prayers, the family's women hurled themselves across the coffin, weeping. Some of the tears were even real.

I nudged my aunt. "Am I supposed to do that?" Grandma hadn't left instructions for this part.

"Baboulas would not lower herself. Litsa was only a wife, and not a devout one at that."

So that was a "no" then.

Every so often I glanced over at Baby Dimitri, who was doing a stiff imitation of womanhood. He was dry-eyed and tight-lipped and he didn't look like himself without white shoes and vicious creases. He stared straight ahead, hands clasped in front of him. Silent. Stone. Elegant and invisible in his borrowed suit and heels.

When it came to disguises, Aunt Rita was a magician.

My heart hurt for the aging mob boss. Maybe he was never in love with Litsa, not enough to make a wife out of her anyway, but it was obvious he had cared deeply about the woman.

Afterwards, the family held a feast for the mourners in the compound's courtyard. Fish was served, and a mountain of *koliva*, boiled and sweetened wheat grains, sprinkled with powdered sugar and silver dragées. I shook hands, kissed cheeks, accepted blessings and gave them on Grandma's behalf. A year ago all I had was Dad. Now I had a family and a village.

My phone rang.

"Katerina, there is a man here who wants to speak with you. One of the local farmers," the compound's guard said. "A Kyrios Agapi."

Agapi was the Greek word for *love*. It was also a popular name. So basically Mr. Love wanted to see me.

"Can't he come in?"

"He does not want to."

"Does he have any weapons?"

"No. He is clean."

Everybody wanted a piece of me and there wasn't enough to go around. Probably I should eat more Greek food to fix that problem.

"Okay. I'll be right out."

Normally when there was a crowd I had to push through, one carefully placed elbow at a time. As Grandma's emissary, the human sea parted without me having to jab a single rib. What did this farmer want, and today of all days? Probably he wanted me to solve a dispute involving beans or olives or whatever grew at this time of the year. I didn't mind too much. Away from the crowd I could breathe again.

The septuagenarian waiting for me was holding a Greek fisherman's cap in his hands and his head was bowed slightly. He smelled like sheep.

"You are not Katerina," he said when he saw me.

"My passport says I am."

He stared at me, long and hard, then he seemed to come to a conclusion. His face broke out in a grin.

"The granddaughter, eh? Michail's girl? I remember your father when he was a boy. I remember your aunt when she was a boy, too." Hands in his pockets, he twisted at the waist, took in the gun-toting cousins. His face clouded over. "Okay, I have a message for you. Tell Katerina I know where she is and I am coming for her. Also, I am going to bury her underground where no one will ever find her, then I will slaughter the whole family as though they are nothing more than sardines." The way he said it, I wasn't convinced he was coming for more than a cup of sugar.

"Cool threat," I said. "Where did you get that? Intimidation R Us?"

His face fell. "You were not afraid?"

"Not even a little bit."

"Was it my body language or my face?"

"Both. Plus you're not really dressed for it."

"What should I wear next time?"

"Well," I said, thinking about it. "You could try a shiny suit. In the movies, men in shiny suits are almost always bad guys."

He didn't look happy. "I cannot afford a suit."

"All black is a good option, too."

"Do the blacks have to match?"

"That's probably for the best. People take you more

seriously when your colors match. I learned that in kindergarten."

"Okay. I think my dead wife left behind some black dye."

"Just asking for a friend," I said, "but who sent you here?"

"Who said anybody sent me?" His face fell further. It didn't have far to go, on account of how gravity had already grabbed his jowls and gone for a jog with them. "Oh. Yes. The terrible intimidation technique."

"It is kind of a giveaway."

He glanced around like he was looking for something. Then he seemed to come to a conclusion.

"I suppose I can tell you. He did not say I could not tell you. Of course, I think he was expecting me to speak with Kyria Katerina and not you." He twisted his hat in his hands. "He did not tell me his name, but he reminded me of somebody."

Very specific.

"How about a description?"

He shrugged. "He looked like a man."

My eye twitched. "That's very helpful."

He smiled cheerfully. "*Parakalo.*" The good old Greek 'please' and 'you're welcome'. "You will give the message to your grandmother, yes? Otherwise I will not get paid."

"I don't really understand what it means, but I'll give her the message. Out of curiosity, what did this man promise you?"

One at a time, he raised his feet, showing off his boots. Old. Scuffed. Soles patched with cardboard. "New boots."

"Nice. Good boots are expensive."

He grinned. "A good prize for easy work."

And then his head exploded in a cloud of red mist and bone fragments.

Chapter 5

I HIT THE GROUND, propelled by about a couple of hundred pounds of hard muscle. Xander. It had to be. No one else was that big and heavy and all-encompassing. Nobody else wouldn't ask if I was okay. Xander had been standing off to the side all day, eyes prowling for trouble from behind dark glasses. Now he'd found some.

Feet echoed around me. Cousins spread out. Takis was barking orders at them. "Find the shooter," he was saying.

Xander gathered me into a bundle and ran, shielding me with his body.

"Is he okay?" I shouted. "Is he okay?"

The old farmer wasn't okay. I managed to get a sneak peek once Xander put me down behind the wall. It was hard to be okay with no head.

"He had a head when we started talking, I swear." I was vomiting words. I couldn't stop myself. "I didn't do it. I didn't shoot him."

Xander didn't answer. He was busy looking me over for signs of imminent death. I was fine. My head was on my shoulders, unlike the farmer, whose head was a Jackson Pollock painting.

"I'm f-f-f-ine." My teeth chattered. My whole body shook. "Probably I'm not going to die today."

He didn't look convinced.

Melas charged out, gun primed. He glanced at me on the way over to the dead man, then he moved on. A tiny shard of disappointment stabbed me; he hadn't asked if I was fine. I was—physically, anyway—but emotions are bossy little things that enjoy pinching logic. Melas was just doing his job, I reminded myself. And right now his job was the dead man and the shooter at large. Before he reached the body he was already on his phone, barking orders. Within minutes, sirens would be climbing the mountain road. This place would be flooded with cops and Family, with a capital F.

Takis jogged over, phone in hand.

"Did you find the shooter?" I asked him.

"Not yet. One of the men found this." He held out a cassette tape in its plastic cover.

"What is this?"

"In the old days, we used to have things called—"

I waved my hands. "I know what it is. I mean what *is* it?"

Elias inspected it. "Looks like a mix tape."

Another mix tape? First the tape at the morgue and now this one? They had to be linked. I hadn't seen a cassette tape in the wild for over a decade.

"What's on it?" I asked.

"Michael Jackson compilation, but only his songs from the 1980s. And some DeBarge." He made a face.

The other tape had songs exclusively from the 80s, too. But what did it mean, other than that someone—most likely the same someone Baby Dimitri was running from—had specific taste in music?

My stomach clenched. I had to get it together. Everyone was looking at me like I belonged in Grandma's shoes.

"What do we know about the dead man?"

"Kyrios Agapi?" Takis shrugged. "He had a farm not far from here. Sheep and olives. What did he say to you?"

"He was just passing on a message for Grandma." Nausea sloshed through me. A man died, and for what? "Jeepers creepers. Some people will do anything to get out of having to pay honest wages for honest work."

My phone rang.

"I heard you have a message for me," Grandma said.

I shot a glance at Takis.

He shrugged. "She is the boss," he said.

Grandma listened while I talked. "Message received," she said when I was done.

"What are you and Dad doing in Athens?"

"Chasing a ghost."

"I think your ghost is here and he likes 80s pop."

There was a long moment of silence. Grandma ended it by resurrecting an old argument. "Maybe it is better for now if you stay in the compound."

"We keep having this talk and it always ends the same way. Do we really need to have it again?"

Freedom is important to this American-born woman. Being told to sit and stay doesn't work for me. As soon as someone barks orders at me, I itch to do the opposite thing. The allergy first cropped up when Grandma ordered Takis and Stavros haul me to Greece against my will. Not that I want to be in danger—I don't—but I'm a person with a life, not a precious doodad to be locked away in a palatial compound, behind a wall, with armed guards scanning the mail for explosives and powered substances.

"If you leave the compound without Elias or Xander I will kill you myself, understand?"

Though she couldn't see me, I saluted. "Yes, Grandma."

"I saw that."

Why wasn't I surprised? Grandma had more eyes than a housefly.

A man had died but Litsa's funeral wasn't over. There were still unsuspecting guests in the courtyard, enjoying the family's hospitality. Someone had to shower and get out there, and that someone was me.

Xander escorted—a fancy word for "followed"--me back to my apartment.

"I can shower on my own," I told him.

He nodded once and headed for my bedroom. When I was done washing blood, brains, and bone out of my hair with shaking hands, I discovered he had laid out fresh clothing—black—and made *frappe*—foamy iced coffee. I wiggled into the clean clothing, then, while I sipped the *frappe*, Xander gently gathered up my hair. Electricity arced down my spine.

"You're good at hair. Have you ever considered a career change?"

Wordlessly, he twisted the ponytail holder, fastening the bundle securely. Not fancy but functional, which was all I needed right now.

I smiled a smile I didn't feel.

"Show time," I said. "Again."

———

Litsa's murder was old news by the time I rejoined the

mourners. Everyone wanted to talk about the new, shiny dead man. Some wanted to give me helpful tips.

"Did you try rubbing alcohol?"

All elderly Greek women dispense medical advice without invitation. Just sneeze or scratch on the way past, and a wealth of knowledge will spray out of their mouths, delivered in sharp, brutally honest tones, designed to give you something to cry about if you aren't already crying.

My eye twitched. "For?"

"That man's headache."

"His head got blown off," I said carefully.

"Vinegar poultice?"

Mime wasn't my strong suit but I tried anyway. "Blown. Off. No more head." I shook my head hard.

"Kaput?"

"Kaput." I drew a grisly invisible line across my throat.

"Then he should have gone to church more often," the old woman said before shuffling away.

I went though the same conversation, same mime, a dozen times before Kyra Mela sidled up to me.

"People are idiots," she said.

"Even the good ones?"

"Especially the good ones."

"Am I an idiot?"

"That remains to be seen. The coffee grounds have not revealed all your secrets." She pinched my cheek and vanished into the crowd.

Yikes.

I approached Baby Dimitri, who was engaged in a staring competition with a large orange tomcat.

"The Care Bear left on your doorstep, what was in the plastic box?"

"Why do you want to know?"

"Because the Greek half of my DNA needs to know everything and it needs to know it now."

"That is a good reason. I suppose there is no harm in telling you, eh? It was a cassette."

"What was on it?"

"Who can say? I did not listen to it, but the track listing told me it was a mix tape. Can I ask you something?"

"Sure."

He held up a slim, black tube. "What part of my face is this for?"

I told him about lipstick and its typically inadequate lasting power, then he took off to find the nearest mirror.

Papou rolled over. "Who was that woman you were talking to? I have to know."

"An international woman of mystery."

He sighed. "I love those."

———

When the sun went down, everyone scurried away after stuffing as much food as possible into their pockets and purses.

"Mama never minds if they take the food," Aunt Rita said when I mentioned it. "Less clean up and less waste. Go get some rest, okay? Everybody knows what to do."

George didn't come by with Tomas. He did message though. Tomas was asleep in his father's bed and George didn't want to disturb him.

Happiness washed over me. Sadness, too. I thought about how Dad wanted to sell the only home I had ever known, the last and only place I had ever known Mom. Could we really inflict Reggie Tubbs on another family? The retired judge was the neighborhood flasher and an unabashed attention seeker. He got up at the crack of dawn and planted himself on the front porch, accidentally-on-purpose waving his wiener at anyone with breasts and a pulse. Come to think of it, probably the pulse was optional.

Everything was changing around me yet I felt as though my feet were stuck in drying cement.

I looked down to make sure that was a metaphor, because in this family, cement happened. But not to me, and not tonight.

After gathering up all the bedding, I crafted a pillow and blanket fort on my bed, and then crawled inside with my phone.

I slept.

———

My phone was stuck to my face. Saliva made great glue. Ask those little birds who made nests out of the stuff, only to have them ripped away to make soup. I had zero missed calls, three text messages, and twelve unread emails wanting me to enlarge my P3N!S with creams, pills, and exercises. The text messages were from Gus, casually suggesting that he really liked muffins and other pastries, and if some should happen to fall into my bag on the way to the morgue, he would be okay with that.

Lucky for Gus, Elias was waiting outside the garage with a white paper bag filled with Stavros' latest offerings.

"When he cannot sleep, he bakes," Elias said like he didn't mind the baking part too much. He swapped me the bag for one of the coffee cups I was holding.

"Your car is ready," my cousin said.

No car. One donkey.

"Very funny."

"Takis thinks so," he said.

"Let me guess. He wants me to get on the donkey so you can upload the video to his YouTube page again?"

My cousin's face fell. "How did you know?"

"I know Takis."

I turned to Elias. "Keys?"

"In the car."

Grandma wasn't around to fuss about us riding in the same car.

"Can I drive?"

Elias grinned. "No, but you can flip off the other drivers while I drive."

As far as deals went, it was a good one. Plus my hands would be free for the important things in life, like eating.

Gus was like a new man now that he had room to perform autopsies without whacking his elbow on a corpse. He whistled while he worked, in between mouthfuls of coffee and muffin. Like everyone else around me, his life was on the move while mine was static.

After work, I sat on the rim of the compound's front fountain, tearing up a leaf, pitching the pieces into the water. Night was still hours away, but I could feel the creep of its cool arrival. I wasn't alone for long. Marika came bustling out, casting furtive glances over her shoulder.

"I have to get away from my children. It is imperative."

"Why?"

She retrieved a large ION chocolate bar from her pocket, the kind with hazelnuts. Not my favorite, but in an emergency I was sure I could choke down the whole thing.

"So I can eat this without sharing." She tore off the green wrapper and bit into the chocolate. Then stopped. "You want some?" She said it like she was asking if I wanted to lose an arm. Seeing as how I was attached to all my limbs, I shook my head.

"I'm trying to quit."

"Good. Chocolate will kill you."

This chocolate would. The most dangerous place in the world was between Marika's mouth and food.

"Want to go for a ride?" I asked her.

She looked around expectantly. "Did you get a new car?"

Crap. I'd almost forgotten about the no car situation. "No. I do have a cool donkey though."

"How am I supposed to ride on the donkey with you? I cannot get on that animal in my condition."

"The Virgin Mary did it while she was pregnant."

"And look how that turned out. She had her baby in a stable, strangers showed up with not-very-good gifts, then thirty years later her son was murdered."

Marika was oversimplifying the situation and completely missing the point.

"She was also apparently a virgin." Somebody involved was a virgin, I knew that much. The details were fuzzy. "Or her mother was."

Marika made a face. "I am not one of those. This body was built to ride in a proper car, preferably one with leather seats and air conditioning."

I sighed. "I don't care about the leather seats, but I would be happy with a proper car. I really liked that Beetle."

"Now that you have a job you could buy one."

As far as ideas went, it was a good one. Okay, so I didn't have my first paycheck yet, but now that my bank knew I wasn't impersonating myself after having stolen my own identity, I could get to the money in my account. Not all that money was mine—not any of it, actually—but I was approximately eighty percent sure Dad wouldn't mind. He didn't know yet that I had helped myself to some of the cash he'd stashed in his safe behind the mirror in the master bathroom back home. What I'd taken was a drop in an enormous green bucket. Thinking about it reminded me that I still had questions for Dad, such as: Where did that money come from, and how long had he been hiding a gun behind the bathroom mirror?

"I guess I could buy one."

Marika brightened up. "I could come shopping with you. I am good negotiating prices. Ask anyone except Takis. He gets angry when I try to negotiate because he is terrible at it. That time he bought that gun from that man under the bridge, I told him I could have got a better price. But did he let me try? No. So what happened? He paid too much for an illegal weapon."

That sounded like Takis. "Okay, I'm going car shopping."

"You mean *we* are going car shopping. I want to know how it works."

"You've never been car shopping?"

"Baboulas provides the family with all the cars it needs. Whenever I need to go somewhere, I can pick up the phone and someone will drive me."

A question popped into my head. "Marika, can you drive?"

"No. Takis did not want me to learn. He said it would make me too independent."

Oh, he did, did he? Well, we'd see about that. "Okay. First we're going car shopping, then I'm teaching you how to drive."

"Takis is going to kill me."

I hugged her shoulders. "Not if you run over him first."

———

Only the fit survive boarding a Greek bus. I was about to put this body and mind to the ultimate test.

Marika and I traipsed the minuscule distance to Makria and waited for the next bus to rattle along. We stood in one corner of the village's parking lot. Opposing us, three widows clothed in traditional black, complete with knee-high stockings. They were ancient. They had walking sticks. They were complaining vocally about their feet and how their children never called, never visited. Maybe it was true; maybe they were totally faking it. I suspected the moment that bus arrived they'd shove us into traffic to board first.

It didn't matter that they knew Grandma and the family: this could be war.

Marika touched two fingers to her eyes, then pointed those same fingers at each of them.

"What are you doing?" I whispered. Smart people didn't wave flags at resting bulls.

"I saw this in a movie with Robert DeNiro. I do it to my children to let them know I am watching them."

"Does it work?"

"Of course. They know I am watching them."

"But do they behave after you do it?"

Marika's shoulders slumped. "My children are monsters."

The widows complained louder. They threw in talk about how this was destined to be the coldest winter in history. Their feet ached … *po-po* … they would be cripples by spring. One of them had a dickey heart from eating radiation-tainted fruit after the Chernobyl incident thirty years earlier.

Was I fooled? Heck no. Greece was Thunderdome and Marika was Mad Max. The widows were the Marauders from *The Road Warrior*. I was Max's Australian Cattle Dog, I'd run out of metaphors.

In the distance, a bus coughed and wheezed. I flexed my fingers. I touched my toes. I jogged in place … in my imagination. Beside me, Marika cracked her knuckles—nothing imaginary about it. The trio of fossilized women leaned on their walking sticks and braced their backs with one hand. Their children never called, never visited. Lawks a-mercy. Woe was them—or was it 'woe were they'?

As I pondered the grammar of it all, the bus chugged around the steep bend, blunt-nosed and in need of a fresh lick of paint. Brakes squealed as the driver wrestled with the steering wheel.

Nobody moved. Not yet.

Slowly, slowly, the bus eased to a full stop. The metal whale shuddered and the rear door hissed as it folded back on itself. Chatter filtered out. Passengers' eyes snapped to the boarding side of the bus; if there was a show about to start, they didn't want to miss it.

"Now!" Marika bellowed. She hurled herself at the steps. One of the widows brought her stick down on Marika's back.

Christ in a Camaro. "She's pregnant!" I screeched, lunging at the stick. "You can't hit her!" My fingers missed. The widow whirled around like something out of a Kung-Fu movie, walking stick twirling, and rapped me across the knuckles. Tears flooded my eyes. Wood beats bone, in case anyone was wondering.

Marika wasn't giving up. She crawled up the steps, kicking at the other two widows, who had death-grips on her ankles.

"Save yourself," I cried out. "I've got this one."

I totally didn't have this one. I was taking a beating.

"I am trying," Marika said over her shoulder.

The widows released her ankles. One at a time, they hobbled up the steps, using Marika's body as a ramp.

I winced as the third widow whacked my knuckles again, and then she pole-vaulted after the others, landing inside the bus.

The doors wheezed shut, Marika stuck between them. I hammered on the glass.

"Open up!"

The conductor shot a look out the window. His face moved into the "oh crap" position. He couldn't get the door open fast enough.

"It is you," he said, lurching forward to help me hoist Marika up.

What was he talking about? "It's me, I guess."

"Do not tell Baboulas that I almost chopped your friend in half, eh?"

Oh. That. Grandma's infamy had struck again. This time it had worked in our favor.

Marika performed her fingers to eyes maneuver again, aiming them at the three widows, who were each hogging a whole two-person seat. There was nowhere to sit so we had to stand.

The women grinned at her.

"I know where you all live and so does my husband," she said. "So keep smiling."

Their smiles broke off.

We rode the bus into Volos, disembarking where the route ended. Apartments mixed with businesses. Parks mingled with car dealers. Smog strangled the clean air and left it for dead. When Volos grew up—and it was growing up fast—it wanted to be Athens. If the city didn't get its clean-air act together, the whole place would become the wrong side of the tracks.

I looked up and down the street. There were several

car yards and I didn't know a thing about any of them. "Where should we start?"

"With food," Marika said.

"I was thinking about starting with the car."

"You cannot shop for a car on an empty stomach. I am sure I read that somewhere."

It had been a decade since I'd bought my Jeep, but I hadn't forgotten the endless wait as the car dealer faked "talking to his boss" to give me a better deal. During that time I made several trips to a vending machine that only sold generic chips and nobody's favorite brands of candy and cookies. It was stocked with bags of candy corn, for crying out loud.

"I guess I could eat," I said.

We trotted over to a nearby *periptero*—newspaper stand--and loaded up on snacks.

Marika dug into a bag of chips. "This will do until we can find some real food."

I peeled open a bar of ION chocolate, the one with chunks of almonds. Europe did chocolate so much better than home. More creamy. Less waxy. "Where now?"

She closed her eyes, stuck her arm out, turned in a half circle. "There."

Really Real Cars wasn't committed to one brand. They had everything from companies I didn't recognize to other companies I didn't recognize, with a few Toyotas and BMWs sprinkled in between. Really Real Cars was a one-man operation, and the one man was really two stuffed into wrinkled slacks and a short-sleeved shirt the color of putty. I wasn't motivated to buy a car but suddenly I was desperate for whatever antidepressant was currently trendy.

The dealer jogged down the wooden steps of the small

shed that was the dealership's office, rubbing his hands and throwing a practiced grin in our direction.

"Come, come," he said. "You want a car? I have cars. So you are in the right place, yes?" He paused while I nodded. "Great. Good. Fantastic." His gaze scanned us. I could almost hear his inner computer doing the math, trying to figure out how much car I could afford and how he could talk me into one with a higher profit margin. His eyes narrowed. He pointed two finger guns at me. "BMW?"

"I don't think so."

"Mercedes?"

I thought about the money in my bank account and how there wasn't much of it. Grandma had gazillions but it wasn't mine to spend.

"Lower."

"Good thing for you we have many very good cars, great cars, for low prices." He squinted at me. "You look familiar. Did you buy a car from me before?"

Marika was wearing her game face. The whopping she took at the bus stop hadn't slowed her down. "Do you get any repeat customers? Because it looks to me like the people who buy a car from you also buy regrets." She shoved a chip into her mouth, chewed like she was imagining it was his head.

The dealer's face flushed. "My cars are the best. Okay, maybe not the best, but definitely second or third best."

Good enough for me, given that my current ride was a literal ass.

"What's the cheapest one that won't blow up as soon as I drive it off the lot?"

"You want cheap and mechanically sound?" Wind whistled through the gaps in his teeth. "Okay. Come,

come." He touched his hand to my lower back, intending to steer me. Marika slapped it away.

"That is sexual harassment," she said. "I bet you do not touch your male customers the same way."

He gave her the side-eye and tried herding me again, this time without getting handsy. "Here is a good one. Very cheap but very reliable, for a certain value of reliable."

"What does that mean?" Marika barked.

He folded his arms. "A cheap used car is not going to perform as well as a new car. Maybe it will last a year, maybe a month, maybe until you run over a drunken tourist. Who can say?"

"I was hoping you could say," I told him. "These are your cars."

He held his belly and blasted out a good laugh. "You are funny." He gestured to a silver compact, about the size of my recently incinerated Beetle. "You like?"

The paint was freckled with rust. The upholstery was grubby. The driver's seat bore an ominous stain I hoped was the result of a *tzatziki* spill. The sticker on the windshield told me I could afford to drive it off the lot but gas would have to wait until payday, whenever that was. Greek gas is taxed out the wazoo. Most villagers can barely afford to breathe a gas station's air as they slouch past on their donkeys.

"I don't like it but I'll take it."

He grinned and shook his hands at the sky. "Good enough!"

Marika stepped forward. "Wait a minute. I did not have a chance to negotiate yet."

The dealer's shoulders sagged. "Why can I not sell just one car without someone arguing with me? The price is the price. Take it or leave it."

"You do not know who this is, do you?"

Marika was gesturing at me. I really didn't want her gesturing at me because I knew what was about to pop out of her mouth next.

"Marika, no."

But it was too late. Marika's ambition had temporarily blocked her ears. "This is Katerina Makris, Baboulas's granddaughter."

I groaned. Not the dealer. He grinned big and wide like someone had just bought his whole inventory for the sticker prices and thrown in a bonus rotisserie lamb.

"Baboulas's granddaughter, eh?" He wedged his body between the dumpy car and me. "You do not want this car."

"I do want this car," I said. "I really do."

"No."

"Yes."

Finger wag. "No, no. For you I have a much better car." He took off at a fast clip to the far side of the car yard.

"See?" Marika beamed at me. "Now we will get you a much better car at a more affordable price."

"I don't think that's how it's going to work," I told her.

"What do you mean?"

"What does Grandma have?"

"A bad temper, a bad reputation, and lots of guns?"

"Besides those."

She thought. Hard. "Money."

"Lots and lots of money. So much money she could yank all of Greece out of debt."

Lights came on in her head. Bright, stadium lighting. "Oh. This is bad. Why did you let me talk?"

Like I could have stopped her.

The dealer was standing next to a sports car, waving to us. "This is my best deal. This is my own personal car, but it can be yours today. I will give it to you, for money of course."

Cherry red paint. Sporty physique. Gleaming black low-profile tires. I peered at the price sticker. It had too many numbers—more numbers than my account balance. More numbers than most people's balances. I walked around to the front, where a black horse was rearing back on a yellow background.

"This is a Ferrari," I said.

"It is a Ferrari," the dealer said. "I bought it from Italy myself and drove it back."

"So you're saying it has a lot of kilometers on it?"

His grin dimmed.

Marika looked way too happy. "You drove a Ferrari once, remember?"

Her memory and my memory were not drawn on the same bank. "I sat in a Ferrari once before I realized I couldn't drive it."

"That is almost the same thing," she said.

Not even a little bit. Ferraris are built for rich people who know about gears other than Drive, Neutral, and Reverse. All those numbers were confusing. And what was that extra pedal for anyway?

"You should get it," Marika said. "Red is our color."

"Who are you?" the dealer asked her.

"I used to be her bodyguard, but now I am an apprentice spy."

The dealer's eye twitched. "Bodyguard. Spy," he said weakly.

There was laughter behind us. I whipped around to see Hera emerging from behind one of the old junkers. She was dressed in skin-tight camouflage fatigues, blond hair tucked up into a dark green beret.

"What are you supposed to be?" I asked her.

"Crazy Bibi-bo," Marika said.

"Bibi-bo?"

"Greek Barbie," Marika explained. "She had a boyfriend named Tzon Tzon. Hera probably has a Tzon Tzon that she stuffs up her——"

Hera shot her in the face with a dirty look. "Finish that sentence and I will cut off your head, making your husband the world's happiest widower." Her attention swiveled back to me. "Now that I have some spare time, I plan to find out what you are up to."

"Where I come from we call that stalking."

"We don't have that here," Hera said. "You could save yourself some time and trouble by telling me what your plans are."

"Right now? Trying to buy a car."

"For what purpose? A car bomb maybe? Or are you going to drive it into a large group of people, possibly school children?" Her cheeks were flushed, her eyes bright. Someone was getting her kicks fantasizing about carnage.

"Neither? I was thinking I'd use it to drive to work and back, like a regular person. That's what most people who buy cars do. Sometimes I might get all wild and crazy and take it shopping."

"Your job at the morgue? That is convenient, yes?"

I tilted my head sideways. "Convenient?"

"Your family is responsible for so many dead bodies, and here you are working at a morgue." She squinted at me. "Do you know what I think?"

"No, and I don't want to. Your head is a disturbing place and I don't want to go there." I figured her head was stuffed with flying monkeys and witches who dug sparkly shoes.

She ignored me. "I think you are destroying evidence at the morgue--evidence of murder. Or maybe you are using the bodies to smuggle contraband. Do you know how much heroin you can fit in the human rectum?"

Something told me she knew. Suddenly I felt queasy. I looked at Marika. "Do you have your guns?"

"Only one, because I am a spy now and not a body-guard. And I do not think it is a very good gun because it is so small." She rooted around in her enormous shoulder bag and pulled out a jar of Merenda, Greece's Nutella. "I carry it in here because otherwise it might get lost. A mother has to carry a lot of things in her bag."

We gawked at her.

"No guns," the dealer said. Sweat dripped from his temples. Wet stains radiated from his armpits. "This is a gun-free zone. We can negotiate just fine without weapons, yes?"

Marika unscrewed the lid, tapped the jar on her open palm. A tiny adorable gun fell out, as benevolent and wee as a kitten. She waved it at Hera, who looked unimpressed.

"The only thing you could shoot with that thing is a toe."

"Is that a challenge? Marika said. "I like a challenge. I have too many children, another one on the way, and I am hungry. So keep talking."

Hera rolled her eyes and turned her back on Marika. A huge Greek insult.

"You and your family are hiding something," she said to me.

"Like what?"

"I don't know, but what I do know is that Baby Dimitri has gone missing."

"Huh," I said. "How about that."

"Do you know where he is?"

"Have you tried his house?"

Her voice sharpened. "Why? Is that where your family kidnapped him?"

The dealer stopped gawking at Hera for a moment. "Are you going to buy this car?" he asked me.

I ignored him. "Kidnapped him? Why would my family kidnap Baby Dimitri?"

"You tell me. Maybe your family does not like competition."

"We didn't kidnap him or anyone else." I thought about it a moment. "We definitely didn't kidnap him."

"The car," the dealer said.

"I do not trust you," Hera said, posing with one hand on her hip. "I'm following you until I get answers."

The dealer was getting testy. "The only answer I want is are you going to buy this car or not?"

Marika whipped around, teeny tiny gun in hand. "How many times have I told you to stop flushing your brothers' heads in the toilet, eh? Get your own drinks and snacks. DO I LOOK LIKE A SERVANT? DO I?" She squeezed off a couple of rounds, hitting the Ferrari dead center in the hood and shattering the driver's side window, taking out the passenger side window on the way through.

The dealer burst into tears. "My car!"

"Marika," I said calmly, "you just shot a Ferrari."

Face worried, she gnawed on her lip. "Give me a moment to let that sink in."

Hera threw back her head and laughed. "Wow, you people are crazy. I cannot believe you are successful criminals. Calling you incompetent would be a compliment."

Yeah, I'd had about enough of her crap. I went rifling through my cross-body bag until my fingers touched what felt like a tube of lipstick. Not lipstick. The tube was a miniature stun gun that packed more punch than its bigger cousins.

Hera grinned. "Let me guess, someone gave you a gun, too? You know that is against the law, yes?"

"Grandma won't let me have a gun. But I do have this." I shoved the incognito stun gun against her ribs. Lucky for me she didn't see it; it was hers, and it was on permanent loan after I found it in her handbag, which was inconveniently wrapped around a dead woman's neck at the time. Jeez, why was everything so complicated here?

ZAP.

Hera collapsed in a camouflage puddle.

I nudged her with my toe. She was out.

"Please tell me you will buy the car," the dealer said, blubbering.

Marika's hands went on her hips. The gun was back in its jar and hiding in her bag. "How much do you want for it now?"

He stuck his finger through the hole in the hood. "With this damage, it is next to worthless."

I dropped the stun gun into my bag. "How much is that in euros?"

Chapter 6

I PARKED the Ferrari outside the compound's garage and honked the horn, restraining my laughter as the cousin on duty's mouth sagged open, his cigarette plummeting to the ground.

"Grandma will kill you if she sees you smoking near her cars," I called out. I could do that without rolling the window down because the Italian sports car's windows were currently tiny pebbles gathered in the footwells.

He approached the door. "Is that a Ferrari?"

"Does it look like one?"

"It is hard to tell without windows and a bullet hole in the hood."

I angled out and went around to help Marika. She was a lot of woman to begin with, and pregnancy was already adding extra cushions to her comfortable figure. The cousin and I each grabbed one of her hands and pulled. Marika popped out with a giggle.

"I love this car. But I think I would like it better without the holes and maybe some windows." She gave the cousin a meaningful look.

"I suppose someone could fix it," he said slowly.

"By tomorrow?" Marika said.

He winced. "The glass, sure. The body work will take longer."

"Good enough." I slapped the keys into his hand. "See you in the morning."

Marika and I set off for the compound's courtyard.

"Hey, Katerina," my cousin called out. "What does something like this cost?"

A grin broke out all over my face. "You wouldn't believe me if I told you."

———

Marika bustled home, leaving me at a loose end. I hung out in the compound for a few minutes, dishing out cuddles to the dozens of dogs the family kept, and nodding at the cats. My goat ambled over, butted me with his head. My goat didn't have a name because all those years ago when I fantasied about having a pet I only thought up names for the usual pets. Goats never made the list. Neither did cows, and I had one of those, too. Come to think of it, I was now the proud of three unusual pets, all of them nameless.

"I really need to do something about that," I told the cats, who were judging me silently from their lofty positions. I made a note for myself on my phone so I'd remember.

Hera's words popped into my head. She mentioned Baby Dimitri was missing. Who else had noticed his disappearance? And who was he running from? An old enemy, yeah, but I wanted specifics. What if someone else with an exploding head showed up? I needed to be prepared.

Preparation was easier with information, and my information well was bone dry.

With Grandma in Athens, there was no one to tell me to leave the room like a preschooler on a sugar high, so I walked into a broom closet at the back of the compound on the bottom floor and turned on the light. Sounds weird, I know, but that was the dungeon's most accessible entrance. There were two others, but this was closest. I rode the escalator down, let myself into the scary, medieval dungeon, then tapped the passcode for the swanky real dungeon inside.

"I have two questions," Monobrow called out. "Who is that and did you bring *loukoumia*?"

"It's Katerina, and I don't have any *loukoumia*."

He chuckled. "Because it is you, and only because it is you, I can live with that."

"You'll have to, won't you?"

The chuckle morphed into a full-bodied laugh—and he was a man with a lot of body, especially around the middle. "What are you doing down here, Katerina?"

"I came to talk to Baby Dimitri."

"Okay. I will eavesdrop, but I can pretend I am not listening if you like."

"Why bother?"

"That is what I always say." His voice had a smile in it.

I knocked on Baby Dimitri's door. "*Kyrios* Baby Dimitri? It's Katerina."

No answer.

"Maybe he's in the bathroom or sleeping," I said.

"Sleeping," Monobrow said. "That man does *kaka* with the door open, and he talks while he does it. Talks! The last thing I want to do is talk to a man who is filling his toilet with *skata*. Very uncivilized."

Knock, knock.

More nothing. It was like trying to communicate with Xander.

"Is he in there?" I asked Monobrow.

"Where else would he be?"

The wily, greasy mobster could be anywhere. Maybe he was slinking around the courtyard after picking the lock again. Could be he was taking a walk through the property's substantial orchard. If anyone could shimmy out a pipe like Tooms from the *X-Files* it was Baby Dimitri. Probably he was crafting a saliva-and-paper nest in the basement right now.

"I don't think he's in here." Panic rippled through me. Baby Dimitri was a voluntary guest not a prisoner, but he was self-admittedly in mortal danger. What if someone had got to him? Despite his flaws—and he had a gazillion—I liked the old gangster. Plus his shoe shop always stocked shoes I liked.

I amped up the knocking and threw in some hollering.

Nothing.

"Keys," I said. "Who's got the keys?"

Monobrow's door flap rattled. A ring of keys fell out.

"You've got the keys?" I said, disbelieving.

"No. You have got the keys." He chuckled at his joke.

I stooped, then I got down to the business of figuring out which key opened this particular door. It took me a moment to realize they were numbered. Duh. Grandma was OCD-lite. No surprise that even her keys were labeled.

With a click, I entered Baby Dimitri's room. His suitcases were on the floor, where Xander had left them. He hadn't bothered to unpack, although one was open. Underwear, undershirts, and white shoes. The bed was folded military-neat and ready for quarter-bouncing time.

There was no sign of Baby Dimitri himself.

I walked back out.

"He's not here."

"Maybe he left," Monobrow said, "although this time I did not hear him leave. He thinks he is very clever but last night I heard him sneaking out of here."

Monobrow was definitely on the ball.

"He came to us for protection. Why wouldn't he let us protect him if this was all his idea?"

"Dimitri is a cunning and secretive old *malakas*. Maybe he slithered down the toilet and out the sewer."

As far as theories went, that wasn't actually bad. It wasn't exactly good either. Plus I'd had it first with the *X-Files* angle.

"But why would he do that?"

"Never underestimate an animal backed into a corner."

Thanks for that, Mr. Miyagi. I wondered if he had anything he needed me to wax on and off, other than the bushy eyebrow stretched across his forehead. "Who was he hiding from?"

"I do not know."

"Beep. Wrong. I know you know."

"It is ancient history, Katerina. Leave it alone."

"Not exactly ancient if Baby Dimitri is running from the same person now, is it?"

A soft chuckle. "There is no fooling you, is there?"

Actually, that wasn't true. My former fiancé had fooled me good. For example, I thought he liked me. Instead, he preferred penis. I couldn't compete with that, not with this innie.

"You may as well tell me, otherwise I'm going to sit here and pester you until you do."

"You can try."

"Great. I love a challenge."

I planted myself in front of his door, turned on my

phone, and stuck in a pair of ear buds. I opened a karaoke app. No one would hear the music except me. But the singing? I was totally going to nail this torture thing.

"Save yourself while you still can," I warned him. Then the first few bars of *Bohemian Rhapsody* played. I channeled my inner Freddie Mercury and gave it all I had, which was painful and excruciating. Poor dead Freddie would have been horrified, but he was such a decent dude probably he would have given me an encouraging thumbs up anyway.

"I love that song but that is the second worst thing I have ever heard in my life," Monobrow said.

I paused. "What was the first?"

"Your grandmother's singing."

"Must run in the family."

I fired up Led Zeppelin. *Stairway to Heaven*.

"Make it stop," Monobrow cried out. "Please."

"Are you going to tell me what I want to know?"

"No. I promised."

"It's your hearing loss," I said, launching into Fergie's *My Humps*.

"You are a monster!"

"It's not easy being me. Who is Baby Dimitri hiding from?"

"I cannot tell you."

"Why not?"

"Because you will go after him if I do."

"Hello, this is me we're talking about. I used to be a bill collector and now I work at a morgue. I don't chase people, unless they've just mugged me or they're waving a gun at my friends. Or if they're Jason Momoa."

"You will," he said darkly, "because you are like your grandmother. He will give you a reason and you will be gone."

My eyes rolled back in my head so hard I almost got a glimpse of my own brain. "Where is Kyria Mela when you need her?"

Monobrow wasn't moved. "Not even that woman can make me talk. She is terrifying, yes, and very good with pliers, but next to your grandmother she is nothing."

"How about if I bring you a crate of *loukoumia*?" Did they sell it by the crate? I could find out.

"Not for all the *loukoumia* in Greece. You are wasting your breath, my girl."

I needed fresh air and I needed it fast. Good thing I had a fast car. After a brief Madonna mash up, I left Monobrow to think about his sins of omission and hoofed it to the garage, where my Ferrari already had two new windows.

"Wow, you guys work fast," I said to my cousin.

"We are magic. We have to be."

Otherwise Grandma might kill them. Okay, she wouldn't really—probably--but they didn't know that.

I jumped in my new car, fired it up. Glee and terror took turns wrestling to be the dominant emotion. I couldn't drive a Ferrari. But look at me: I had a Ferrari.

Now, how did I do this again? Foot on clutch. Gear in first. Slowly ease foot off clutch.

The sports car bunny hopped forward, then it stalled.

I stuck my head out my new window. "You aren't laughing at me, are you?"

"No, but I am recording this for Takis' YouTube channel."

Of course he was. This was a conspiracy and they were all in on it.

My eyes closed. I could do this. Countless people— people less coordinated than me—had mastered the art of the standard transmission. All I needed was divine intervention. Given my shaky relationship with the Big Guy upstairs, my expectations were low.

Bunny hop.

Stall.

A shadow fell over the hood. It moved, and then the passenger door opened. Xander angled his body in. He leaned back in the seat. He looked better in my new car than I did. Probably he even knew how to drive it. Here was my divine intervention but it looked like the devil, so naturally I was suspicious.

"Do you want to drive?" I said helplessly.

Xander got out, came around to my side, gave me his hand so I could make a semi-elegant exit. We swapped seats. He worked some kind of driving voodoo and soon we were out on the open road, speeding to God only knew where.

I leaned my head back on the headrest and watched him shift up and down between gears, following Mount Pelion's tight twists and turns. There was something seriously sexy about watching the man's forearms as he shifted gears. My mouth dried up. I closed my eyes, purposely avoiding the view. "I don't care where we're going, just go there."

He went. That was the nice thing about Xander: he did stuff without a bunch of questions. I opened one eye. Still sexy. I closed it again. Xander was one of those problems a woman needed occasionally, but not too often otherwise she would wind up with a urinary tract infection.

After a while, Xander cut the engine. The purring stopped. Wherever we were, there we were.

Big field. Trees sparsely littered around the edges. Not a building in sight. Or people. Or anything. Just me and my new wheels. Oh—and Xander. He was here, too.

"What is this place?"

Xander didn't say a word. He got out, came around to my side, tugged me out and dusted me off. Out of his coat pocket came a wand thingy. Yowza. It wasn't a sex toy, was it? In the dark it definitely resembled something designed to show someone a good time, if they liked that kind of thing. Sometimes I liked that kind of thing, especially after wine.

He started at one end of the car and began running down the length of the body on one side. Then he did the same thing with the other.

So ... not a sex toy. More like some kind of bug detector.

Disappointment stabbed me. I shooed it away with a question.

"Are you going to do me next?"

That was a yes. He ran the wand over me, then shoved it back in his pocket. He grinned, wide and lazy and sexy as all get-out.

"Right now, that Ferrari is too much car for you. So I'm going to teach you to drive that thing," he said in actual, out-loud words. He held the door open for me. "Get in."

Xander's voice was exactly what you'd expect: deep, warm, sensual. Every time he spoke I felt like a hard cookie dunked in hot coffee.

"Not that I'm not grateful, but why teach me?"

"Everyone should know how to drive a standard." His grin widened. "Plus you look good in a Ferrari."

"Will there be a test at the end?"

"Do you want a test?"

"Tests aren't really my thing."

"No tests," he promised.

I spent the next hour embarrassing myself. Xander stayed cool, calm, relaxed. "Let's do it again," he said as the Ferrari lurched forward and crapped out for the hundredth time.

To my astonishment, the bunny hops soon slowed. Somehow—probably sorcery was involved—I eventually managed to slide through the gears without Xander weeping for the Italian-made machinery.

Sometime later, he stopped me. We got out of the car. It was one of those clear Mount Pelion nights where the stars appeared to be within plucking distance. I stretched. Yawned. A headache was blooming behind my eyes and my leg was cramping from all the clutch work.

My discomfort didn't go unnoticed. "Let's walk it off," Xander said.

We traipsed a short distance across the field. That short distance evolved into a longer one. Despite the faint whisper of crisp air and the close proximity of the stars, the night felt thick and ominous. Or maybe it was me. With Grandma gone, a man murdered, and Baby Dimitri on the run, I felt like a tiger was crouched behind the next corner, waiting to bite off my face.

"How bad are the winters here?" I asked Xander. We were standing on one of the mountain's edges, overlooking a blanket of darkness, with the occasional sequin stitched onto the fabric.

"Do you like snow?"

"I like snow when I don't have to go out in it."

"One winter, there was so much snow the villages below went without electricity for days."

"That's a lot of snow."

"Some winters Makria does not get any."

I quickly flipped the switch on the conversation, hoping to shock an answer out of him. "Who is Baby Dimitri hiding from?"

Xander grinned down at me. "Nice try."

"Thanks. I was hoping it would be more fruitful. Or any amount of fruitful."

"You have a lot to learn, grasshopper."

"Yeah, like who Baby Dimitri is hiding from and who shot off that poor man's head yesterday."

"A bad man."

Like I didn't know that. Nice people didn't go around shooting people in the head for fun. "What's his name?"

"That is enough for tonight," he said, cutting me off before I pitched more questions at him. "It's getting late."

"Can't handle any more of my driving, huh?"

His lips quirked. "There's nothing wrong with your driving that practice can't fix."

The night was cool but his approval was a warm, fleecy blanket. We walked back to the waiting Ferrari.

Xander's hand snapped out. His warm fingers clamped my wrist.

"Wait," he said.

Something cold tiptoed up my spine. A worried Xander meant trouble.

"What?"

He moved forward without me, going straight for the sports car's hood.

Holy cannoli, had someone stuck a bomb to my car? No. Obviously not, because Xander was raising the hood.

"Virgin Mary," I said. "Someone stole the engine!"

Xander looked at me.

"Just kidding. I know it's in the back."

Like the original VW Beetles, the Ferrari's engine was definitely in the back. That didn't mean the trunk at the front wasn't empty—oh no, I wasn't that lucky.

There was nothing to see here.

Except the dead body.

"Not sure if you noticed," I said politely, "but there's a dead person in my trunk."

"It's more than that. It's a message."

Greece didn't have the highest literacy rate in the world but still I expected better. Sign language. Hieroglyphics. Interpretive dance. Possibly it was a message, but not a very good one because I didn't have a clue what it meant, except hey, this guy really needed a trip to the morgue and possibly close inspection by a cop.

"A message? Why would anyone send me a message like this? I didn't do anything."

"It's not for you," Xander said. He reached into the trunk and withdrew a small plastic box the size of a pack of playing cards.

"Who is it for then? Wait, I bet it's for Grandma. This seems like the kind of message she's used to getting."

He held up the box. It was a cassette tape. Another one. "It's for me."

Chapter 7

"THAT'S NOT the first cassette tape I've seen lately," I said. "Or even the second." My voice didn't have the hysterical edge it did a few weeks ago when someone sent Grandma a severed penis, followed by other body parts. That's because this was the world I was living in now, one where people sent corpses instead of text messages and bouquets of dicks instead of flowers.

"How many have you seen?"

"Counting this one? Three. Who is doing this, and what do the tapes mean, besides the fact that the sender loves 80s pop. It is 80s pop, isn't it?"

Xander glanced at the cover. "Hair metal from the 80s. Tell me about the third tape."

He didn't waste any time bundling me into the Ferrari while I spilled the brief beans on the tape from the morgue. Despite my hour or so of lessons, Xander took the wheel and I let him. My hands shook in my lap. For Xander or not, why had someone stuffed a body in my car, and when did they have a chance?

"Someone must have followed us up here and placed

the body while we were walking." Xander was reading my mind. I pictured him naked. He didn't react. So not a real mind reader then. Good to know.

"Tell me the truth. Who is this guy? Is he the same one who has Baby Dimitri on the run?"

"Yes." Xander glanced over. "You okay?"

"No. Does it ever get any easier? Dealing with crime, finding bodies, that sort of thing, I mean."

He went silent for a moment, and I thought this was it, end of our verbal communication until the next time he got a wild hair to talk to me.

Then he said, "No." His eyes were on the road.

"What now? Do we call the police? Wait—you are the police. So who do we call?"

"Kyria Katerina."

"Grandma? She's in Athens with my father."

He pulled out onto the road. "I know."

"So who is that in my trunk?"

No answer.

"Are you going to tell me?"

No answer.

"Are you going to tell me this creep's name?"

Nothing.

I slumped back against the seat. "That's so 1940s, that thing you do where you clam up when you don't want to answer a question. It's toxic the way men do that. Keep everything bottled up and one day you'll flip out and shoot up a post office or wind up with a drinking problem."

More silence.

"You know I'm right."

Xander gave the Ferrari more gas. He broke the silence. "I'm taking you home."

"Then what?"

"Then nothing. You stay away from me, that's what."

"Why? What's going on? Who is the dead guy? Why won't you tell me?"

His lips quirked. "That's another thing I like about you."

"What?"

"That thing you do where you don't blindly accept orders."

"I'm not used to taking them. I wasn't raised in your world."

"No," he said. "You're weren't. The dead man is nobody—not to me, anyway. To somebody he is probably everything."

"So, an innocent?"

"Close enough."

He went silent and stayed that way for the rest of the drive back to the compound. When we pulled up, Takis was waiting. He was holding a military duffel bag in one hand and a large coffee in the other. He set down the bag long enough to open my door.

"What's in the bag?" I asked him.

"Tools." His eyes cut to Xander. "Where is the body?"

Yikes. I knew what Takis could do with an axe and a sack.

Xander popped the trunk. Takis peered in. "This will not be easy. A Ferrari's trunk is small and that is a lot of man." He set the bag on the ground, unzipped, pulled out a pry bar.

I let out a sigh of relief.

"What?" Takis grinned. "What did you think I was going to do with these tools?"

"Cut him into bite-sized pieces," I said truthfully.

"The cutting comes later. First I have to get him out."

Acid bubbled in my stomach.

Takis wedged the pry bar between the trunk and the

man's shoulder. "You should leave." He gave an almighty heave. The body didn't move.

"Are you kidding me? I have to watch this. What if my luggage gets stuck one day?" Things had definitely changed since I wound up in Greece and started working hard for the money in the city morgue.

"I cannot believe you have a Ferrari," Takis said. He heaved again. The dead man wasn't going anywhere.

"Your wife helped me get it." Not mentioning the gun and the subsequent shooting seemed prudent.

"*Gamo ton kerato sou*," he swore. Why Greeks loved doing the horizontal mambo with a horn, probably I would never know, but for some reasons horns featured heavily in their colorful sexual descriptions. "Marika never helped me get a Ferrari."

"Maybe if you let her get a driver's license she would."

Laughter roared out of him. "Let Marika drive? You are a joker."

"Why not?"

"Because she is a woman. Women do not have a temperament for driving, especially not my wife."

Could he be more of a chauvinist pig? "We'll see, won't we?"

"What do you mean?"

I went into full hands-on-hips mode to show him I meant business. "I'm going to give Marika driving lessons."

Takis yelped and bore down extra hard on the lever. The corpse's arm popped out. "If you teach my wife to drive, I will kill you."

"*Tsk, tsk*. I'll tell Grandma."

"Heh. I did not mean the murder kind of killing."

Like there was another kind? I raised my eyebrow at him. He responded with a nervous cough and got busy yanking on the dead man's arm. When that didn't work, he shoved the lever under the corpse's other shoulder.

Five minutes later, the three of us were looking down at the dead man, who was laid out on the compound's cobblestones.

"Good thing he was not shot," Takis said. "Blood is hard to get out of upholstery. Normally we have to strip it out and replace it." He nudged the dead man with his boot. "You know him?"

The guy on the ground was thirty-something, with a recently self-inflicted buzzcut. The cut was uneven, and in places he'd stuck Band-Aids to the 'do. Olive skin. Crooked nose like he'd won second place in a fistfight. He was naked from the waist up and camouflaged from the waist down. He was wearing military boots and loved My Little Pony, according to the tattoo on his chest. His heart belonged to somepony named Twilight Sparkle.

"No."

"I never saw him before either," Takis said. He shoved the pry bar back into the bag and pulled out some kind of electric saw.

"You can't cut him up with that!"

Marika's husband grinned. "You are right. A reciprocating saw always chokes on the bone."

Thunk!

I passed out. I woke up a moment later to Takis slapping my cheek.

"I'm fine," I said, not fine at all.

Xander scooped me up and set me on my feet. My head felt light and my knees were weak. Corpses are one thing, but cutting them into fun-sizes pieces is a different matter.

"Why do you have to cut him up?"

Xander and Takis traded loaded glances.

"Easier to burn," Takis said. "This way we can stack the body parts like logs."

"Why do you have to burn him at all? Why can't you call the police?"

Takis laughed. "'*Yiasou*, Kyrios Policeman, can you come and get the corpse that was in my car? By the way, my grandmother is Baboulas, but I am sure that is not related.' Or maybe you could call your little friend Nikos and spend hours answering questions. I know you and Nikos had a little lovers' quarrel so I bet that would be very uncomfortable for you both."

He had a point, and it was even a good one.

"It wasn't exactly a quarrel," I said defensively.

"This way is better for everybody," Takis said, "except maybe this one, whoever he is.

———

Takis took off in the direction of the garage, leaving me with Xander and the dead guy.

"You really don't know him?" I said to Xander. "But you knew the tape was for you?"

Xander didn't do anything at first, then he nodded.

"Did it have your name on it?"

Chin up-down. *No.*

"Whoever killed this guy and stuffed him into my car, are they coming after you?"

Xander shrugged.

Was that a yes? A no? Oh, my freaking God, who was this bad guy? My sympathetic nervous system wasn't happy about any of this.

Takis rolled up in a black van. He and Xander loaded the dead man onto a rug and rolled him up.

"I thought they only did that in movies," I said.

Neither man looked back. They jumped into the van—Xander took the driver's seat—and sped off, tires kicking up dust as they hit the long driveway.

I had nowhere to be, a head full of questions, and my new car was a dumping ground for the dead. What to do?

Carbs. Carbs were simple and sweet, and the sugar would kick my brain into gear or slow it down to a stupor.

Grandma wasn't home but her hovel was unlocked. I let myself into the kitchen, where half a dozen containers were lined up on the counter, all of them brimming with baked goods. Twisty *koulourakia*, *finikia*, *kourabiethes* steeped in powdered sugar, and other things I didn't have names for. But if they had sugar they had to be good, right?

I loaded up my plate with one of everything, then helped myself to the kitchen table, where I checked in on the Crooked Noses Message Board, a forum dedicated to organized crime aficionados. The Greek board was hopping with the news that Baby Dimitri had vanished. The godfather might be a humble—*cough, cough*—shoe and souvenir salesman but he was also a vicious mobster of ill repute. Naturally the Crooked Noses' minds turned first to murder. Most of them were convinced Baby Dimitri was lying in a ditch somewhere, gutted like one of the oilier fishes.

For all I knew, he was.

My mouth stopped. Here I was fretting over a missing person when I could easily roll the compound's security footage and get a glimpse of how Baby Dimitri made his stealthy and unannounced exit, and which direction he'd taken after his crafty escape. As soon as I was done with all these pastries that's exactly what I would do. I didn't think Grandma would want me leaving crumbs in her sensitive computer surveillance equipment.

In the meantime, I went poking through the message

board's archives. Before today I'd never had a reason to pick through Baby Dimitri's past. He was just a curiosity, one of Greece's colorful creatures ... who also happened to be more crooked than a dog's hind leg. Now the cat hair in my DNA was wiggling, and I was itching to know more about his past. Maybe the Crooked Noses would know whom he was running from. They seemed to know everything, even when they were completely wrong. The message board also had its own wiki site, an encyclopedia on the subject of organized crime. Grandma's page was longer than Santa's Nice and Naughty lists.

Oooh, I had a page, too.

Was I supposed to be flattered or offended? Ugh. Someone had thoughtfully linked to Takis' YouTube page, where you could watch me yell on a chair and make obscene hand gestures at a bus driver on repeat. Good thing I loved Marika and didn't want her children to grow up without a father-shaped thing in their lives.

Baby Dimitri's page wasn't much shorter than Grandma's. He ran an empire of crime, focusing on drugs, prostitution, strip clubs, organ sales, and a growing interest in counterfeiting and other financial crimes. His siblings were all dead, rumored to have been eliminated by Baby Dimitri himself, who didn't want to share his mountain of money. He had a half sister and nephew, although I wasn't sure about the half-sister anymore, on account of how she was a murdering, porn-peddling nut. As for the nephew, I hadn't seen Donk since he busted out of the dungeon, where he'd been hiding out because he thought someone would kill him for banging Litsa. The loon who'd killed Litsa was his mother, so he was probably safe there.

Now here was something interesting.

Baby Dimitri had a wife, although she hadn't been seen for thirty years. Her whereabouts were currently unknown.

Rumor had it she lived in Piraeus—or used to. The couple's marriage had produced one child, a son, who died when he was an infant. I wondered if the wife had left after they'd lost their child. Only a rock-solid relationship could withstand that kind of tragedy.

As far as old enemies who were supposed-to-be-dead-but-weren't-really went, Baby Dimitri's wiki page was a dry haul.

I crammed a piece of *koulouraki* into my mouth and chewed.

My message board inbox said I had one new message. My username is FarFarAwayGirl—a silly name, thought up on the fly. *Makria* is Greek for a distance far away, so I thought I was being clever at the time. In reality it's a ginormous clue, waiting for someone with too much time and an endless supply of Mountain Dew and Doritos at their disposal to go digging. I have one "friend" on the board, another poster who calls themself BangBang. He or she seems like the levelheaded sort, who often wades into the fray with a dose of common sense or a handful of more accurate facts. The waiting message was from Bang-Bang, who was currently online.

You won't find anything in the wiki.

Wait--how did BangBang know what I was doing on the board?

I shot off a message, asking that same question.

The reply came back fast.

I own the board.

Boy, oh boy. Not good.

A bead of sweat rolled down my forehead. My heart picked up its pace. I logged out as fast as I could. I wasn't any kind of computer whizz, but even I knew if BangBang owned the Crooked Noses Message Board, he or she would have access to things like IP addresses. May as well stick a big red pin in my forehead, with a note declaring HERE I AM, AND BY THE WAY, I'M BABOULAS'S GRAND-DAUGHTER.

There had to be a way to cruise the site without giving away my location and identity. Probably Grandma had something like a Virtual Private Network installed in her underground bunker. For now, it could wait. I was more interested in the compound's security camera footage.

I washed and dried my plate and fork, and returned them to their proper places. When I was done, I went out to the front yard, stood on a particular area of the concrete and pressed the invisible button that lowered me into Grandma's control center. From here, Grandma could see the public areas of the compound, as well as any number of strategic locations around the country and possibly the world. Aunt Rita had showed me how to pull up older footage, so within minutes I was watching foot traffic to and from the dungeon. Spoiler alert: there wasn't any outside of the usual meal deliveries and housekeeping. Baby Dimitri was diminutive—not that I'd say that to his face—but even he couldn't fit on a dinner tray or in a small bundle of sheets. According to the cameras he had never left but he wasn't there.

I messaged Grandma.

Is there a camera inside the dungeon?

Why?

Baby Dimitri isn't there.

Long pause. Then: *What else is going on that I do not know about?*

Someone left a corpse in my new Ferrari.

My phone rang.

"Where did you get a Ferrari?" Grandma wanted to know.

"Where does anyone get a Ferrari? From a car dealer."

Gus was in the locker room, inspecting a new arrival when I rocked up. With all the long-term residents moved to the mortuary or already placed in the ground, the thermostat was hovering on the cool side of normal, which meant I could shed the thick winter coat. A light cardigan would suffice. I didn't have one of those but it was on the list.

"Who is that?" I peered at the deceased's face. Seventies, or in the ballpark. Skin like a mistreated leather jacket, which was unavoidable in parts of Greece, thanks to the heat and salt air. His scalp was visible between thick salt-and-pepper strands.

"No identification. An old woman found him this morning like this, outside a shoe shop."

"Like what? Dead?"

He whipped back the pale green sheet. The dead man's penis was stuck in a Mr. Potato Head. "She loaded him onto her donkey and brought him to the hospital."

"Argh! Give a woman some warning."

Gus was muttering himself, shaking his head. "Who does that to a man?"

"An angry woman?"

"Very angry," Gus said, covering up the dead man. "Probably he cheated on her. Why else would you put *Kyrios Patata Kefala* on his *poutsa*?"

When Todd cheated on me I definitely considered whacking off his wiener with an array of household objects such as plastic spoons and slivers of paper—castration by paper cut would be horrifying and painful and h-i-l-a-r-i-o-u-s—but shoving Mr. Happy into Mr. Potato Head was a new level of twisted.

Gus slid the dead man back into the chilled locker with a metallic clang. "The police will be here soon. They have questions and I need to have answers or a good excuse about why I do not have those answers."

My heart didn't technically skip any beats because otherwise I'd be passing out and maybe even dying, but it did a good imitation of a stopped pump.

"Which cops?"

"Probably Detective Melas and Constable Pappas. You are friends, yes?"

Oh. Great. That wouldn't be at all awkward.

"Um … would you look at the time? I'm going to do some work before you fire me," I said, without any real clue what my actual work was besides answering phones. Now that the extra bodies were gone and I wasn't required to yell at orderlies doing their jobs, I was questioning my usefulness here.

"Everything okay, boss?" Elias asked. He was sitting behind the reception desk, arms folded, body relaxed, not missing a thing except the dead guy in the back room with a Mr. Potato Head on his wiener.

"Really?" he said when I mentioned it. "*Kyrios Patata Kefala*?"

"A vintage one, by the looks of it. Say, do you know what I'm supposed to do?"

"About what?"

I gestured at everything. "My job. What am I supposed to do when I'm not answering phones? Gus doesn't need me to chase away new arrivals now."

He took stock of the office, then shrugged. "You could file something. Receptionists do filing."

The filing cabinet. It had an odor like old feet and *casu marzu* cheese from Sardinia. Something was in there-- something more insidious than paper and yellow manila folders.

"I was afraid you would say that."

"At least pretend to file something and look busy."

I glanced around. The place was tidy. The paper inbox was empty. Conversely, the wastebasket was overflowing with what looked ominously like vanquished paperwork.

"Probably I should file this." One piece of paper at a time, I emptied the wastebasket, flattening each piece into file-able shape.

Gus stuck his head out. "Do not throw that out."

"I didn't. It was already in the garbage."

"I had to put it somewhere. The filing cabinets are full."

On some other planet, that made sense.

"Should I reorganize the filing cabinet?"

Gus sagged against the wall, relief spreading across his face. "Please, I am begging you."

"Probably that's a good idea because there's a weird smell coming from them."

"It has been that way for a year," Gus said. "Maybe longer. It was not so noticeable when this place was colder, but now that it is warming up it will become a problem again." He vanished. The little guy really needed a bell around his neck.

The filing cabinets ran from ceiling to floor, taking up reception's entire back wall, because parts of Greece were still mired in some long lost decade where a single computer filled a space the size of a gym and had the processing power of an electric can opener. These filing cabinets weren't ironically retro.

I tugged one open, peered inside, tried to close it again. My full bodyweight wasn't doing the job.

"That's a problem," I said.

Elias grinned. "Big problem."

Whoever had done the filing before hadn't done the filing before. Their idea of filing was to stand on other side of the lobby and drop kick paperwork into the open drawers. Then they had forced them shut, possibly with a crowbar.

Christ with a pet canary.

"This is my job, right?" I said hopelessly.

Elias moved to make two coffees, bless him. "I think so, boss."

I rolled up my sleeves, then rolled them down again because it was still chilly down here. "How hard can it be?"

Chapter 8

I WAS on my hands and knees sorting paperwork into alphabetical piles when Detective Melas and Constable Pappas walked out of the elevator.

"Is that *sovraka*?" Pappas said, squinting at the pile.

It was underwear—traditional Greek underwear—and someone had filed it, for some inexplicable reason, under *omega*, the last letter of the Greek alphabet. Traditional Greek underwear was one small step up from Mormon's magic underthings. It was big. It was baggy. It was all encompassing. I wasn't sure whether to file it under *sigma* for *sovraka* or toss it in the hospital's Lost and Found—if it had a Lost and Found. If this were my underwear I would lose it on purpose.

"If you think that's weird, Gus has a guy out back with Mr. Potato Head stuck on his *poutsa*," I said.

The cops looked at me.

For crying out loud, I'd forgotten to translate. "*Kyrios Patata Kefala.*"

Pappas winced. The constable is a big barrel of a guy. Stoic is probably his middle name, and he always has food stains on his shirt. I used to think he was a messy eater until I met his wife, Irini. Irini snacks while she irons; and because Pappas adores his tiny kewpie doll of a wife, he cheerfully tolerates the food stains. His wife is also Hera's sister—allegedly. They share the same parents but I'm not convinced; Hera is at least part Gorgon.

"A real *Kyrios Patata Kefala*?" he asked.

"Whoever stuck it on there must have cut a hole …"

Pappas paled.

Not Melas. The detective was focused on that wall over there. He inclined his head. "Let's go," he said to his best friend and regular partner in solving crime.

They vanished down the hallway. I heard Gus greeting them, then low, objective voices.

"*Gamo tin putana sou*," Melas said suddenly. Nothing objective about that. Someone had just got an eyeful of Mr. Potato Head and thought cursing sex workers would take away some of the mental sting.

"You would think he'd never seen a *Kyrios Patata Kefala* on a *poutsa* before," I told Elias. I looked at the files on the floor, looked at the corridor's open mouth. My nerves twitched. "I can't help myself. I have to see their reactions, otherwise I'm going to pop."

My bodyguard laughed. "You are more Greek than you realize."

I grinned and trotted down the hall to watch the grown men cry. They weren't actually weeping but Melas was rubbing his eyes and Pappas was looking down at the ground, hands on his hips, shaking his head.

"You know, I'm shocked that whoever did this didn't give *Kyrios Patata Kefala* the surprised face," I said.

Gus doubled over laughing. "I love my new reception-ist! She is funny and she makes coffee."

"And I reorganize filing cabinets."

"The last five receptionists never did that," he admitted.

"I figured that out," I said. "Did you know there was underwear in there?"

"Probably there are a lot of things in there." Gus shuddered. "Terrible things."

Melas got busy snapping photographs of the dead guy. He made a motion with his hands. "Turn him over."

For a human matchstick, Gus was strong. He rolled the body over. We all winced. The killer (I presumed) had stapled a note to the dead man's back. *Hello. My name is George George. You killed my family. Prepare to die.*

English.

Melas and Pappas looked to me for a translation. Well … Pappas looked at me. Melas's gaze was glued to my shoulder. He was doing a passable job of pretending I was there.

"I don't know who or what a George George is, but the rest is a mangled quote from a movie," I said.

"What movie?" Pappas asked.

"*The Princess Bride.*"

"Can you translate?" Melas asked my shoulder.

He typed on his phone as I waved my magic wand and turned the words from English to Greek with as little loss of context as possible.

"Who is this George George? Anyone? Is he a bad guy I should know about? I feel like I should know about someone who goes around pinning movie misquotes to dead people."

Nobody answered me. They were busy learning forward to take a closer look. Not wanting to be left out, I took a gander, too. The thoughtful person who'd stuck the corpse's johnson in a Mr. Potato Head had also jammed something between his butt cheeks, and it wasn't a dollar bill.

"What is that?" Melas asked.

I knew the answer, so I raised my hand. "Cabbage Patch Kid. Where's the head? Because they usually come with a head."

The cops looked at me. I looked back.

Oh. *O-o-o-o-h.*

I winced.

"Why would someone shove a Cabbage Patch Doll up a dead man's *kolos?*" Melas said.

"If he put it up there post mortem," Gus said helpfully.

"To be fair," I said, "it's just the head."

———

The cops bailed without telling me anything about anything. Why would they? Like crime, law enforcement was in my veins, not on my ID badge. That didn't stop me muttering as I resumed emptying the filing cabinets and rearranging their contents into alphabetical piles.

"You okay, boss?"

I held up a squashed thingy of dubious origin. "What is this, and does it belong in a filing cabinet?"

Gus appeared. "That is supposed to be in the personal items boxes."

"Personal items boxes?"

"That is where we store things that were on the bodies, until their families come to claim them. But …"

Greece's financial woes had all kinds of unexpected side effects, including, but not limited to, their ability to give their dead relatives a forever home in their local cemetery. Nobody claimed the bodies so it made sense that the same nobody claimed their accessories.

"We have personal items boxes?"

Gus waved his hand in way that made me think he wanted me to follow. By the happy chirping noise he made when I got up off the floor, I figured I was right. He led me into one of the rooms deeper in the morgue—one I hadn't been in before, mostly because at the time it had been packed with bodies. The bodies were gone now, which meant I could see three out of four walls covered with what appeared to be safety deposit boxes of varying sizes.

Gus yanked open one of the boxes. A stick-on dildo fell out. He picked it up, stuffed it back inside, used his back to slam the metal door shut.

"Personal items boxes," he said.

I eyed him suspiciously. "Just out of curiosity, whose job is it to maintain those?"

"The morgue has not has a receptionist for a while now, as you can see."

I stared at him. He stared back.

"So you're saying that's my job?"

He winced. "Yes?"

Between the filing cabinets and the personal items boxes, there was weeks' worth of work here. I'd be sorting, filing, and tossing things from dusk till dawn.

"Has anyone ever tidied them?"

"I do not think so," he went on. "Nobody has sorted them since before I started working here. Maybe not ever."

That reminded me I had another question. "What happens to the old files? I'd like to make room for new ..." what was I supposed to call the newly deceased? "...intakes."

"Sometimes things get moved to the archives."

"Can you define 'sometimes'?"

"When the cabinets are overflowing and we have a receptionist to pack the old files into archive boxes."

Well, all righty then.

I went back to the filing cabinets, setting the underwear and random other assorted non-paperwork items (a chocolate bar, a toy goat, a stack of old teen magazines called Manina) in a separate pile. While I was sorting out the lives of dead people, I thought about Mr. Potato Head. Whoever was responsible they'd bought vintage not new.

Vintage. 1980s era. There was no way that was a coincidence.

I went to find Gus. "The Cabbage Patch Kid," I said. "Did you remove it from his--you know--yet?"

He gestured to a metal tray with a green cloth thrown over the top. "You want to see it?"

"No, but also yes."

"Take a look."

I raised the cloth. Swearing on my own life was out of the question, but I was pretty sure the doll was one of the original 1980s Coleco creations. The 1980s were a recurring theme this week, what with the mix tapes and now the toys. Either Greece was stuck in the recent past (as opposed to the 1950s) or some sinister character had a boner for that particular decade. Some weirdo psychopath named George George, according to his note.

"How was he killed?" I asked Gus.

"He choked."

"On what?"

"A wad of tape."

Using a scalpel, he held up a long brown glossy snake of plastic covered with magnetic coating.

"From a cassette?"

"It was tangled up in his throat and wrapped around his uvula." He made a face. "I cannot even think about it without wanting to gag."

That made two of us. "What happed to the tape we found the other day?"

"I took it home. Nothing will ever separate my mama from her cassette player. She uses my bookcase for her cassettes."

"And your books?"

"One winter she needed to start the fire. Now that I think about it, she needed to start the fire a lot of times that winter."

Yowza. His mother was a bona fide book burner. I thought those only existed in Nazi Germany and some southern states.

"I don't suppose you know who the dead man was?"

"Not yet, but the police will tell me sooner or later, if they find out."

For the next hour I sorted files, moving anything older than two-years-old to a different pile. The mess wasn't taking shape yet, unless a nebulous blob counted, but one day, before I perished from old age, I hoped to have the filing cabinets in some kind of functional condition.

Then, blissfully, lunchtime happened.

Elias followed me up the steps to the ground floor. "Where are we going, boss?"

"Someplace where people don't have relations with children's toys. There's something strange going on, Dr. Watson, and I intend to find out what that is ... as soon as I've had lunch--preferably souvlaki. How does that sound to you?"

"I do not know who or what a Dr. Watson is, but souvlaki does sound good."

"Then today is your lucky day, because I'm buying."

The sliding doors parted and the arm air mugged me. My antiperspirant got to work. We headed for the employee parking lot.

"There is someone following you," Elias said. "Someone annoying and not as smart as she think she is."

"Hera? Still? How can she not be bored out of her skull?"

His head tilted sideways. My head swiveled. Through my dark lenses I could see Hera peeking out from behind a tree across the street. There was a short row of them. Poor things; they were struggling to turn convert smog into oxygen.

I looked both ways, jogged across the street with Elias behind me.

"Aren't you bored yet?" I asked her. Hera was all dolled up in a dress with a fippy hem and cute wedges. She looked almost human. I wasn't fooled.

"If my personal life was not amazing I would hang myself, that is how bored I am. Your life is stupid. Have you considered jumping off a tall building and ending it all?"

"Only when I look at your face. Do you put all that makeup on with a shovel or a tattoo gun?"

Hera shuddered. "One of these days …"

"Are you sweating? I didn't know you could."

"I do not sweat, I perspire."

Well, la-de-da. "We're going for lunch now, so don't get too excited when you watch me eat."

"I love watching you eat because it reminds me not to eat junk food."

Ouch.

"Listen," she said, "I am only telling you this because I do not like competition, especially when it comes to catching criminals, but there is someone following you. I tried to tell you earlier but you would not listen."

"Is this one of those things where you talk about your-self in the third person?"

"No, I mean someone else is following you. She is not very good at it though."

"Who?"

"Two o'clock. Your two o'clock."

At two o'clock, directionally speaking, there was a convertible snugged up to the curb. Unhappy traffic was cutting around the car, flipping it off, even though its driver was absent. As I watched, a head peeped out from behind the wheel, then vanished again.

Oh, brother.

I jogged over to find Dina, Dad's ex, crouched down behind the rear tire. Dina is a top-heavy garden gnome with fake black hair and more hang-ups than Oprah's closet. She didn't look happy to see me, but then she never does. If Dina could wriggle her nose and make me vanish, she would. I'm walking, talking, breathing proof that Dad had sex at least once with someone who wasn't her.

"Are you following me?"

"*Nyet.*"

That was weird, even for Dina. "What are you doing on the ground?"

"*Nichego.*"

"What's with the weird language?"

"What weird language? There is no weird language. You are imagining things. Crazy must run in your mother's family, who or whatever they are. Maybe they are dogs, I do not know."

The face was Dina's. The voice was Dina's. But the accent was straight out of a cold war movie.

"Is that a Russian accent you're doing? Because I have to say, that's pretty weird, even for you."

"*Nyet.*"

Dad was NIS. Grandma worked for some police agency or another hooked up to Interpol. Xander was NIS and a henchman. The people in my life had a knack for duality. If Dina were something other than a crazy Dad lady, I wouldn't drop dead from the shock.

"Are you KGB?"

Just joking. If Dina was KGB then I was a superhero— and I was not a superhero.

"I could tell you but then I would have to kill you," she said in her fake-o Moscow accent.

"Kyria Dina …"

"Call me Natasha. Natasha Boris."

Woo boy. "Natasha Boris, what is going on?"

She sat on the ground and looked up at me. "Okay, okay. I am working for a man who is KGB."

"And he wants you to follow me?"

Her eyes darted left to right. "That is what he said."

"Why?"

"He did not say."

Something about this was stinkier than feet in jelly shoes during August. "How did you meet this man?"

"He approached me.""

How convenient and interesting. "This man … what does he look like?"

She shrugged. "He is tall and he wears big shoes. You know what that means?"

"That he has big feet."

"A big *poutsa*. You know who else has big feet? Michail."

Gag me with a fork. Michail was my father. Nobody needed that scar on their psyche. "Can we not talk about my father's genitals please?"

"I keep forgetting he is your father."

Yeah, right. "What have you told this man so far?"

Shrug. "Nothing. You are very boring. You go to the hospital and you go back to the compound. When I was your age I spent my time going out, visiting people who could put spells on Michail to bring him home to me. I traveled. I met people. I got to see the whole Volos area."

"It's a gift," I said.

She leaned close. Her perfume clubbed me over the head and mugged me. My eyes watered. "Did you know somebody is following you?"

"Yes, and there are two of you." I waved at Hera, who raised her middle finger, shattering her wholesome image.

"No." She glanced around furtively. "There is someone else. It is my job to see these things. Do you know what I am going to do with the money I make following you?"

"Do I want to know?"

"My plan is to open the world's only Michail Makris museum."

It was official: Dina had lost her damn mind. I shook my head, hoping to shoo away the crazy. Last time a string of people decided to follow me, they were assassins and I was the target. Fortunately they couldn't decide who would get the honors; and while they were arguing their bosses were picked off, one at a time. One of those assassins was Elias, my now-bodyguard.

"Can you just tell me who is following me?"

"Some boy. He is hiding in the trunk of your car. He has been there for an hour now. Lucky it is not August."

I marched back across the street and popped my trunk. Donk was hunkered down inside, crunching on a bag of potato chips, sweating like a camel's armpit.

"What's aaaaaaap, biatch?"

I ignored the teenager's appalling attempt at English and focused on the important stuff.

"Why are you in the trunk of my car?"

"Why am I in the trunk of your car? I don't know. Can you just tell me the answer?"

"It wasn't a riddle!"

Elias grabbed him by the scruff of the neck and lifted the teenage Snoop Dog wannabe out. Donk wolf-whistled at the Ferrari.

"Nice car."

"Your uncle's pal blew up my other one."

Suddenly I remembered that someone was out to get Baby Dimitri, which meant Donk was probably in danger, too. I hugged the skinny teenager tight. He grabbed my butt with both hands. Squeezed.

I shoved him away. "Do that again and I'll have Elias cut your hands off. Come on. Get in the car."

Donk looked at Elias, who was thumbing the blade on a nasty-looking knife. He gulped. "Can I drive?"

"No."

"You let me drive the Ferrari last time."

"What happens in Naples stays in Naples. The includes unlicensed teenage drivers."

Donk wasn't miffed. He grabbed his shades out of his pocket and jammed them down on his nose. "Can you drive slowly along the *paralia* from here to Agria and back again? Ferraris are an aphrodisiac. The girls will go crazy when they see me in it."

"Not a chance."

"You are boring, did you know that?"

"I try." I have him a big toothy grin. "Get in the car."

"Where are we going?"

"Somebody wants to kill your uncle," I said. "There's reason to believe they'll come after you, too."

"Cool!"

Donk angled bonelessly into the Ferrari's passenger seat and leaned his arm on the open window. His desperation was palpable. I felt for the kid. He had been raised with money and position, but how happy could his life be? I was starting think I was the most stable force in his life.

"It's not cool." The gears made a metallic weeping sound. My driving skills were sad and they knew it. In the rearview mirror I glimpsed Hera and Dina leaping into action. Hera drove her usual car. Dina struggled to keep up on a moped. Elias shoved them into the next lane, taking up position behind me. "It's not cool at all. Someone might try to kill you, so I'm taking you back to the compound."

"Why?"

"Because my family can protect you there."

"Cool."

I was starting to think he didn't know what that word meant. "You want to tell me why you were sweating in my trunk?"

"I was working and I needed a good hiding place."

I glanced at him. He seemed serious. No point telling him a dead man had been wedged into that same space hours earlier. "Working? Doing what? Because that's not how you deliver a newspaper."

"I am a spy."

For crying out loud. "Not you, too."

"Who else is a spy?"

"Lately? Everyone."

"Women love spies. Have you seen James Bond? All the women love James Bond."

"Well, the spying is on hold until no one is trying to kill you. Who are you spying for?"

"I could tell you but then I would have to kill you."

This whole thing was starting to sound circular, like a table saw.

"It's not a Russian, is it?"

His face fell. "How did you know?"

"Lucky guess. Who is he?"

Shrug. "I don't know. He did not say."

"You're working for someone who didn't tell you his name?"

"He is KGB."

Something told me if this guy was KGB then I was a moose.

We went back to the compound, where I marched Donk down to the dungeon.

"Oh look, it is the boy with the sock," Monobrow said. "I hope you brought two this time."

Chapter 9

BABY DIMITRI still hadn't returned to Grandma's protective fold.

"Does the name George George mean anything to you?" I asked Monobrow.

His face gave nothing away. "No. Is he a pop star? Because that sounds to me like a pop star's name."

It did have a certain repetition to it, the kind that wouldn't be weird in the music industry.

"I don't know."

"Where did you hear that name?"

"Stapled to a dead man's back."

"I hope he was dead before they stapled it to his back. Katerina …"

"Yes?"

"You have a look on your face."

"That's just my face," I said.

The man with a ferret stapled across his face chuckled. "I know that look. I have seen it before on your grandmother's face."

"Before or after she stopped moisturizing?"

"Both." He waved his hand at me. "Get out of here. And when strange bodies show up at your work, leave it alone. That is why we have the police."

George George.

My gut was telling me he was Baby Dimitri's resurrected nemesis. The 1980s angle and the tape in the dead man's throat were a giveaway. Now I needed to dig.

Unusual name. His parents didn't hate him—he was simply Greek. Real name: Yiorgos Yiorgiou or something similar. All I needed to do now was Google Greek men named George George who were obsessed with the 1980s.

Half of Greece's male population was named George. The internet wasn't going to cut it. I had time to kill before heading back to work so I decided to kill it with legwork and bribery. But first, I wanted to make sure Baby Dimitri hadn't skipped the compound to hide out at home. His house wasn't cut out for subterfuge.

———

Baby Dimitri lives in a geometrical mansion that is seventy percent glass and thirty percent steel, stone, and white paint. No grass. No garden. What he does have is gravel. If you ask me, it's just cruel to have all those tiny rocks lying around with so much glass in plain sight. I was dying to pitch one at the windows.

The Godfather of Shoes and Tanks wasn't home. I knew this because the pinheads at the gate told me so. Like Grandma, Baby Dimitri employs a small army to keep his property safe. Unlike Grandma, his security isn't family so he has to pay big for all that loyalty. Grandma isn't stingy but she walks softly, carries a big chainsaw, and isn't afraid to hack a wayward branch off the family tree. Or so the rumor goes.

So he wasn't here. I still wanted in. What if there was a list of super-secret hiding places stuck to Baby Dimitri's fridge with a magnet?

"I know he's not home," I told the guard. He had a big gun. He was jacked. From the way he was blinking, I figured he wasn't one of the world's great thinkers. "I just want to look inside."

"Nobody goes inside."

I stepped closer. Big? Check. Foreboding? Also check. Good thing I was used to big and foreboding, thanks to Xander.

"What if you need to use the bathroom?"

"Bushes."

Liar, liar, pants on fire. There were no bushes on Baby Dimitri's patch of Greece. His property was a rock farm.

"Look, Baby Dimitri came to my family for help. I'm trying to help him."

He looked me up and down. "Why would he need your help?"

"Because I'm helpful."

The gears turned slowly. "Help how?"

"I don't know. I'm looking for something, anything, that would help me help him."

He didn't look convinced. I really needed to work on my convincing skills. Maybe Grandma would give me lessons.

"Pretty please?"

"No."

"Is that your final answer? Do you want to use one of your lifelines? Maybe call a friend?"

He went back to his gate.

I guess he didn't have a friend. With that winning personality, I wasn't surprised.

What now?

Baby Dimitri's house was off limits, but it wasn't his only hangout. With Elias following, I tootled down to the waterfront, cutting the engine outside the shoe and souvenir shop. Baby Dimitri's chair was empty. Laki's chair wasn't. Laki was in his usual seat, rolling a cigarette. The decrepit henchman grinned his golden grin as I stepped up onto sidewalk.

"Why do you want to drive that Italian garbage when I gave you a good Greek car?"

"This one doesn't keep trying to eat my lunch."

He cackled silently, then his grin slid off. "You looking for Dimitri?"

"Any idea where he is?"

"He is late today."

"When was the last time you saw him?"

A cloud passed over his face. "I … I do not remember."

Guilt kicked my shin. This wasn't the first sign of dementia Laki had displayed. Baby Dimitri knew and kept a close eye on his friend and henchman, but Baby Dimitri wasn't here.

"I can't remember when I saw him either," I lied. "Greek time is slippery. All the days seem to smear together on the calendar."

Laki's mouth smiled. His eyes didn't shine. He was worried and so was I—for both men.

"He came to the compound the other day, in his tank. He asked Grandma for protection."

He thought about that for a moment. "What did Katerina say?"

"We took him in. He went to Litsa's funeral, and then he vanished." I was about to prod a sick old man for information, which made me a monster. "You've known Baby Dimitri a long time, right?"

"Since he was born. My father worked for his father."

"Did he own a shoe shop, too?"

The grin came back. "Chairs."

"Normally he doesn't seem like he's afraid of anyone, except maybe Grandma. The other day he seemed scared. Who has that kind of power over him?"

Puff, puff. "Now? Nobody."

"In the past?"

Laki sucked on his handmade cigarette until nothing was left except butt.

"Who can say?"

"Does the name George George mean anything to you?"

"Do not dig, Katerina Makris-with-an-s."

"Why not?"

"It is bad for your health."

Said the man squashing the cigarette's damp corpse under his heel.

"Like smoking?"

"Everybody needs one bad habit. It keeps you from going crazy in this world." He pulled out the packet of tobacco and the little box of papers. He lined up the brown flecks in a neat row. Then he paused, eyes downcast, as though he didn't know what to do next.

I took the paper from him, rolled the cigarette, ran my tongue along the seam the way I'd seem him do a dozen times now. Butt first, I handed him the finished product. Not too shabby for my first hand-rolled cigarette.

Baby Dimitri didn't have much family left, mostly because he had killed them all. But he did have Laki, and Laki needed him.

"I'll find him," I said. "I promise."

———

Despite Grandma's notoriety and the Greek blood in my veins, my contacts in Greece were limited. The number of those contacts who were willing to talk about Baby Dimitri was even fewer. But there was one person who might cough up some pertinent information—if I fed her right.

I had just made a promise. Keeping it was the right thing to do.

So I bought gyros; the deluxe kind that included fries tucked inside with the shaved meat, the tomato, the feta, the *tzatziki*, and onions. I bought *loukoumia*. I purchased the last of summer's good tomatoes and an assortment of cheese. Elias and I ate a gyro apiece and a handful of *loukoumia*, then drove a short distance along the coastal road, until we found Penka sitting on her stoop, shaking her head at the increasingly barren beach.

"I should move to Mykonos," she said. "In Mykonos people are always at the beach and they always want classy drugs."

Penka sells prescription medication for Baby Dimitri. The Bulgarian woman insists that there are levels, and that selling classy drugs puts her above those grubby dealers who sell *sisa*—Greek meth—to school children. Instead of targeting kids, Penka dishes out Ambien and Ritalin to their teachers and other pillars of Greek society.

"I don't think people on Mykonos care if their drugs are classy or not." I helped myself to a concrete step. "Business still bad?"

"Terrible. I am thinking about selling myself, but only to classy customers."

If Penka sold herself by the pound she could make a fortune. Today she was wearing a strip of red lycra around her lower half with a green and white T-shirt that was meant to be an XL. On Penka it was a second skin.

I handed over the food. "Present?"

She peered into the bags. "You brought food." Her eyes narrowed. "What do you want?"

"Information."

"I can recite the literature on every prescription medication I sell. Which one do you want to know about?"

"Baby Dimitri's past. His enemies in particular."

"I know nothing."

"I brought food, remember?"

She made a reluctant but agreeable noise. "You did bring food, I suppose. And not just Greek food. You brought tomatoes and cheese. Very Bulgarian." Penka went diving in the bag. "People like Baby Dimitri, all they have are enemies. Even their friends are enemies waiting to happen."

"Friends into enemies ... sounds like middle school."

"They are the worst kind of enemies because they know where to stick the knife. There are many ways to make an enemy out of a friend, but a betrayal is the worst, yes?"

She had a point. Todd lost me fast when I discovered him on his knees, worshiping the almighty corndog. At that point I would have sold him into sex slavery if I'd known any human traffickers. Now that I probably knew several, Todd was lucky I didn't hold grudges forever.

"Are you saying Baby Dimitri had a friend he betrayed and that friend turned into an enemy? Was his name George George?"

Penka shrugged. "I don't know. I just heard this enemy took something that belonged to Baby Dimitri, and so Baby Dimitri went after him."

"And what happened?"

"This is Baby Dimitri we are talking about, yes? He killed his enemy."

Apparently he didn't kill his foe hard enough. "No

wonder he's freaking out. I'd freak if I killed someone and they came back from the dead."

"Sounds like a zombie to me," Penka said darkly.

"Who would know more, do you think?"

"Talk to Laki."

"I already did. I don't think he's well."

"That would make sense," Penka said. "The other day I saw him talking to a can of olive oil for a whole hour."

"My grandmother does that, only it's my dead grandfather in the can."

"Greeks," Penka said. "I should go to America. My cousin lives in Florida, where people are sane."

Someone had never heard of Florida Man. I left her to her cozy delusion and drove back to the compound, wondering how Grandma fit into the George George and Baby Dimitri vendetta. Perhaps this George George character knew she had granted him sanctuary at the compound. As far as theories went, that one didn't feel right. Although he hadn't mentioned George George by name, Xander was convinced the stupidly named man was gunning for him. Then there was the cryptic clue Monobrow dropped before Grandma booted me out of the dungeon so the really old grownups could talk in private. Monobrow said Baby Dimitri wouldn't be the only one the Big Bad was coming for.

Netflix was convinced my favorite movie categories were thrillers and crime fiction. Now my whole life straddled those genres. What I wouldn't give to be living something more wholesome and less deadly. Maybe a nice romantic comedy.

The idea of dredging through all the filing cabinets alone was daunting, so as I turned down the compound's driveway I decided to muster the troops.

Minutes later, I was knocking on Marika and Takis'

door. Marika met me with a grin and a glass of cold water with a lump of vanilla mastic inside, clinging to a spoon. The smile was for me; the vanilla was for her and she would rip off my arm if I made eye contact with the spoon.

"Want to earn some money?" I asked her.

"I do not need money but I could use more snacks. Why?"

I told her about the mess in the morgue and how it required an expert touch. Marika's kids might be zoo animals, and inmates waiting to happen, but everything in her house had a clean and organized place.

Marika's face lit up. "I will bring the rubber gloves, the wooden stakes, and the holy water in case zombies happen."

"There's no such thing as zombies."

Her eyes narrowed as she sucked on the spoon. "Would you bet your life on it?"

Good question. Logic said zombies weren't a thing— yet—but fiction had its hooks in my psyche. Watch too much TV, read too many books, and you'll believe anything is possible. "No."

"Then I will bring the supplies. I still have them from last time I went to the morgue."

"What are the rubber gloves for?" As far as I knew, the undead were resistant to rubber.

"To protect my hands while I clean."

Not the answer I was expecting.

"Where is Elias?" she asked after she'd gathered her supplies and we were good to go. "Someone has to carry my bag. It is too heavy and I am pregnant, you know."

Marika was about five minutes pregnant, and I was starting to suspect she was going to drag the pregnancy to the nine-year mark before producing a child.

I relived her of the bag. It hit the floor, taking my arm with it.

"What did you pack—rocks?"

"Spy tools."

"What kind of spy tools?"

"A spy never tells."

I peeked in the bag. Guns. "It's just filing and organizing. What are the guns for?"

"When you are a spy you never know when you will need a gun."

"What happened to the small one in the Merenda jar?"

"It is in there, too. But a good spy needs choices. What if I find myself in a situation that calls for a bigger gun? It could happen."

Muttering to myself, I hoisted the bag onto my shoulder. Now I was leaning distinctively to the right. "Just so you know, I've got people following me."

"Again? What people?"

When I told her, she grinned. "This is why it is good that I am a spy now instead of your bodyguard. Bodyguards have rules. Spies can steal an ambulance and ram it into the criminals without repercussions."

Yeah, I was pretty sure that wasn't how the spy business worked.

Gus groaned when he got a load of Marika. "The hospital cannot afford to pay for another employee. Believe me, I would love another one, but unless you are okay with indentured servitude you cannot work here."

"I am a mother and a wife," Marika said. "Indentured servitude is my life."

"Perfect." Gus rubbed his hands together. "You can stay."

We got to work. Well, I got to work. Marika planted herself in my office chair and rifled around in her bag. Her hand emerged with a fistful of plastic-wrapped chocolate cakes, the size and shape of American Twinkies, but with fewer chemicals and more frosting.

"I cannot work on an empty stomach," she said.

My stomach liked the looks of that chocolate. "Me either." I perched on the desk, peeling plastic wrap off the cake Marika gave me. I wanted to snarf it down before she changed her mind.

We munched on chocolate cakes and stared at filing cabinets and the stacks of files and other assorted non-files on the floor. The chocolate was magic. It made the wheels in my head spin. George George was supposed to be a dead man, and maybe if people had mistaken him for dead he'd been processed in this very building. It wasn't a huge stretch; the Volos Hospital was the area's main morgue.

Gus was in the back room, scraping under the Mr. Potato Penis's nails. He had removed the plastic potato and, as far as I could tell, the Cabbage Patch Kid.

"What happens to the old files?" I asked him. "You said something about archives, right?"

"How old?"

I did some mental math. Ten years wouldn't be ancient history. Most people walked around in shock that ten years had happened. Heck, most people were horrified that *Die Hard* was about to turn thirty. I went for the middle ground.

"Twenty years."

"Files older than two years go into the archives, like I told you." He made a face. "But it has been much longer than that since these files were archived."

"Where are the archives?"

"The hospital keeps them offsite, in a warehouse. Why?"

"I wanted to poke through them, hoping to uncover old secrets."

He gave me a thumbs up. "Nice."

"So where's the warehouse, any idea?"

Gus gave me an address. The warehouse was on the edge of Volos, not far from Grandma's airstrip. I filed it away for a rainy day. Greece didn't have many of those but eventually one would crop up.

Say, was that a rain cloud?

If I squinted it could be.

———

Baby Dimitri's untimely disappearance on the heels of his begging for sanctuary bothered me. It bothered me back to the compound, where Marika and I found Donk hanging out with Marika's boys. They were playing video games on the huge screen in Marika and Takis' living room. Donk being Donk, he was trying and failing to buy a virtual hooker.

"You're supposed to be hiding," I told him.

"I am hiding."

Onscreen, the prostitute throat-punched his character. Marika's boys hooted and jeered.

"He is safe here," Marika told me. "Nobody would come in here on purpose. Even I would not be here if someone offered me a chocolate factory."

"Did Tomas ever open that safe for you?"

Recently, Takis stashed a small safe under the bed he shared with Marika. She had employed the family's tiniest safe-cracking prodigy to break into the impenetrable box.

"No. But that is okay because the boys are going to spit in his food. They already agreed." Marika beamed. "Sometimes I love my children more than chocolate."

"Mama," one of her boys said. "We're hungry. Get us some snacks."

She slapped him on the back of the head. "You have two hands, get it yourself."

Her son—the eldest, perhaps—peeled his backside off the couch, slouched into the kitchen. He looked around, blinking and dazed like this was his first time in the food-making room. Marika rolled her eyes at me.

"Sit down, *re*. I will fix something."

Marika was right: nobody would venture into her apartment if they had any kind of will to live, so I left the teenager to his game and headed back to my car, searching the Crooked Noses board along the way. Nobody in the site's wiki fit the information I had. George George wasn't part of anyone's mob.

Elias materialized beside me. He was good at that.

"Going out, boss?"

"I was thinking about driving to a probably haunted old warehouse and digging through old morgue archives. I'm picturing something out of *Raiders of the Lost Ark*, but creepier and with more dust. Want to join me?"

"I go where you go. What are you looking for?"

"Dirt."

Like me—sort of—Elias was new to the family. Grandma paid his salary but he considered me his boss. Which meant he didn't get up in my face and wag his finger at me for wanting to dig up old bones.

"You take me to the best places," he said.

In our separate cars we drove to the dark rim of Volos, where it was impossible to tell abandoned houses from the occupied. Strange lights danced in some of the windows. Fowl made offended noises in their sleep. Everything was in a state of disrepair; earthquake damage from days of yore, when rebar and concrete weren't mandatory.

The warehouse wasn't exactly a warehouse. It was more like an old factory with its guts ripped out to accommodate old paperwork that no one was ever likely to need ever again. Except here was little ol' me and, by golly, I really wanted that paperwork, if it existed. There were no guards. No staff with plastic badges, peering down their noses to see if I had a similar badge pinned to my shirt. The place was locked but these days that isn't much of a deterrent. Aunt Rita had bought me a set of lock picks, and YouTube could walk a person through opening most kinds of locks.

There was no electricity to shine light on the situation, so Elias drove his car through the open warehouse door and left the engine running and the lights on.

"In case we need to make a quick getaway." He took stock of the warehouse. There was a lot of it to take stock of. "Where do you want to start?"

Heck if I knew. The warehouse was an enormous cavern filled with horrors. Spiders the size of toy poodles crouched in webs larger than grown men. Dust-crusted boxes were draped with empty snakeskins. The only thing thicker than the dust was the dense, stale shadow that refused to be chased away by the car's light.

"Outside?"

Elias raised his eyebrows. "Scared of a few spiders?"

"Those are not spiders, they're mutants. I have a mutant problem, especially when they look like that." Elias suppressed a smile. "The 1980s. That's my target."

"That was a long decade."

"Ten whole years," I said.

As we moved deeper in the warehouse the light thinned out. Elias brought out his flashlight, a heavy-duty metal tube meant to double as a whacking stick, if the need for a sound beating arose.

We located the 1980s in bankers' boxes against a far wall, under a shroud of cobwebs. Someone, at least, had taken care to file things in something that tipped its hat at alphabetical and chronological orders.

"*Gamma … gamma …*"

"*Gamma*," Elias said.

With the sound of a Y—and occasionally a G--and the looks of a twisted Y in its lowercase form, *gamma* is the third letter of the Greek alphabet.

For the next hour we moved boxes around, searching for a man who was dead but wasn't. A person who enjoyed 80s music and shoving 80s memorabilia in places guaranteed to void any resale value.

"I wonder how often anyone comes here," Elias said.

"If you're wondering when they'll find our desiccated corpses, I don't know."

After the clock struck nine, and the witching hour and those spiders over there crept closer, we uncovered a mass grave in 1985. Twenty adult Yiorgious and no children. George George was one of the many. Like the rest of his family, he had died of multiple gunshot wounds.

Dead. Multiple gunshot wounds. I read the words over and over.

Whoever was responsible for today's dead man, it couldn't be the real George George. Not unless he was a zombie, in which case I owed Marika and Penka apologies for doubting them.

My phone rang. I might have yelped and shouted, "SPIDER!"

Grandma's name appeared on the screen.

"Grandma?"

There was a long, shady patch of silence.

"What is it, Grandma?"

"We have a slight kidnapping problem," she said in an embarrassed sort of tone that wasn't like Grandma at all.

As Scooby Doo would say: Ruh roh. "What's the kidnapping problem?"

"We have been kidnapped."

Christ in a cup of coffee. "Kidnapped?" My voice had a bright edge—the sound of early onset panic. "Who? How? Where? Are you okay? Is Dad okay?"

"Your father is fine but I am going to rip off somebody's *archidia* as soon as I get a chance."

Balls. She was going to rip balls. Under the circumstances, ball ripping sounded good.

"And the other stuff? Who kidnapped you and how?"

"Our kidnapper is a ghost, a person I believed was long dead."

"Is his name George George, by any chance? Because George George is dead. I'm looking at his morgue file right now. It seems pretty conclusive."

"George George escaped death somehow." Suspicion tinted her words. "How did you know his name?"

"Found it stapled to a dead man's back at work. Your guy is a real sicko."

"Sick would be an improvement."

"Where are you?"

"In my lair," a voice in the background said. A voice I didn't recognize. George George, presumably.

"In his lair," Grandma said, voice dripping with disdain.

"Is that George George?"

"That is *Kyrios* George George to you," the voice said. "Hurry up, Katerina."

Hazard of sharing a name with Grandma: were they talking to her or to me?

"I cannot talk long," Grandma said, answering that

question. "George George wanted me to tell you that you have twenty-four hours to turn over Baby Dimitri, otherwise we will die."

"You and Dad?"

"No," she said. "This *malakas* wants to kill the whole family, and to be honest, I have it coming. That is what he told me to tell you."

The phone went dead.

Chapter 10

My fingers drummed the steering wheel.

The second I got Grandma off the phone I called Aunt Rita. She promised to muster the troops, rouse the cavalry, toss a cat into the snoozing pigeons.

"We have a contingency plan," she told me. "I will meet you in the courtyard."

By the time I screeched to a halt outside the garage, the family was gathering near the pool. Xander, Takis, Stavros stood at the front. They had questions. I didn't have a lot of answers. I told them everything Grandma said and then I told them again.

"George George?" Takis said. "George George is dead. George George has been dead for decades."

"Apparently not," I said.

He snorted. "Marika keeps talking about zombies rising from the dead, and now I am starting to think she is not completely insane."

A window above the pool opened.

"I heard that," Marika yelled."

"There's no such thing as zombies," I said, not entirely sure.

Takis grinned. "Have you looked in the mirror lately, or ever?"

I scratched my nose with my middle finger. Laughing, Stavros slapped Takis on the back. The most badass mobsters in Greece were overgrown, hirsute frat boys.

"What's the next part of the plan after Takis' lame and unfunny comedy act?" I asked my aunt.

"We rescue Mama and Michail, then we find George George and kill him again because the first time did not take."

I drew a circle in the air. "I think you missed a step there. How do we find Grandma and Dad?"

She hugged me around the shoulders. "Sometimes I forget that you have not always been here with us. Mama has a chip. All we have to do is turn on the GPS and follow the directions."

"A chip? Grandma has a chip?"

Something told me she wasn't talking about the potato kind.

"At the time I told her she was a paranoid, but now? Very smart." She grabbed my hand. "Come on."

"Wait—where is the chip?"

"They put it in her arm, but who knows where it is now. Apparently those things travel. I like to think it is in her *kolos*."

I turned around to the others—which was pretty much everyone, minus their wives and kids. "Get ready."

Takis kicked Stavros's shin. "She wants you to fix your hair."

"Get ready to go the moment we have a location," I said, giving Takis my best stink-eye. "How do we do this?" I asked Aunt Rita.

She whipped out her phone, pressed her manicured fingertip to a plain black icon on the screen. The app had no name, just the monochrome square. A map appeared.

"Turn right at the next intersection," the talking map lady said. I hated the talking map lady. She was a real nag. Smug, too.

"Please tell me you can turn off the voice setting."

"Baboulas likes the talking map," Aunt Rita said, her downturned lips telling me she didn't think much of the bossy bitch either. She consulted the part of the map that didn't have a big mouth. "We are going to Delphi. That gives us two hours to figure out how we are going to kill George George and save Mama and Michail." She hugged me. "We will find them, I promise."

"What is this 'we', Kemosabe? I'm coming, too."

Aunt Rita pulled me aside. "You have to stay here. Do not worry, Xander will be here with you."

"Xander's not going either?" Now Grandma and Dad were done for.

"Believe me when I say it is best if Xander stays here."

"Because you don't trust me?"

She smiled. "I trust you with my life. But I do not trust George George. If anything goes wrong, you will be safe with Xander."

"Is George George after Xander, too?"

She paused. A battle happened inside her head. Finally, she seemed to come to a decision. "We will talk later, okay?"

Not okay. But they had a thing to do and not nearly enough time to do it.

They left—all of them, except the guards, a couple of snipers, and Xander. Elias stayed behind, too. He was watching over Tomas, who was asleep in his father's bed.

Just because I was left behind, didn't mean I had to stay

that way. There was work to be done. Someone with sharp detective skills had to find Baby Dimitri, dish him up, and present him to George George within twenty-four hours or otherwise Grandma and Dad would be dead meat. I didn't know anyone like that, so it was up to me.

———

George George. Definitely not a ghost. What was he then? According to the morgue's paperwork he was a dead man. According to all the other evidence, including the fact that he was alive and walking around, kidnapping decent people—okay, well, Grandma and Dad—would suggest he was alive. Greece wasn't so good at paperwork. The country's bureaucrats loved to wrap up bundles of paper with red tape then shove them into dank warehouses. A little thing like mistaking someone for dead was bound to happen sooner or later.

George George.

I plugged the name into my browser again, in English and in Greek.

Nothing.

I slumped against the back of the chair in Grandma's kitchen and contemplated the goodies on the counter.

Although I was terrified, I knew the family would find Grandma and Dad. This George George bozo sounded like he wanted them to be found. What worried me was the next bit. What would happen after Aunt Rita and the gang rescued them?

What would happen if I couldn't produce Baby Dimitri?

Would I, even if I knew where he was?

Hardly. This George George sounded like a real bully. No way was I going to hand Baby Dimitri over to him.

But I had to find Baby Dimitri, and not just for Laki's sake either. Something told me he was the key to ending George George's deadly shenanigans. He was definitely a guy who knew a thing or two about this character. Where had he vanished to? He was thin. He was short. He could fit in places smaller than a breadbox.

The greasy godfather's shop and house were dead ends.

Where else could he be?

I combed over Baby Dimitri's wiki page at the Crooked Noses site. The old guy owned a bunch of strip clubs and a warehouse that was apparently legitimate and housed his shoes and souvenirs, possibly after they fell off the back of a boat.

Wait a minute.

What about the tank?

Maybe Baby Dimitri was hiding out inside his rolling metal box. Too bad the tank had vanished the day he had arrived at the compound. Grandma had stashed it away somewhere. The compound was big and featured a lot of hiding places, some of them underground.

Who would know where she had hidden the machine? Whose wheels were easy to grease?

Papou. Duh.

I cast a longing look at Grandma's baked goods and headed up to Papou's second floor room. Weird for an elderly man in a wheelchair, yes, but he didn't want to be at ground level. Probably he was afraid of potential Turkish invasions; at his age there was a good chance he had seen a few of them.

I knocked twice. The door flew open. Papou rolled out, grabbed my arm.

"*Psst*, Katerina. Come and look at this."

"Why are you *pssting* at me?"

"Come in already before the Turks get us."

He rolled backwards, leaving me enough room to crab walk into his apartment. Every surface was covered in plastic wrap and punctuated with tall potted trees, and … was that a fish tank?

"That belongs to Yiorgos," he declared proudly when I asked. "He likes to go fishing."

A dozen or more fish darted around their tank. They had no idea they were dinner. Yiorgos had no idea either. He was perched on a plastic-covered recliner, eyes closed, ignoring the oblivious prey.

"I am thinking about bringing in a rabbit hutch next. Maybe let him do a little rabbit hunting."

"That worked out well for Elmer Fudd."

Said no one ever.

"Who is Elmer Fudd? Some American *malakas*? Who cares? Check this out." He clapped. The lights went out. He clapped again. The lights came on. Someone had been watching infomercials. "You like it?" *Clap*. Lights out. *Clap*. Lights on.

"Congratulations, you bought a clapper."

"I could do this all day," he said.

Clap. Lights out.

"And I do."

Clap. Lights on.

"You should get one."

This conversation was headed towards Home Depot, and I was naturally allergic to home improvement stores. Buy one can of paint, next thing you know you were tearing out a wall and installing shiplap—and I really hated shiplap.

"Where would Grandma hide a tank if she had one?"

Clap.

"What kind of tank?"

Clap.

"A big one."

"Why you want to know, eh?"

Clap.

Light flooded the room. Yiorgos was pecking at his stuffed and mounted sibling. My eye twitched.

"I like big tanks and I cannot lie," I said.

Papou's eyes went beady. "Are you going to drive it?"

"What? No. I can't drive a tank." Probably it was like driving a house.

"That is too bad," he said. "I would have like to have gone for a ride. I have never ridden in a tank before."

"Me either," I said. We stood there for a moment, quiet in solidarity.

"Rita would know."

I messaged Aunt Rita. Her answer shot right back. Grandma had moved the tank to her airfield.

Papou farted. The lights went out.

———

The night was dark and cool, like a walk-in refrigeration unit. The only thing missing was the hanging meat. Knowing the family, probably the meat was around here somewhere. There was a good chance it was human.

I wasn't looking for meat, although now that I thought about it, I could eat.

Going out without an escort would make Grandma's eyebrows rise and her lips pucker, but Grandma wasn't here. Grandma and Dad had been kidnapped and now I had less than a day to find them, and hopefully Baby Dimitri. I needed a miracle, and that miracle, I hoped, was in the tank. The lucky version of me would find Baby Dimitri hiding out in the war machine, possibly wearing an adult diaper. That was the best scenario my brain could conjure up. He was alive somewhere. He had to be. Without him, the family might be doomed.

Nobody was manning the garage. Or maybe the cousin on duty had snuck off for a covert smoke. So many vehicles, so many choices. Times like these, I called on the big decision-making guns: eenie meanie, miney, and mo. They selected a small black Toyota, which suited me just fine. The garage was organized by someone with a mild obsessive-compulsive disorder and so all the keys were kept on tiny hooks on the wall, carefully labeled with each car's make, year, and plate number. I grabbed the Toyota's key and eased out of the garage.

The guard eyed me when I stopped at the gate.

"Are you supposed to be leaving?"

"Did anyone tell you I couldn't?"

He thought about it a moment. "No …"

"Great answer. Be a good man and push that button, would you."

"I don't know if I should."

"Push the button, cuz. You know you want to."

"I do want to, but I also don't. Everybody is leaving."

My ears pricked. "Who else left?"

"Xander."

"When?"

"About thirty minutes ago."

"Where was he going?"

He patted his shirt pocket. "Let me find his itinerary."

I waited. Then I realized someone was being a smartass and it wasn't me.

"Clever."

My cousin grinned. He pushed the button. "Be careful out there, eh?"

That was the plan. Okay, I didn't actually have a solid

plan beyond scouting out Baby Dimitri's tank and hoping he'd left a mobster-shaped breadcrumb in the glove box, but it was all I had tonight.

Grandma's airfield consists of a small hangar, a carport, an airstrip, and her jet. A while back she scored a police helicopter, but wherever she keeps it it's not here. Word on the cobbled street—okay, the compound—is that she has other planes, but they're not here either. Tonight there was something else sitting behind the hangar, hidden from casual view: Baby Dimitri's tank.

Excellent.

I parked the Toyota, grabbed my bag, and hoofed it across the parched dirt to check out the metal beast. Wherever my tails were hiding, they were doing a good job. The smell of eau de skank perfume was imperceptible tonight.

The Toyota had come with a flashlight and an array of other goodies useful in event of a breakdown or an emergency quickie burial, so I'd grabbed it out of the glove box. I shone the blue-white beam at the tank. Very tank-y. Lots of doodads and thingamabobs. All of it was painted a flat utilitarian green that made me wish I could curl up on the couch with a bag of chips while I watched Tom Hanks save Private Ryan one more time instead of hunting ghosts and smoke.

I clambered up the side, to the top. The hatch was smaller than I remembered. What if I got stuck? My weight was fine but my hips were Greek. Ridiculous. Men bigger than me got in and out of these things all the time. Men with shoulders wider than my hips. But this was an old tank, one from the days when people—even men—weren't as big as they are now. My head really didn't want me squeezing into that itty-bitty cramped space.

What would Grandma do?

Bake cookies then dive in, of course.

I grabbed the handle and yanked. No can opener required, the lid opened with a low squeal. I peered in. The flashlight slipped out of my hand. There was a loud, echoing clank as it hit the tank's floor. Everything went dark.

"Baby Dimitri? Are you there?"

Silence.

Wow, that mouth was big and black. All the better to eat me with. Feet first, I wriggled down into the tank. It wasn't so bad. There was room to move … sort of.

Something warm and large and human—oh gods, please let it be human and not a Greek bear—slid past me. The lid clanked, plunging me into full darkness.

There was laughing, soft and deep and male.

Holy crap on a cracker, someone was definitely in here with me—a real human and not that Greek bear I was so worried about a moment ago. I scrambled toward the hatch, but I was going nowhere fast. Someone had their fingers through my belt loops.

"Omigod, get me out of here!"

There wasn't room to do the windmill, but I did it anyway. All the fancy Kung Fu and karate in the world can't compete with the good old windmill.

"Katerina! Stop," Xander said.

My windmill devolved into slaps. "Xander? What the hell is wrong with you? I could have windmilled you to death!"

"To death, huh?"

Light flooded the small space. Xander had brought his own flashlight to the party. He reached past me to pick up the flashlight that had fallen and dropped it into my lap. Like me, he was dressed in black. Me because I was technically in mourning for someone I'd barely known, and Xander because it was his favorite color.

"You scared the life out of me," I whispered. "What are you doing here?"

"Never driven a tank before. Thought it might be fun."

"Really?"

"No."

I waited for a real answer. Didn't happen. So I elbowed him.

"Are you going to tell me why you're really here?"

"You first."

"I thought Baby Dimitri might be here. When I realized he wasn't about ten seconds ago, I decided I'd look for clues."

"Are you saying you're clueless?" His lips were grim but his eyes were smiling.

"Be serious. I am on a very important and serious mission here."

"So am I." The flashlight's beam moved. "There's nothing here, if you're looking for clues."

Lucky freakin' me. "Nothing at all?"

"Baby Dimitri didn't leave so much as a hair."

"It's all the Brylcreem," I said. "It keeps the whole thing in place like a greasy helmet."

We looked around.

"What are you really doing here?" I asked him.

"Same as you. Looking for something—anything. I want to get to Kyria Katerina and your father before George George kills them."

"Isn't that what everyone else is doing?"

"George George is smarter than that. He escaped death while convincing everyone he was dead, and he did it for decades."

"What do you know about George George?"

Xander shrugged. It was big shrug because he had an

abundance of shoulder to put into the movement. "Not much."

"Not much meaning you don't know, or not much meaning you don't want to tell me?"

"Yes."

I shook my hands at the tank's ceiling. "What is wrong with you people? You never tell me anything! And you should—you really should—because what I don't know can, and almost has, gotten me killed."

"You're a civilian."

"And you're a big poopyhead."

He raised an eyebrow. "Poopyhead?"

"It loses something in translation."

"I know what it means," he said. "It's colorful."

"It's brown. Brown isn't colorful."

He exhaled. "What do you know?"

"About George George? Not much. He and Baby Dimitri used to be friends. Then they became enemies, so Baby Dimitri had him killed. Also I think he has some kind of weird 80s fetish."

"George George screwed Baby Dimitri."

"How?"

"He stole something from Baby Dimitri."

"What kind of something? Was it shoes or souvenirs?"

He shook his head, a faint smile lurking around his lips. "Do you know how difficult it is to find the perfect boots?"

A laugh bubbled up and out of me. "For a mute you're pretty funny."

Outside, a vehicle approached. My breath caught, and my bladder squeezed, a rude biological reminder that I should have gone to the bathroom one last time before driving out here. Xander's smile dissolved. Maybe his bladder was doing the same thing.

The vehicle sped up. The engine's hum faded to silence. My bladder relaxed and quit nagging me.

"Gone," I said.

Xander clapped a hand over my mouth—his hand, thankfully. In this family it was important to make that distinction. With his spare hand, he reached over, took my phone, and flicked the switch to silent mode, then he stuck it in my bag. Slowly, he pulled his hand away. Lucky for him, because I was this close to licking his palm.

Xander touched his ear, pointed up.

I held my breath. He was right, there was somebody outside.

Hera and Dina, I mouthed. *They've been following me*.

Chin up-down. The good ol' Greek no.

Clank.

I jumped. "What was that?"

Nothing from Xander. The man was a violin string, yet somehow relaxed.

Clank.

Was someone trying to get in?

I shot that idea down. If that were the case, they would be on top with a jumbo-sized can opener. Everyone knew tanks opened like a can of Pringles. This clanking was ground level.

There was a new sound, too. Whirring, like a propeller plane or a helicopter. Moving closer. Probably this was how canned goods would feel when they heard the rattle of an oncoming shopping cart, if they were sentient.

Clank.

"We've got to get out of here," I whispered. I tried to stand but Xander pulled me back down.

"Buckle up."

"What?"

The whirring was getting closer. Was it Grandma's helicopter? I hoped so because I really didn't like being trapped in this tin can.

I felt around. There weren't any seat belts. There wasn't anything to hold onto except my handbag or the steering wheel, and that was on Xander's side.

Xander reached over and curled his arm around my waist, reeling me closer until I was tucked into that safe nook between his arm and body. Problem solved, more or less. Less, I suspected.

"It's going to be okay," he told me.

Was it? Because nothing about this felt okay. "What's going on?"

The whirring was directly overhead and moving lower.

The tank jerked. Everything tilted.

"We're going to die!"

"Not yet," Xander shouted over the noise. Boots braced against the tank, he held me tight against him. "We're going up."

"What is that? A helicopter?"

"Helicopter," he confirmed.

How was that possible? This tin can was huge and heavy. "A helicopter that can lift a tank?"

"This an older tank, and a light one at that. Could be a Halo, a Chinook, a Super Stallion up there. There are others that can handle this kind of load."

"Military?"

"Military or someone with deep pockets. I'm betting on the deep pockets."

"Whose? Please tell me you have a theory."

"George George's pockets."

"How deep are they?"

"Deep enough that he convinced the best that he was dead and managed to hide for years."

With an almighty groan that reminded me of me

trying to leave the table after Thanksgiving dinner, the tank left the ground.

"What are we going to do?"

"We wait."

"For what? For that helicopter to drop us into the sea?"

Xander fell silent. That scared me more than the whole being hauled across the country in a tank attached to a helicopter.

I prodded him with my elbow. "Are we going to be okay?"

His arm tensed. I wiggled closer and laced my fingers through his. If we were going to die it would be nice to have some kind of human contact on the way out. With my head on his chest, I could feel his heartbeat. In the moment my fingers touched his, his heart picked up its pace.

Xander exhaled, ruffling my hair with his breath.

"You feel good," he said.

My head tilted back. Our gazes collided. Things happened below the waistband of my sensible mourning clothes. Probably this kind of tingling was against some kind of Greek Orthodox custom. Right now I didn't really care. The church wasn't stuck in this tank with us. Like Santa Claus, God allegedly saw everything, but if he saw we were hovering over hard, non-elastic land in a metal box with caterpillar tread and not doing anything about it, then I was okay with feeling hot and bothered by the proximity Xander's body and its appealing parts.

"So do you," I said.

His fingers closed around a handful of my hair. "I want you."

The smile in his eyes was gone. They were serious now, filled with desire that I was pretty sure was for me, given that I was the only other warm body around.

"I did always want to go for a ride in a tank," I said carefully.

And then I kissed him.

Fireworks exploded in my underwear. My hormones cheered; lately I'd been a disappointment to them. Xander worked his way from my mouth to my neck. My everything was going up in white-hot flames.

"I can hear your heart beating," I murmured. "Are you part robot, because it sounds like a lead pipe banging on a chain-link fence."

Yikes. My dirty-talk skills had seriously eroded.

Xander pulled away. The banging continued.

"Wait a minute," I said suspiciously. "Is that someone knocking on the hatch?"

Xander reached up and twirled the knob. He knocked once then flipped the hatch upward. A face appeared, followed by a pair of skinny arms. Donk tumbled through the hole in a tangle of limbs, saggy pants, wind-whipped hair, and a grin that didn't go with the decor.

"What's aaaaaaaap?"

At least that's what I thought he said. It was hard to tell with all the helicoptering going on overhead. Xander pulled the hatch down and spun the lock.

I shook the teenager by the puny shoulders. "Donk? What the hell are you doing?"

Grin slathered across his face, he took stock of his new surroundings. "I am following you, remember? I climbed into the backseat of your car while you were not looking. I have never been inside a tank before. Now I can say I have ridden in a tank being transported by a helicopter. I bet none of my friends have done that."

You have friends? I almost said. Guilt got to me before it could roll out. Donk didn't have much in the way of people in this world. If anything happened to Baby Dimitri he would be down another relative.

"Why did you leave the compound? I told you to stay there, where it's safe."

"Relax, I am safe with you and this guy, right?"

This guy, AKA: Xander, was back to his usual silent self. It was one thing for me to know his vocal cords worked just fine, but Donk wasn't known for his discretion.

"We're in a tank, dangling on the end of a chain—"

"Four chains," Donk said. "At least."

"—on our way to God only knows where. I wouldn't call that safe."

He grinned. "But no one is shooting at us, eh?"

"No one is shooting at us—yet." I had a nasty feeling guns and bullets were in our future; these days they almost always were, because I was just lucky that way, I guess.

"Good thing I brought my own gun then." He whipped out a small cannon from the back of his pants. As soon as it appeared Xander snatched it out of his hand.

"Awww man," Donk said in thickly accented English he'd picked up from *Dora the Explorer*'s light-fingered fox. "That was my gun."

Xander looked at him. Hard.

"Okay, that is not my gun. But I had it so it was mine, yes?"

"According to that logic, the gun belongs to Xander now," I said. "And you should never stick a gun down the back of your pants because you might shoot your *kolos* off."

"But that is what they do in the movies."

"Life isn't a movie."

He glanced around at the tank's cramped and drab interior. "This is a bit like being a movie."

He had a point, damn it: this was too much like a movie. Question was: would it have a happy ending? For us, I meant. Not for George George. I was less invested in his happiness.

"Did anyone see you?"

Two thumbs up, Fonzie-style. "Heeey, I am the Donk."

"Yes or no?"

He shrugged. "No. I am good at being sneaky."

"Okay. Sit back and be quiet."

He was quiet. For … oh … about thirty seconds.

Then: "Can you move over? There is not much room …"

"That's because we're in a tank. Nobody buys a tank for its roominess."

"Where did you get this sweet tank anyway?"

"It's not mine. It belongs to your uncle. He left it at Grandma's place and she moved it to the airfield."

He whistled low. "My uncle had a tank? Ma-a-a-a-n, nobody tells me anything."

I rolled my eyes. Beside me, Xander was relaxed. His arm was still around me and Donk's gun was resting on his lap. The gun looked kind of familiar—as familiar as a gun can look. They all look about the same to me: L-shaped, black, and deadly. There was a telltale smudge of chocolate on the grip.

"Is that one of Marika's guns?"

He went shifty-eyed. "No."

"It is," I said. "It is one of Marika's guns. Don't lie to me. Look: crumbs in the barrel." I leaned back, closed my eyes. "You're going to be in so much trouble when she discovers you've been poking through her bag."

"It is just one little gun."

I texted Marika. *Missing something?*

Her reply shot right back almost indignantly. *Some* kolopetho *stole my cakes!*

"You stole Marika's cakes, too?" I left out the part where she'd called him a butt child.

"Just one or two. I was hungry. That old man in the dungeon eats all the sweets. What else was I supposed to do?" His shoulders slumped. The kid looked bummed out. I'd be bummed out too if someone ate all the sweets.

"Why didn't your KGB buddy give you a gun and a snack allowance?"

Xander tensed up. He shot me a questioning look.

Between my big mouth and everyone's subterfuge, it was hard to keep track of who knew what. I really needed an app for this. "Some guy pretending to be KGB hired Dina and Donk to follow me. Although, if you ask me if he's a lame employer if he doesn't give you money or weapons." I swiveled to look at Donk. "What are you getting out of it, anyway?"

"Bragging rights and exposure," Donk said.

This time I paired my eye roll with a groan. Teenage boys were so predictable.

"Exposure is the last thing a spy needs," I told him.

What had this so-called KGB guy promised Dina besides money? A romantic dinner with Dad? Dad was already avoiding the first one he had agreed to. Now, I thought, panic welling up in me again, he had a legitimate excuse to avoid the date.

My chest tightened.

God, Virgin Mary, Jesus Christ, and all the saints who names I didn't know—Saint Valentine and Santa Claus were two of them, right?—I had to find Dad and Grandma. Going down the abduction road again ... I didn't think my heart and head could take it.

George George was good. George George was so good that he got one over on Grandma and Dad—that's what I was up against. My skills weren't mad; mostly they were non-existent.

Where are you?

Marika again.

With Xander.

Winking face. *Do not do anything I would do.*

It was pointless getting her riled up, telling her what was going on. Nobody could do anything. They weren't around to do anything. Saving Grandma and Dad was their main priority right now—and mine. We were scattered, working toward the same goal. The compound was mostly empty of anyone trained to wield a deadly weapon.

The compound was *vulnerable*.

"Christ on a cruise ship," I yelped. "We have to go back!"

Xander raised his eyebrows. His silent act was driving me up the wall.

"Now is not the time," I said. "Grandma and Dad are gone. Everyone else in the family has gone after them. We're up here. Who is left at the compound? Wives, children, and a handful of armed men. A handful when there are usually dozens. The compound is completely exposed. What if that's what George George wants?"

Just a theory, but it felt like something a villain would do.

Xander stood up. His head connected with the tank's ceiling. He plopped back down. The colorful string of curse words was right there on the tip of his tongue, I could tell. He sat with his head between his knees, rubbing his head.

"Want me to curse for you?"

He glared at me.

"I've got this," I said.

I didn't have gangster skills but I did have some sense.

Not common sense, otherwise I wouldn't be stuck in this tank, but maybe uncommon sense. I texted Elias, told him to wake up Tomas and get the little guy to show everyone —women and children—the way into the dungeon. Underground, in the space few knew about, they'd be hidden and safe. Something told me Monobrow was more than Makria's only homeless person. Something told me he was a man with his own set of secrets and skills besides "most pieces of loukoumia crowded into a human mouth at the same time".

Elias didn't waste time asking questions. He shot back with two words: *Okay, boss.*

Relief rippled through my body. The menfolk could protect themselves; they were soldiers, they were armed. With the vulnerable stashed safely underground they'd be able to do what needed doing—if it needed doing. Could be I was worrying about nothing, but I didn't think so.

What about the police, should I call them?

Who was I kidding? I meant Detective Melas. I wanted to call him … and I didn't. He walked away from me. Avoiding me was his choice. I couldn't—and wouldn't—call him now.

On the other hand—good thing I wasn't cursed with more than two—the family was the mob, but Grandma and Dad were law enforcement, so it wouldn't be the wrong thing to contact the police. The compound couldn't have too much protection, under the circumstances. The family and the Family were my family. There was no level to which I wouldn't stoop to save their souvlaki.

I texted Melas, told him to get to the compound and have a casual look around to make sure everything was okay.

Then I waited. Would I get a reply or had he stripped me out of his phone as well as his life?

My phone blinked. My heart skipped a beat because it was an idiot and also guilty that minutes ago I'd been ready to take my first lap ride in a tank with Xander.

Already on my way. Where are you?

In a tank, suspended from a helicopter.

It was a serious question.

Obviously my answer didn't sound serious to him. A year ago it wouldn't have sounded serious to me either.

Wait—why are you at the compound? Who called you?

Xander texted me.

"Thanks for making me look like a tool," I said to Xander.

From the confusion in his eyes I realized it didn't translate well.

"It's like a *malakas*, but without the … well, you know."

Xander raised his eyebrows. There was a smile in his eyes—a dirty one. Then his face changed again. His muscled tensed.

I held my breath. Listened.

The blades were slowing.

We were going down.

Chapter 11

WHEN I WAS A KID—AND an adult—I watched a million war movies. Not because I wanted to but because Dad was a junkie for any movie that featured camouflage. The movies he liked best were set in submarines, tin cans with propellers that shunted them around the oceans. Invariably, at some point in the movie, the captain shut off their engines and the crew held their tongues, plunging the submarine into an eerie silence. Sometimes they lived, sometimes they died, but one thing was constant: ghostly metallic noises outside the sub. The same spooky sounds I was hearing now. Metal grinding against metal. Faint, high pitched squeals as alloys collided. A haunting groan as someone walked over what was starting to feel like our way-too-early grave.

The tank touched ground with an almighty thump. Like a bunch of skittles, we bumped around. Donk grabbed my boob.

I elbowed him.

"It was just there," he said.

I made a grabbing motion with my hand. "While you were going like this?"

"How did you know?"

I elbowed him again.

Xander zipped his lips, held up his finger.

"Quiet," I whispered to Donk, in case he didn't understand basic hand gestures.

Chains rattled.

CLUNK.

Everything went quiet.

Then someone with one X chromosome and a serious cigarette and Metaxa habit said, "Come on out, it is safe out here. Nice evening, in fact. A good night to discuss business."

We kept our traps shut.

Metaxa and Cigarettes snapped his fingers. "I almost forgot the music. Life is better with a soundtrack."

There was a click, and then *Eye of the Tiger* shredded the silence with its 80s power. Another coincidence that wasn't a coincidence at all. Which meant there was a strong chance that voice belonged to none other than the Man Who Lived: George George.

"That does not sound good to me," Donk whispered. "I think I will stay here."

Great idea. I wanted to do that. Too bad I couldn't.

"Okay," I said, giving myself a pep talk. "You can do this, Kat. This is what Grandma would do."

I climbed up and out of the tank, hoping my bladder wouldn't betray me.

The voice's owner was waiting in a pair of neon parachute pants, straight out of the late 1980s. His skin said he was vintage too, from one of the early Baby Boomer decades. Lots of potholes and crepe ditches. He wore a tightly permed mullet dipped in a bucket of midnight dye, a neon ski jacket that clashed with his pants, and high top LA Gear sneakers. Someone had been on ice for thirty years. Did he know KC and the Sunshine Band weren't top of the charts anymore?

He clicked his fingers again. "Somebody get her down from there."

A young guy in rushed over to help me down. Military boots. Black T-shirt. Black cargo pants and accessories. If it looked like a henchman and took orders like a henchman, it was probably a henchman.

On firm ground, I managed to get a look at my surroundings.

Holy crap on toast.

Apparently the super-duper helicopter had airlifted us all the way to Athens. Currently the tank and I were perched upon the Acropolis, home to the Parthenon. The place was a national treasure and completely breathtaking. How it had never made any of the World Wonders lists was mind-boggling. Dumping a tank on the hilltop was a travesty, but apparently this clown didn't care about things like rules and probably laws.

"Cool Parthenon," I said, trying not to be all giddy with excitement over my first up-close glimpse of the architectural and historical marvel. The city stretched out before me, millions of lights pressed into its darkness.

Hand shielding his eyes, he swung around to look at the ancient stones. At night, the whole hill was strategically lit. "Thank you. I made it myself."

"You look old," I said, "but not that old."

He quit looking at the Parthenon and swung his attention to me. "You are funnier than your grandmother."

I shoved my hands into my pockets—well, part of my hands, seeing as how pockets in women's clothing are inadequate, at best. "Don't let her hear you say that. Are you George George?"

The washed-out wannabe smirked. The smirk didn't look pretty on him. You had to be a certain kind of man to work a smirk without it coming across as sleazy. George-by-two was not that kind of man. "You have heard of me?"

"I read a note on a dead man's back, and I also saw what you did with a Cabbage Patch Kid and *Kyrios Patata Kefala*."

He crossed himself, forehead to chest, shoulder to shoulder. "I love the 1980s. They were the best years of my life. I was young …"

I raised an eyebrow, then the second one. This was a two-eyebrow situation.

" … younger. I had money. I had ambition and a burning desire to take over the whole world. Who can blame a man for wanting to hold onto the good life, eh?"

"You put the doll's head up his *kolos*. That's weird and messed up."

"I did not," he said. "Someone else did it for me." He pointed. "That one over there, I think. Was it you?"

The henchman raised his hand. "It was me."

These people were deranged, even for criminals. "You're holding two of my favorite people hostage. Well, one of my favorite people, and my grandmother. I don't see them, by the way. Where are they?"

He shrugged. "Not here, and they are not hostages. I just have them somewhere for safekeeping."

So basically they were hostages.

Survivor gave way to Loverboy, who begged someone to turn him loose.

"Where?" I asked.

"One of my favorite places. Do not worry, you will see them eventually in hell."

"Greeks don't really believe hell as a location, you know that, right?"

Geriatric MC Hammer held his substantial belly and laughed. "Come over here, Katerina, and bring your friend."

"Friend? I came alone."

"I want to see the boy."

Donk. Why hadn't he listened to me and stayed behind, where it was safe? Well, safer than this.

"What boy? There's no boy."

He pulled out a Nerf gun. "The boy."

"That's a Nerf gun."

"I know. This gun is one of my favorite things from the 1980s."

"The first Nerf gun came out in the 1990s."

His hands jerked. "You are wrong."

"No … I'm right. I was a child of the 90s. I know these things."

The canyons on his face purpled. "Get the boy now."

"Donk," I called out.

Donk popped up like a meerkat, eyelids blinking at the hilltop's bright lights. "What's a-a-a-a-p?"

The moldy oldie laughed. "Who is that creature?"

I felt my forehead crumple. If I ever got Botox, Greece would be responsible. "That's Donk—Yiorgos—Baby Dimitri's nephew."

He grinned. "His nephew, eh? Must be Vikki's boy. Do not worry, I will kill him later. Where is the other one?"

"Other one?" I asked. "What other one?"

The grin fell away. "Do not play the *vlakas* with me."

Playing stupid? Hardly. This nutcase was missing a few *souvlakia* from his picnic. No one sane discussed kidnappings to a carefully curated playlist. There was only one warm body in that tank right now, and if Xander hadn't revealed himself yet there was a reason. Did he need time? I could give him time to play whatever card was up his tight, black sleeve. The only question was whether I should exaggerate my smart side or my inner idiot.

I scanned George George. In that outfit, he didn't strike me as someone who appreciated women for their brains.

All righty. Idiot it was, then.

"I'm not playing. I really am stupid. Ask anyone in Greece. Have you seen Takis' YouTube channel? He's my cousin's cousin's cousin. Anyway, Takis has a YouTube channel, a really popular one, and he loves putting up videos of me doing crazy things. I get a lot of Likes, or whatever they're called on YouTube. And now that I'm thinking about it, I'm wondering if Takis is monetizing that channel, because I'm thinking I'd like a cut, seeing as how he's making money off of me." I pulled out my phone. "Here, want to see? I don't know if you have a phone or anywhere to put it in those pants". I eyed his pants. He was a walking fashion Don't. "Speaking of pants, those are cool—or they used to be. You do know the 1980s are over, right? I'm just checking because sometimes people your age get confused. They have places that can take of that now, you know. Back in the USA they even have a nursing home where it's all set up like a real neighborhood with little porches in front of the patients' doors. Maybe your family can find you something like that, but with 80s references. *Little House on the Prairie*? That house from *The Goonies*? Oh! I know! The *Poltergeist* house. It's so you. Anyway, this is YouTube. Oh, and I have Takis' channel bookmarked. With this bookmark I can easily go back to his channel anytime I want to watch myself being an—"

He grabbed his tightly permed hair, so I guess you

could say I was succeeding at being a royal pain in the butt. "*Gamo ton kerato sou*, do you ever *skasmos?*"

"All the time. I'm normally quiet, but right now I'm feeling especially talkative. You really bring it out—"

"Xander," he said between gritted teeth that may or may not have been real. "Where is Xander?"

"Tall, dark, and silent? Kind of sexy? Really loves the color black?"

George George looked at me. It wasn't a nice look.

"Haven't seen him." Girly shrug. "Not since—"

Click.

Xander appeared behind George George, arm extended, gun to the back of his mullet-covered head. Whoa. Slick. Did the tank have a backdoor?

"Well, since just now actually." I waved cheerfully. "Hey, Xander, this *malakas* was just asking about you. And look, what a coincidence, you're here."

George George was old but spry for a guy with forty extra pounds and about ten years left on his lifespan—if heart disease didn't get him first. He whipped around, knocked the gun out of Xander's hand using his Nerf gun.

Xander was the best of boy scouts and he'd come prepared. He pulled out Donk's pistol and aimed that at the old guy.

George George raised his hands. "Xander, I am your father," he said dramatically and a lot like Darth Vader, but without the heaving breathing issue. Also, technically he said, "Xander, father your I am." Like Yoda, Greek to English wasn't always linear.

Then his words drip-filtered through my translation center and entered the part of my brain where I processed impossible things.

Oof.

Bees set up house in my ears. Or maybe they were wasps. Possibly flies.

"His father?" I raised a pair of horrified eyebrows at Xander, who was as relaxed as a pillow and as expressionless as a recently shaken Etch-a-Sketch. "If you get this crazy old weasel anything for Father's Day, I will personally kick you in the shins."

My mind performed cartwheels. Xander had told me himself that Grandma raised him after killing the man who had kidnapped him from his birth family. If someone had kidnapped him from George George, I could understand why. George George was a real douche, and not in a fresh vinegary way.

"Not just funnier than your grandmother—you are almost as charming," George George said. "I cannot wait to watch you die when you cannot produce that *malakas* Dimitri. For you I will choose one of my favorite songs. A big hit. You like Madonna? Of course you do. Everybody loves Madonna." He did a little dance while he hummed a few bars of *Papa Don't Preach*.

Xander said nothing. God, he was good at it. The man had serious self-control. I'd last about five minutes before I popped my mouth off.

I was terrified but I wasn't about to give George George the satisfaction he'd get if I showed it. So I stuck my chin out and leaned against the tank, channeling my inner cool cat. "No offense—not that I really care much about offending you because you're kind of weird and also rude—but Xander doesn't look anything like you."

"That is because his mother ate too much fruit while she was pregnant."

Yeah, genetics didn't work like that. But why argue? At times, elderly Greeks weren't big fans of things like science.

Xander slowly moved around to the front, gun trained on George George.

"Why did you bring us here?" I said.

"You and the child were collateral damage. I only wanted my son. But now that I think about it I am glad you are here. I can use you as an insurance policy. If my son here decides to shoot me, my men will shoot you."

"He's annoying and those clothes are atrocious, so feel free to shoot him," I told Xander.

George George looked down at his clothes. "What is wrong with my outfit?"

"Nothing, Baklava Ice."

His face fell. "I was going for Michael Jackson."

"More like Germaine."

"*Gamo tin putana*. Is that the oily one?" He whipped out a cell phone, tapped on its screen. "*Gamo tin putana*, it is the oily one. I do not like you. You should leave. I have what I want. But I will see you tomorrow night before I kill you and Baby Dimitri's nephew here, okay?"

I looked around. "Leave? How are we supposed to do that?"

"Take the skinny boy, get in your tank, and drive off into the sunset."

"There's no sunset and I can't drive a tank."

"Oh, okay." He waved his arm at something or someone in the distance. A Trans Am pulled up, chauffeured by a David Hasselhoff lookalike, complete with leather jacket and fluffy hair. He turned around, looked me in the eye. "Find that *voithi* and bring him to me."

"I don't even know what that is."

"A *voithi*? A filthy animal."

"You know my family, we have a lot of those. You're going to have to be more specific."

"Baby Dimitri," he said, exasperated. "You have

twenty-four hours." George George heaved his non-boda-cious bod into the Trans Am. "Hurry up, son. Get in before I get you in—and you do not want me to get you in."

Xander placed Marika's gun in my hand, closed my fingers around the warm metal.

"I'm not leaving here without you," I said.

He folded me up in his arms, lips moving against my hair. His words were lower than a whisper but I heard them anyway. "It's going to be okay, I promise. Trust me. Go." He pushed me away gently and angled into the Trans Am's backseat. It was a small backseat and he was a lot of man—all of it muscled and tan.

"Wait." I waved the gun at the 80s reject. "You stole something from Baby Dimitri years ago. What was it?"

"What he deserved to lose," George George called out. "Everything."

"Why?"

"We were friends, and then he fucked me in the *kolos*."

This was Greece so I had to ask. "Literally or figuratively?"

"He betrayed me. Nobody betrays George George."

Greeks were maddening. Or maybe it was just the Greeks I knew. "If someone could be specific for once, that would be great."

"You want to know? Ask Dimitri. If he is a man he will tell you."

"Can't," I said. "He's missing."

"I know." Big oily grin. "Then this is good incentive to find him, yes? This and the salvation of your family."

What I had to do now was plot. First I had to get Donk out of here and retreat to the family compound, where I could muster the troops and hope one of them had a good idea about how to extricate Xander from George George's clutches. Yes, Xander had told me it would be okay. Yes, he was a tough guy and I had no doubt he could handle himself. But could he save himself from the fruitcake that believed he was Xander's father? Also probably yes.

But I wasn't about to risk his life based on "probably". There were no sure things in this world except death and taxes, and taxes were optional if you were Greek or an American corporation, but I wanted Xander's safety to join the ranks, because Xander would never let anyone take me—not without a fight.

And while I was doing all that, I was going to hunt down Baby Dimitri. That cunning old gangster couldn't hide forever. I needed to find him if I was going to save my small piece of the world and the people who mattered to me. Handing him over to George George was out of the question, but maybe we could trick the old goat somehow.

"See you in twenty-four hours, Katerina," George George said. Before he rolled down the window, he handed me something.

"A mix tape?"

"Music is life," he said. "And the 1980s had the best music."

The car bumped away to the whimsical pop beat of Karma Chameleon, leaving me with Donk, the tank, and a dozen henchmen.

Xander didn't look back.

That didn't stop me from waving until the car was out of sight.

I blew out a long, frustrated sigh. "Can we go now?"

There were whispers. I couldn't see faces but the dawn wasn't that far away so I was getting a load of shrugging shoulders.

"Anyone? Bueller?"

A lone voice spoke up. "Sure. We guess."

Now wasn't the time for withering gaze, although I was certainly in the mood to put on my best bitch-face. I gave the accommodating henchman a thumbs up. "Thanks!"

"No problem!" There was a pause, then: "Do you need a ride?"

"Is there a bus stop around here?"

"Down at the bottom of the hill."

"Thank you," I said.

With Donk beside me, I set off in the downward-pointing direction, leaving Greece's most famous landmarks and Baby Dimitri's tank behind me.

"Wait."

I turned around. The helpful henchman was standing there, black cap in hands.

"On a scale of one to ten, how helpful was I? My boss rewards positive customer satisfaction."

"About a ten."

He beamed at me and gave me a business card. "Thank you, thank you. If you need hired muscle, call and my boss will give you a good price."

I didn't bother telling him that my grandmother was Baboulas and she already had all the muscle she needed. Donk and I set off down the winding path.

There really was a bus stop at the bottom of the hill, which was no huge surprise given that the Acropolis was one of the world's most recognizable and famous locations. Tourist season was over in the Pelion region, but Athens was still flooded with the kind of people who knew that if you have to slog through a smoggy city to look at architectural wonders, this was the time of the year to do it, when summer's blade had dulled.

Which was a long way of saying the bus was already crowded when I dragged Donk onto the back end and paid the conductor to take us as far away as we could get from the Acropolis.

Definitely not a Pelion region bus. Everyone was polite. Nobody whacked me with their bags, and nobody paid us any attention. Tourists were so nice. I almost shed a tear.

"A bus? Why do we have to catch a bus?" Donk whined.

"Because if I rent a car right now I'll ram the first annoying pedestrian that crosses my path."

"We could have taken the tank."

"I can't drive a tank."

His chest puffed up. "I bet I can."

I snorted. "Until this morning you had never been in a tank—and neither had I."

We got off the bus, then got on another bus. Using the power of the internet, we got on and off buses until we found a bus that would take us to Volos. Along the way, I messaged Elias. I didn't call in case everyone was still in hiding.

He called me.

"Everyone is fine, boss. Kyria Rita got back from Delphi an hour ago."

I heard Aunt Rita's voice in the background. "Is that Katerina? Katerina, where are you?"

"It's a long story," I told her when she grabbed Elias's phone. "It involves a tank, Donk, Xander, George George, and a lot of buses."

"Too many buses," Donk said in a gloomy voice. He wasn't too bummed out, though. Three seats ahead of us there was a cute teenager with a pulse who was completely ignoring him, which made her totally his type.

"Did you get Dad and Grandma?" I asked her.

"No. They are there somewhere—Mama's signal says

so—but we could not find them. Takis and some of the others are still there, searching."

Still missing. Less than a day to go.

"Change of plans," I told Donk, whose eyes were glued to the cute teenager. "We're going to Delphi."

His eyes were glazed over. "Huh?"

Ugh, never mind.

"Aunt Rita, is it true that George George is Xander's father?"

Her laugh had no funny in it. "What? No. Why?"

"That's what he told Xander before he took him."

"George George took Xander? That is not good."

She ended the call.

"That was weird," I said to Donk. "I would like one week that isn't weird."

We changed buses again. The trip to Delphi took three hours and change. The bus stopped at the Friendly Cafe along the way, then we all bundled back onto the bus again and rattled toward Delphi.

Under crushing pressure wasn't the way I wanted to see Greece. The scenery scampered past. It was green and brown. Leafy in places. Look—a squirrel!

Nope. Just a discarded plastic bag. Never mind.

I called Melas. "What's going on?"

"Nothing to report. Everyone in your family is fine."

"And people in Makria?"

"Fine."

His voice was all cop and no Nikos. My heart was a bowling ball: heavy, with holes in it.

"Is this how we are now?" I asked him.

"You lied. How can I trust you?"

"Do you tell me everything?"

"I am a policeman. Some things are confidential."

I eyed Donk, who had scooted forward. He was stalking the girl.

"So are certain people we both know, which means I couldn't just tell you about the surveillance equipment."

Melas sighed. "Not now, okay?"

"Why not? I'm on a bus with some time to kill."

"Why are you on a bus?"

"Grandma and Dad are a little bit missing."

Silence.

"Melas?"

"Since when did they go missing?"

"Since a crazy man named George George picked them up and stashed them away somewhere in Delphi."

"George George is dead. He died thirty years ago."

"How can you think that? You were there in the morgue when we found that note on the man with the--"

He cut me off. "When I saw the note in the morgue I figured it was a hoax or someone with the same name. That happens a lot in Greece."

"Everyone keeps saying that, but I saw him myself. I don't think he likes me very much."

Melas chuckled. "Probably because of that mouth of yours." He went silent again. Then: "Did you see someone left a tank next to the Parthenon?"

"Huh. It's amazing where people will dump their junk. What do you know about George George?"

"George George was bad news. If he really is alive he is still bad news. Where are you now?" he asked me, suspiciously.

"On a bus. I already told you that."

"A bus to where?"

"Delphi."

"Alone?"

"Donk is with me, but I may as well be alone because he's trying to pick up some girl."

The teenager in question was smoothing his hair and rearranging his ball cap.

"If George George has Baboulas and your father, leave it alone. They can handle it. I want you to turn around and come home. George George is a desperate man. If he is still alive, he has been waiting for his revenge for decades."

"Revenge for what?"

"Baboulas killed his whole family."

My mind reeled. I knew this story. Grandma had told me herself. Once upon a time, she killed her enemy and his whole family, except for a child she took home and raised. Then Xander had filled in some of the blanks for me. Grandma had rescued an infant Xander from the man who had kidnapped him. I'd had it all wrong. George George was the kidnapper.

Which meant George George was not Xander's father. Ha! I knew Xander couldn't have sprung from that fruit-cake's loins. What an ass. George George didn't even have Darth Vader's tiny shred of integrity.

"Xander," I said. "That's where Grandma found Xander."

"Yes."

The bus chugged into Delphi. We were almost there.

"Time to go," I said.

"Come home," Melas said. "I do not want you to get hurt."

"No. This is my family. None of them would abandon me if I was kidnapped."

I ended the call and looked at Donk, who was this close to letting the girl know he existed. By lunchtime he might have even worked up the courage to speak.

I scooted forward and crouched down beside him. "Do you trust me?"

"Why? Do you want to take advantage of me? Because I would let you."

I pressed some cash into his hand and folded his fingers around it—about a hundred euro. "Stay on the bus until you can get one headed to Volos. Go back to the compound. You'll be safe there."

Donk folded his arms. "Forget it. I have to stay with you. The man said so."

"The KGB man? If he was KGB then I'm a mongoose."

"What's a mongoose? Is it a sex thing?"

I didn't know the Greek word for mongoose, so I tried winging the description. "It's a furry little animal that kills snakes."

"Kind of like a sex thing then."

"It's not a sex thing, okay? My point is this. Probably your KGB guy isn't a KGB guy. Whoever he is, probably he's some kind of criminal. Strangers usually are these days."

"But he promised—"

"Prestige with the ladies, I know. Trust me on this. I've been around the block a few times." Different kind of block, different kind of country, but Donk didn't need to know that. He was fifteen or sixteen, for crying out loud. "Stay on the bus. Go home. And by home I mean the compound."

The bus stopped.

I got off.

Donk stayed behind. Back at the compound, surround by my family, he'd be safe.

For now.

Chapter 12

DELPHI, population 1500 and change, was postcard pretty. Not exactly the kind of place you went to murder decent people, or even people like Grandma and Dad. The streets were narrow. The houses were the stucco-covered two-story houses you'd find anywhere in Greece. The awnings —and there were a lot of them—were pale. Businesses mingled with homes. Everything was in one state of disrepair or another, yet, the effect was charming. I could see myself falling apart here and being happy about it.

I stopped at a *periptero*, where a moon crater with a couple of teeth and a gray monobrow grunted at me.

"Have you seen any strangers in black cars?"

She pointed the way with her nose. "They went to the ruins."

"How far are they?"

"Not far."

Distance is as nebulous as time in Greece. Could be twenty miles, could be one. Lucky for me, my phone's map was more specific. Not far, in this instance, was accurate.

I bought four bars of ION chocolate, two bottles of

water, and set off on foot for Delphi's famous ruins. Within minutes I had passed the museum and made my way over to a Greek Quasimodo with a walkie-talkie who was pelting the ruins with her finest stink-eye.

"They made us close down the ruins," she muttered in my direction. "Very bad for business."

Athens' Acropolis usually hogs the limelight when it comes to cool old stuff in Greece, but Delphi is no slouch in the beauty department, with its endless green view of the valley. Weather-stroked pillars point at the sky. Fragments of ancient stone, interspersed with pale brown dirt, serve as a reminder that people have always enjoyed building things but trying to get contractor out to make repairs in a timely fashion has always been nigh on impossible.

I marched up to where Takis and Stavros were huddled around a cell phone off to the side of Delphi's Temple of Apollo—the Olympian god, not the cute one from *Battlestar Galactica*. Apollo was the god of lots of things, including medicine and the plague, which meant he was a lot like a medical research company—possibly the Umbrella Corporation. Neither Takis nor Stavros looked happy. Mostly they looked sweaty and frustrated.

Takis glanced up. His ferret face crumpled up. "What are you doing here?"

"Sightseeing. Did you find them yet?"

"Of course we did," he said sarcastically, waving his hand at all the nothing they'd found. "Did you hear somebody left a tank up on the Acropolis?"

"Huh. How about that."

He looked past me. "Is Xander with you? We need him."

"Xander is with George George."

Takis sandblasted Delphi with curse words. Apparently

he wanted the Virgin Mary (a virgin in name only, apparently) to take a horn up the butt, after she'd penetrated Jesus with a goat and several olive trees.

"Keep your fantasies to yourself," I said.

Stavros laughed. Takis nailed him with an elbow. Happy families.

"According to Aunt Rita, Grandma's transmitter says she's still here."

"It is a mystery," Takis said, clearly unhappy about mysteries.

"Where did you look?"

"Everywhere."

"And the signal?"

Takis pointed. "Over there."

His finger was pointing at the Temple of Apollo. I didn't need binoculars to see Grandma and Dad weren't there, party because we were standing six feet away and partly because we were the only ones here. The family had the kind of clout that could lockdown a national treasure for the day.

"Nobody there," I said.

Takis slowly clapped. "Give the girl a *koulouraki*. No, they are not there. Nobody is there. And nobody has seen anything."

"Did you check the underground chambers?"

A long uncomfortable silence happened. Then: "What underground chambers?"

My relationship with God was "It's complicated". When Mom was dying, and after, I turned to philosophers for explanations and excuses. God had remained silent; I'd never quite forgiven Him for that. The Greek philosophers had all kinds of things to say about death though, and you don't brush up against a philosopher without scrapping off a bit of history. One thing lead to another, and now here I was in Delphi with more knowledge under my belt that all of my Greek relatives.

"Don't any of you know anything about history?"

"Of course. We went to school."

"You went," I said, "but did you learn anything?"

Takis feigned shock. "Is that why I was there? I thought school was for chasing girls."

I oinked, and then immediately felt bad because pigs are clean, sweet, smart animals that really suffer from bad PR.

"There's a rumor, backed up by conjecture, myth, and legend, that Delphi has underground chambers," I said. "There's a real science-verified pair of fault lines that run through the area and intersect almost directly under the temple. Gas used to seep up through the cracks—allegedly. Or it used to—still allegedly—because an earthquake sealed the cracks and stopped the gas leaks, rendering Delphi useless and the sibyls out of a job. The young women, the sibyls, used to hang out in the underground chamber, where they would get high on the gas and babble the way you do when you're super high. Then priests" I made air quotes "would interpret the babble to serve their own purposes because that's the patriarchy for you. It's not the only alleged underground chamber—there are others, also allegedly—but that's where the signal is coming from, I bet."

"Son of the bitch," Takis said in English. "How do we get under there?"

Good question.

I blinked.

Oh.

He was looking at me like I had all the answers. I didn't. I was just the person who read a book or two.

I shrugged. "Ask someone who works here."

"Good idea. You should do that." He turned his back on me and got busy talking into his phone. The other family members trickled toward where we were standing, ready to receive orders.

"Okay," I said to no one in particular. "I'll just go find someone who can help."

I trotted down to the bottom of the hill, where Greek Quasimodo was waving her broom at the tourists. "We are closed," she shrieked at a cluster of bright-eyed elderly women in loose capris and sneakers. They looked like the kind of women who usually spent their days on the couch, knitting and clucking and drinking milky tea. They also seemed to be confused. A lot of clueless glances were being exchanged. One woman was leafing through an English-Greek phrase book from some bygone decade.

"What's the old buzzard talking about then?"

"I don't know but she doesn't look happy, does she?"

"Reminds me of a pile of rocks, she does."

I hid my smile in a fake cough. The women weren't American or Canadian. Definitely some flavor of British. I didn't know enough about Great Britain to make a more educated guess.

"I think that's how she always looks," I said helpfully.

Relief swept over their faces. "She speaks English."

"Good English, too."

"Can we really call Americans English?" one of them said. Pretty rich from a woman sporting a denim fanny pack.

Uh oh. Things could turn ugly fast if someone brought up the whole tea-tossing thing. I changed the subject fast. The English were touchy about tea.

"Do you need some help translating?" I asked them.

Their attention shifted back to Greek Quasimodo. "We thought Greeks were always cheerful."

"Avoid the ones in black," I told them. "That's a good rule of thumb. They'll peck out your eyes."

"Like magpies in the springtime." A round of polite nods. "Can we come in, then? We really want to see Delphi."

"That's kind of a problem," I told them. "See, my grandmother is one of Greece's infamous mobsters, and she's been kidnapped, along with my father. We have reason to think they're being held underground by an elderly lunatic dressed like Germaine Jackson."

Were they bummed out and afraid at the prospect of crazed criminals and abductions?

Nope. These women had steel spines, honed by the messy decades after World War II. They weren't afraid of anything except maybe bad tea and stale biscuits. Their wrinkles plummeted to new depths as their faces broke out in rashes of smiles.

"Oooh, we've never seen that before, have we? Do you think we could come and watch? My mum will never forgive me if she finds out we missed a chance to rub elbows with real life mobsters."

I glanced back at Takis, who was standing around, hands on his hips, metaphorically counting his balls. "I don't think that would be a good idea."

"We won't be a bother, will we? We'll stay out of the way. You'll hardly know we're there. Quiet as church mice."

"They have guns," I explained. "Sometimes they go *bang*."

"We've never heard a gun go off before, have we, luvs?" They exchanged excited glances. A shrill chorus of British-tinted "No's" echoed around Delphi.

"They're louder than you'd expect," I said.

"Never mind that. Most of us can't hear as well as we used to. Betty can't even hear herself fart, can you Betty?"

A woman, who I assumed was Betty, cupped her ear with one hand. "What was that?"

"I said you can't hear yourself fart, can you?" the woman said at the top of her lungs. She turned back to me. "Can't smell them either, or so she says."

"*Vre*, Katerina, what are you doing?" Takis called out.

Right. The chamber. I turned to Greek Quasimodo, who had whipped the whiskbroom out of its hiding place and was currently sweeping a clean patch of stone. I told her what I needed. She stared at me like I'd sprouted two heads.

"What chamber?"

"The chamber under the temple. You know, where the sibyls used to go to huff gas."

She clicked her tongue against her teeth. "No chamber. A rumor only."

"There's a chamber," I said, hoping no one would make me swear on my life that a chamber existed. "That's where Grandma's GPS says she is."

"Maybe is just her body. Could be somebody dug up the dirt and put her in it."

"That's cheerful."

"But I do not think that is what they did."

"Why not?"

She touched her watery, jaundiced eye. "Do you see this?"

"Your eye?"

"My eye is magic. The doctor calls it cataracts but now I see better than ever before. I see secrets and crimes and worms wiggling beneath the earth. And let me tell you, if someone had buried bodies up here I would have seen them digging."

"But you didn't see them dragging one old lady and one man up here and cramming them into the chamber?"

"There is no chamber."

"There's a chamber, and I'm going to find it."

She wagged her finger at me. "You cannot find something that is not there."

We'd see about that. Grandma and Dad were under there somewhere, and I was going to find a way in.

I waved Takis over. "How soon can you have some kind of digging equipment here? Maybe a backhoe or whatever digs big, destructive holes?"

Takis was a jerk and a dumbass but he wasn't stupid. He immediately cottoned on to where this was going. "Half an hour. For Baboulas? Even faster."

Greek Quasimodo cackled. "Baboulas schmaboulas, you cannot scare me. I survived the Turks, the Italians, the Turks, the Germans, and the Turks again."

Takis whipped out his phone. "Stavros, excavation equipment." He listened for a moment. "Okay. Dynamite is even better."

This time the color bled out of the canyons in Greek Quasimodo's leather upholstered face. "You cannot blow holes in Delphi."

"Watch me," Takis said.

"Okay, okay, there is a chamber. But you cannot get to it easily. Very dangerous."

"Show us," I said. "Please. It's life or death, and I don't want it to be death."

"That will go very badly for you," Takis said to her.

"Takis," I said.

He held out his hands in supplication. "Just show us the chamber, eh?"

The old woman waddled up to the temple, slippers slapping against the uneven stones that were almost as old as Greece itself. "There." She pointed to a wide, flat stone. Square. Unassuming. Like so many things in Greece, you'd never know it was hiding secrets. "Lift it and you will find your chamber. My eye tells me it is there."

"Crowbar," Takis called out.

A crowbar appeared in his hand. The cousins could be efficient. No wonder they were so good at crime. It took Takis and Stavros both with crowbars to pop the stone up. Four cousins hauled it aside. Takis shone his flashlight in.

"Okay, that is a chamber," he said.

"Told you so." I crouched down beside him. "See anything?"

"I hear something."

I could hear it, too. "Sounds like hyenas."

"Greece does not have hyenas."

"Yeah, because they're all down there." I stuck my head into the hole. "Dad? Grandma?"

More cackling.

Takis' head popped up. "*Re*, what are these *malakies*? There are old underpants with faces here. Why are there old underpants with faces walking around when I paid good money to keep them away?"

The British tourists had wandered up to the temple and were oohing and ahhhing. Their phones were out and they were holding them up like tech savvy meerkats in stretchy pants.

"They're harmless," I told my cousin's cousin's cousin, hoping that was true.

"*Gamo tin putana*. I am holding you responsible if they breathe." Takis shone the flashlight into the hole in the ground again, then he sat on the edge and slid in, bone-lessly. He didn't howl in pain, so I slid down after him.

He grabbed me by the scruff of the neck.

189

"What are you doing down here? You cannot come. Baboulas will kill me if you get hurt."

"No problem." I pulled out my phone. "Let me call Marika …"

"You play very dirty, you know that?"

"Who me?" I gave him an angelic smile. "Which way?"

He rolled his eyes and pointed with his flashlight. "There."

The chamber wasn't a single chamber; it was a series of low ceilinged rooms that reeked of sweet, rotting fruit.

"Ethylene gas," I said. There must have been a quake here recently that reopened the ancient fissures. "Dad? Grandma?"

A rash of giggles broke out.

"Dad? Grandma?" Grandma said in a singsong voice.

"Dad? Grandma?" Dad said, laughing his big, stupid head off.

They were in the next chamber, doubled over, tears streaming down their faces. Grandma was old; I wasn't sure all this mirth was a healthy lifestyle choice, but for now they were both alive.

Relief flooded through me. I hurried over.

"Takis?" I said. My cousin's cousin's cousin had already jumped into motion. He threw me his flashlight, then he went for backup. The flashlight's beam scanned Grandma and Dad. They were fine, uninjured. George George had left them down here with a twenty-four pack of bottled water and a crate of chip packets.

"Look," Dad said. "It is Katerina! Katerina!" He did a little *tsifteteli* dance. *Tsifteteli* is basically belly dancing. Nobody wants to see their father belly dance. "Katerina! Katerina! Shake, shake!"

Grandma waggled her finger at me, and then she closed her eyes and stood like a statue. "Greece is the donkey of the world. Ever will it be until we pull our fingers out of our *kolos* and beat down the Turks."

"That's not weird or anything," I said, checking her over.

"The Russian will come. He will meet his end at his beginning. Not yet, but soon," she said.

"I hate to tell you this," I said to Dad in English, "but your mother is losing it."

Grandma wasn't done. "The father will kill the son …"

"That was a whole season arc of Angel," I said. "And if you ever saw it you'd know it was a lie made up by a time-traveling demon."

That didn't stop Dad. This gas was a real trip. "Did you bring any food? If I see another chip I am going to cut somebody." He leaned against the ancient wall and laughed himself sick.

Oh boy. I dug around in my bag and handed him one of the ION bars.

There were sounds behind me. Takis was back with Stavros and a handful of the other cousins. They bundled up Dad and Grandma and steered them toward the entrance. Someone smarter than me had thought to bring a ladder to this party. Grandma looked at Stavros and giggled. There was something screwed up about watching a mob boss and high-ranking intelligence agent giggling. It lacked gravitas.

"If a sausage has hair around it, do not put it in your mouth or you will go blind," she told him. "Never spank a monkey or it will spit."

Takis cackled. "I wish I could take video of this without Baboulas killing me and burying my body in a shallow grave." He handed Dad off to a couple of the cousins and accompanied Grandma to an SUV parked at the bottom of the hill.

"What is wrong with them?" Stavros wanted to know.

"Happy gas," I told him. "It turned Grandma into a prophet and Dad into a loon."

My phone rang. It was Gus wanting to know if I was coming in to work today.

"Not this morning," I said. "Slight case of kidnapping."

"I hate it when that happens," he said cheerfully, "but I am happy you did not quit."

"You couldn't pay me to quit."

"Good, because we cannot afford to lose you."

I blinked in the sunlight, sucked in a lungful of clean air, the kind that wouldn't have me babbling in tongues or predicting the flexible future. We had less than a day before Hurricane George George struck. Grandma and Dad were safe; now I needed to locate Baby Dimitri. And Xander.

"Yoohoo!"

It was the British tourists and they were waving at me. I jogged over to see what was up. They tapped and scrolled. A lot of frowning happened. A lot of "Oo, er, I lost my pictures." "Never mind, here they are. Look at that, I lost them again." "Remember the old days when everything wasn't stuck in a storm?" "A cloud, Mary. A cloud."

Clearly they didn't know I might have less time left on in my hourglass than they did.

"Can I help you?" I said.

"Do you want to see our pictures? We took hundreds. We've never watched a rescue before. Was that your grandmother, the infamous mobster?"

"She seem like a little old grandma to me," one of the others said. With her tight white perm and comfortable walking shoes she looked like she was rubbing noses with eighty.

"Don't judge a book by its cover," I said. "Grandma could cut off a grown man's head with a look."

"My nana could do that, too. She was a right old bitch."

The first woman jumped in. " You want us to send you those photos? He said we should takes lots of pictures, so we did."

My ears pricked up. "Who?"

"A man."

"What man?"

"Mutton dressed as lamb, wasn't he?"

A chorus of agreement.

"I don't know what that means," I said.

"I forgot you're one of those Americans. It means he's an old goat dressed twenty years younger. A bit sad, really. And he's not even famous."

"He might be famous," one of her friends said. "It's not like we know Greek stars."

"Oooh, wouldn't that be something, us brushing up against a Greek movie star and we didn't even know it?"

Sad. Old goat. Mutton and lamb. Sounded like George George to me.

"He's not a movie star." Their faces fell. "But he is a homicidal lunatic who manipulated you into taking photos, for what reason I don't know."

"Oooh, exciting!"

These old buzzards were really something. One of them patted me on the arm.

"Don't feel bad, luv. Meeting a homicidal lunatic is almost as exciting as meeting a movie star."

"Sometimes it's the same thing," another one said.

If George George asked them to take photos, maybe he was around here somewhere. "Did you see where he went?"

"Went down to the museum, didn't he?" The others nodded. "He said he wanted to see Cletus and Biter, whoever they are."

I jogged over to Stavros. "I'm staying here. Can you leave one of the cars and I'll meet you back at the compound later?"

"Why?"

"I was thinking I might check out the museum."

His face brightened up. "I love museums. Let me call Takis and I will come with you."

Having someone tag along while I hunted for George George wasn't my first choice, but I liked Stavros and the company would be nice. Plus, he was handy with a gun if shooting needed to be done.

Wheels slowed alongside us. Automatic windows whirred as Takis lowered the passenger window. "Look, two *malakes*."

Grandma rolled her window down, stuck her head out. "Watch out for the twins with very small *poutsas*, otherwise your death with not be as beautiful as theirs."

Dad joined the party. "Always wear clean underwear before you go out because you never know when you will be trampled by a donkey."

"Takis," I said.

"What?"

"Get them out of here before I shoot you with this gun Xander gave me."

The windows rolled up. The SUV sped away. Hopefully Takis had the air conditioner going full blast. Grandma and Dad needed the oxygen.

My phone rang.

"You found them."

The voice oozed through the phone, that's how I knew who was on the other end.

194

"Nice try, George George. I want to speak to Xander."

"Xander does not speak."

"Okay, so let him mime at me over Facetime."

"Mime is for losers, and my son is not a loser."

Not your son, Bozo the Clown. "Pretty please?"

"What will you do if I do not comply?"

"Probably use a bunch of bad words and fling some empty threats in your general direction."

"Okay. You should do that." He ended the call, the big doody head.

A car pulled up alongside us. Trying to keep up behind it was Dina on her moped. Hera rolled down her window. Dina pulled off her helmet. Her fake hair went with it.

"Pretend you did not see that," she said, cramming the wig back onto her head.

"Saw what?"

Either Stavros played dumb or he was clueless. "Kyria Dina, I did not realize you were a balding old lady. Is it the hormones? You can tell me."

Dina ignored him. "Where are you going now?"

"Why would I tell you?"

"Because if you do not, the KGB man might kill me."

Hera rolled her eyes skyward. "KGB."

Dad's old girlfriend was a pain in my rear end but I didn't want her to get killed. "Museum."

Dina and Hera revved their engines.

"Wait," I called out.

"What?" Hera said.

"How did you find me?"

"Magic. Did you hear there is a tank stuck at the Acropolis?"

"One of these days," I said to Stavros as she trundled down to the Museum parking lot.

"One of these days, what?"

"I don't know, but I'll think of something. Maybe a pie to the face."

"That would be a waste of a good pie. How about *revithia?*"

Revithia—chickpea soup—sounded like a better idea.

"This is why I love you," I said. "You have all the best ideas."

"You love me?"

"Maybe a little bit."

Stavros whipped a large handkerchief out of his pocket, dabbed his eyes. "That is the nicest thing anyone has said to me lately. I am so glad we kidnapped you and dragged you to Greece against your will."

I hugged him around the waist. "Come on. Let's go find George George."

We trotted down to the museum, where clusters of tourists were grumping about the ruins' closure. The museum was blocky and sand colored, a seamless transition from the stones around the building to the building itself.

"They ruins are open again," I said to the cashier. Everybody heard me. They surged outward in one awkward wave. A few remained behind to take in the museum's artifacts.

I approached the museum security guard, a woman with a baton and a face like she was itching to use it on anyone with a pulse.

"Have you seen a man in his seventies, who looks like he's a reject from the late 1980s?"

"Look around. You are describing half these people."

Good point. This late in the season, the tourist trade skewed towards the retirement set. And like most of Florida's snowbirds these people weren't in any hurry to leave their youth behind. Every other body was trapped in the wardrobe of decades past.

"Thanks."

For nothing.

I paid the entrance fee for both of us, took a map, and spent several seconds wrangling with the paper. Where were Cletus and Biter, if those were their real names? Which probably they weren't, seeing as how this was Greece and not the Deep South. Reluctantly, I went back to the security guard and hoped she wouldn't whack me for asking a stupid question. She rolled her eyes and gave me Cletus and Biter's real names.

"What are Kleobis and Biton?" I asked Stavros.

"Statues of two men. Brothers."

"What's so famous about them?" My history and mythology skills were decent but these two were missing from my brain-o-pedia.

"They helped their mama with an important task, and after, because they were such good sons, she asked Hera for a gift. So Hera killed them."

That was Hera the goddess, not the temporarily suspended NIS agent. Although it seemed to me like there was a pattern here with women named Hera. "Wow, their mother should have kept the gift receipt."

Stavos clapped his hand over my mouth and glanced furtively from side to side. "Shhh! She might hear you."

"Hera?" I said against his hand.

He nodded. "It was a mercy killing. In the time of the gods it was considered better to die peacefully, untouched and unscarred, than maimed in war."

Oh. Well. That made it totally okay then. "Where do we find them?"

After several seconds of peering, he jabbed the map. "Here."

We found the room where the two statues stood poised on their pedestals. There was no sign of George George.

"He's not here." I squinted at the poor, unfortunate brothers who had been cursed with more than one crappy gift. "Why are Greek statues always hung like mice?"

"Because Ancient Greek men liked sex with other men and smaller ones hurt less."

My eye twitched.

Wherever George George was, he wasn't here. Which meant he could be anywhere within a fifteen minute radius. We were never going to find him. He'd have to find us.

Unless …

George George had called me. Caller ID had registered a number. I dialed his number.

Axel F blasted out of a nearby phone, startling me.

My hand jerked, smacking my phone into Kleobis—or was it Biton? There was a crack, then a hard, echoing snick as the statue's itty bitty chipolata hit the ground.

Oh my God. *Oh my God.*

This couldn't be happening. I'd just destroyed a priceless piece of art and history.

I looked around. Nobody was in the vicinity except Stavros and me, and Stavros was busy wiping tears of laughter off his face.

"You knocked off his *poutsa*," he said through breathless guffaws.

I crouched down and snatched up the penis. It was cool and hard and felt bigger than it looked. With the knob in my hand, I scurried around to find the source of the ringing phone. It was behind one of the statues, taped to its rock solid butt cheeks. For safekeeping, I stashed the wiener in my pants pocket.

I ripped off the tape, took the phone. A burner phone

programmed to play the *Beverly Hill's Cop* theme as its ring-tone. Nothing fancy. Nothing on it except my number and the one call George George had made to me.

My phone rang. Aunt Rita was on the other end.

"Did you know there is video of you putting a marble poutsa in your pocket?"

"Video," I said weakly, because of course there was.

"It is on Takis' YouTube channel."

"Takis isn't here." I looked at Stavros, who was over the laughter and playing with his phone. "Stavros …"

He looked up. "What?"

"Did you send a movie of me to Takis?"

Guilt sprinted across his face. Like a dog that had just pooped on the couch, he hung his head. "No, I swear. I did not send anything to Takis."

I held up my phone, which was currently playing me stuffing a marble dick in my pocket on repeat. "Then how did it get on YouTube?"

"Takis gave me his login and password and now I can upload things directly without having to send them to him first. Technology is amazing, yes?"

"Take. It. Down," I said through gritted teeth.

"But it already has fifty thousand Likes!"

Refresh. He was right.

"Fifty thousand!" I yelped. "How is that possible?"

"When I upload my cooking videos nobody Likes them except Elias and my mother."

"You have a cooking channel?"

"Naked Cooking with Stavros."

My brain shut down. It crawled into a dark closet and assumed the fetal position, rocking slowly back and forth.

"Please tell me you wear an apron."

"Of course. Ever since I cooked bacon naked that one time."

Yikes. What could I say to that? Nothing. Nothing was best.

Well, we were out of options. George George had fled the premises and here I was with the star of Naked Cooking and this marble penis.

"I don't suppose you have any glue?" I asked Stavros.

"No. No glue."

We looked at the ragged stone edge where the penis used to be.

"I have an idea," I said. "Not a good idea, but an idea."

———

Halfway back to Volos it was already headline news.

Kleobis's Poutsa Found in Museum Donation Box.

"Good thing it was small," I said, reading the headline to Stavros on my phone.

Hera and Dina were behind us. Hera's mouth opened and closed as she drove. She was singing along with the radio. The women clung to our backside all the way into Volos and up the mountain, breaking off at the far end of the driveway, outside the massive gate.

Dina got out, tried to follow me. Had to give the woman credit: she did it with I'm-with-her attitude.

My finger wagged at her. "No, no, no. You stay here with the rest of the garbage." Hera won herself a pointed look from yours truly.

Dina clutched her bountiful hips. "I am practically family and you cannot keep me out."

I snorted. "You will never be part of this family."

She shifted her weight, stuck out her pointy chin. "We will see."

Everyone was at Grandma's place, gathered in the

yard. It looked like business as usual, except for the Xander-shaped hole in the crowd. My chest tightened. George George still had Xander, but where, and was he okay? To me, Xander always seemed invincible, like a modern day Talos (without the single fragile vein that lead to the bronze automaton's doom) circling the compound instead of Crete. The idea that he could be hurt, or worse, was unthinkable. Yet here I was thinking about it. Stewing. And I was pretty sure there was an alien about to bust its way through my chest.

"Good work, all of you," Grandma was saying, obviously over her bout of gas-induced precognition. "Now we have work to do. George George is still out there."

"And he has Xander," I said.

She pulled me aside and spoke in a low voice. "If he has Xander, it is only because Xander wants to be there."

"Are you saying Xander believes George George is his father and wants to enjoy a little family reunion? I know Xander isn't his son but does Xander know that?"

Grandma was stone. The woman could look death in the eye without flinching.

"Believe me when I say Xander is exactly where he wants to be at this moment." She said it slowly and carefully. "The good news is that the body from your car has been identified."

"Who was he?"

"A solider. He was born in this area, then he went missing as a boy. Now I have to tell his parents that he has been found." She shook her head. "What a world we have made to live in."

My heart ached. "So what do we do?"

"We prepare and we wait."

"For what?"

"War."

"How did George George get you?"

"Luck." She didn't elaborate.

"What about Baby Dimitri?" I looked at my phone. The family had sixteen hours to produce the Godfather of Disappearing Acts and Kitten Heels.

"Forget about Dimitri. Believe me when I tell you that old *malakas* can take care of himself."

Grandma got down to business. She grabbed a mixing bowl, a wooden spoon, ingredients, and then she beat it.

"But George George is going to kill us all if we don't produce him."

"Baby Dimitri or no Baby Dimitri, George George will kill us anyway."

I gulped. "What should I do?"

"Go to work. Live your life. Taste this *koulouraki* dough."

"Really?"

"No. If you touch my dough I will cut off your hand."

———

Grandma's war preparations left me with a headful of loose ends. Work wasn't a cure but it was something I had to do. I needed to think, and the cool, dry air in the morgue, the tedious drudgery of sorting files, and the bottomless pot of coffee were good fuel for my thinking cap.

Coffee wasn't the only stimulant.

All that bumping through the Ferrari's gears jogged something loose. If finding Baby Dimitri wasn't possible, what if I found a different target? I wanted to find Xander, and Xander was with George George. Find George George and I might be able to save Xander and the rest of my family. He could be anywhere, but I was willing to bet he had come home to the Volos area to roost.

When I rocked up to the morgue, Marika was already there, whipping files into alphabetical shape. She threw her arms around me.

"I am so glad you are okay! Lucky I am a spy because you are going to need my help."

Gus rushed in. He joined us in the group hug.

"Help?" I asked Marika.

"Finding George George before he comes for us, of course."

Gus broke out of the hug. His face was pale. "George George? *The* George George?"

"You know him?"

"No, but I heard the stories. They brought the bodies here you know, after the murders."

Not news to me. I'd read the files.

"Why would you be looking for George George?" Gus went on. "He is dead and buried and has been for decades."

"Alive. Very alive," I said. "He kind of kidnapped me, while I was in a tank."

"Funny. There was a tank at the Acropolis this morning."

"How interesting," I said. A shadow passed over Gus's face. "What's wrong?"

"I hope George George does not come back here for his things."

My ears perked. "What things?"

"In the personal items boxes. Nobody in the family was left to collect the bodies, so someone from your family took them and buried them. They only wanted the dead, not their things."

Begging would have been tacky, so I asked nicely. "May I see them?"

"Since you are a morgue employee you can look at anything you like, provided you do not sell dead people's valuables on the internet. The hospital does not like it when we sell personal property on the internet—it prefers to do that itself so it can pocket the money."

"I am coming, too," Marika said. "What if there is something there from a hostile foreign government? You will need a spy if that happens."

"Is she really a spy?" Gus asked me as we paraded down the corridor.

"You can be anything you want to be," I said. "That's what my mother almost always said."

Gus herded us into the room filled with lockers. He crouched down, keys in hand, and when he rose he was holding a large metal box.

"I was not working here when the Yiorgiou family was killed so I do not know what is inside."

"Stand back," Marika said, stepping in front of me. "Who knows what is in that box? It could be anything."

Elias had something to say about that. "I hate to say this but Marika is right. I will open it."

"Then who will protect Katerina?" Marika puffed herself up until she resembled a large, black-clad marshmallow. "I am a spy, so I will do the spy things."

"What if there's anthrax or something in there?" I said.

Marika raised her hands. "I am not opening that box. I have children and another one on the way. Probably better if I stand over there and have a little snack while I watch."

Elias's eyeballs swiveled toward the ceiling.

Anthrax or no anthrax, Gus didn't waste any time popping the box open. "Jewelry, wallets." He waved a black brick at us. "Look: an old *kinito*."

A cell phone the size of a small baby.

"Money. More money. These people had a lot of money." My boss held up a wad of drachmas. "George George's things are in their own envelope."

The envelope in question was the yellow manila variety, but smaller, with a bulge at the bottom.

"If George George wasn't killed that night, why are his things here?

Gus shrugged. "Who can say? I was a child when it happened."

"Who was doing your job back then?"

"Kyrios Agapi. He retired ten years ago and took over his family farm on Pelion."

Another non-coincidence. It had to be the same Kyrios Agapi who'd come with his hat in hand to the compound on the day of Litsa's funeral.

Marika hoisted up her bag. "Then we will go and talk to this Kyrios Agapi."

"I don't think he'll be in a talking mood," I told her. "He doesn't have a mouth anymore. Or a head."

Everyone except me crossed themselves.

So Kyrios Agapi's death wasn't entirely senseless—only mostly senseless. A picture was forming and it wasn't a pretty one; but then I'd never been much of an artist. George George was shot to pieces, and between that night and today, somehow he went on living. Either Kyrios Agapi patched him up and nursed him back to health—or some variation on that theme—or there was enough life in George George for him to slither out of a body bag and into the night. Probably the former. Why else kill Kyrios Agapi unless he was privy to George George's mortal secret?

"What's inside the envelope?"

Gus showed me the contents. "A key."

"A key to what?"

The key looked like a key. Small. Dull. Unmarked. It swung from a Michael Jackson keychain.

"What did George George do for a living? Besides being evil, I mean. Because the man is obviously some flavor of evil."

Gus dropped the key back into its envelope. "All I know is that he had a warehouse up on Mount Pelion. After his death, the place mysteriously burned to the ground."

More like Grandma had the place razed. It wouldn't be the first time she had sanctioned arson. Back home, I'd rented my first apartment and was this close to giving Dad the bad news about my imminent move-out date when he vanished and Takis and Stavros hauled me to Greece. My apartment had caught fire shortly afterwards. There was no apartment for me to return to.

"What's there now?"

"They say there is a graveyard in its place."

"Was George George buried there?"

"I thought you said he was still alive," Gus said.

"That doesn't mean I don't want to know where he's buried."

Marika stopped chewing long enough to lob a question at me. "Are you thinking what I am thinking?"

"What are you thinking?" Ten bucks said it had something to do with food.

"That we should dig up his grave to see what he left in there instead of himself."

My mouth dropped open. I stared at her in horror. Who did that sort of thing?

"Are you sure you weren't born a Makris?" I asked her.

"I am a little bit curious," Gus said.

My horrified gaze swung around to Gus. "Are you kidding?"

He shrugged. "No."

"We should do it tonight," Marika said. "The sooner the better."

"I have a shovel," Gus said.

Elias was slouching against the wall, lost in thought.

"Can you believe this?" I asked him.

"A few weeks ago I would have said no. Now? There is nothing I would not believe."

My hands sat on my hips. "We are not digging up George George's grave—if there's even a graveyard there. We already know he's alive, so what's the point?"

"Somebody must have been buried in there," Gus said. "What if it is someone completely innocent whose family thinks they are missing? We could give them closure."

No way. No now. "I'm not digging up anyone."

Chapter 13

I‍t wa‍s midnight and I was holding a shovel that wasn't mine. Marika, Gus, Elias, and I were at an unmarked cemetery in the wilds of Mount Pelion, on a spot that used to be part of George George's property. Elias was the designated lookout.

On the drive up, I managed to squeeze raiding a grave-yard into my master plan to find George George. What if there was a clue to his whereabouts up here? I would kick myself if I let little things like squeamishness and decency get in the way.

"We have company," Elias said. Headlights—double and single—dimmed not far from where we were.

"Dina and Hera? At this point they're harmless stalkers."

"I could shoot them if you like," Marika said.

"You brought guns to excavate a grave?"

She held up two fingertips, an itty-bitty space between them. "A small one, because a spy never knows when they might have to shoot someone."

Gus gulped.

Marika hoisted her bag higher. "Speaking of graves, which one do you think it is?"

"Let's spread out and look," I said.

We had flashlights and we weren't afraid to use them, seeing as how it was darker than the inside of a dog out here. The moon was out but it was in one of its mostly useless phases. Vines snuggled up to gravestones. Grass and brush had covered the graves years ago, which meant I was stepping all over dead people. *Eww*, and also, *sorry*. Most of the headstones were good marble and the names were legible once I nudged the greenery away with my booted toe. Beloved fathers, mothers, grandparents.

No children.

Small mercy, but I'd take it.

"Do you notice anything strange about these grave markers?" Gus called out.

"They are not very fancy," Marika said, sniffing. She had a point. A Greek cemetery was the final chance for remaining family members to show the world how much they loved their dead relatives, even when they didn't. *Especially* when they didn't. Greeks were good at overcompensating, and they did their overcompensating with big displays of crucifixes and statues and pedestals slathered in white paint and gold accents.

Not wanting to stand on the dead, even at a distance of six feet, I crouched beside a gravestone, angling the beam so I could read the name: Yiorgiou.

"George George's own personal family cemetery," I said.

"This one has a different last name," Marika said. "And this one."

The flashlight's beam cut across several more headstones. Different birth years, same use-by date.

I sat back on my haunches and blew out a sigh.

"Henchmen, probably. They were all killed on the same night." Of course they were. Grandma had collected the whole set, minus one Joker.

Gus's voice cut through the dark. "Here he is."

We gathered around George George's not-so-final resting place.

"Wait—how do we know it's *the* George George and not a different George George?" Marika asked.

Greek naming conventions meant that every family over a certain size produced multiple people with the same names. Names passed from paternal parents to the first grandchildren, then the mother's parents got their turn. I was Katerina Makris because that's Grandma's name and Mom didn't wasn't in the mood to put up a fight, seeing as how the OBGYN had just stitched her from front to back.

I focused the flashlight on this George George's birth year. A relic from Grandma and Baby Dimitri's generation.

"This is him. Or rather, isn't him."

We leaned on our shovels. Not much digging happened, and it didn't happen fast.

"I cannot dig," Marika said. "It might hurt the baby. I will swap places with Elias."

She disappeared into the night. Elias didn't look happy when he showed up, carrying Marika's shovel.

"She *is* pregnant," I said.

"I am starting to think she is just fat," he said.

My phone shuddered. "Tell your bodyguard I heard that," Marika said on the other end.

"Pregnancy has really done wonders for her hearing," I told him. Elias crossed himself, then he slammed the shovel against the dry dirt, breaking ground. Gus and I jumped forward to help him. Elias assigned me to flashlight duty.

"Baboulas will kill me for sure if I let you dig up a grave," he said.

The men worked quickly. Two feet later, metal struck metal.

"There's something here," Elias said.

"Not a casket." Gus tapped with his shovel. "Those are usually wood.

"Stand back," Elias said. Gus clambered out. I kept the flashlight steady while Elias scraped away the dirt from a metal cube, about two feet in each dimension. It had a rusted lock.

Marika stuck her nose in. "What is it?"

"Aren't you supposed to be the lookout?" I said.

"It is the middle of the night, there is no one out here except for us."

"What about Hera and Dina?"

"Somebody slashed Dina's tires, I do not know who. And somebody else, I also do not know who, called Hera and told her that her mother died in a strange and sexual *souvlaki* accident."

Holy cannoli. Marika looked like a soft, plump marshmallow but the woman was hardcore.

Elias tapped the lock with the shovel. "Locked."

I dangled the Michael Jackson keychain under his nose. "Key."

We crowded around the box. Elias brushed away the dirt and slid the key in. A few wiggles later, the lock popped open. I did my part and angled a blue-white beam of light at the contents.

Cassette tapes. Someone had packed them in neat rows, alphabetized by artist and album. Elias hauled the box back to my car. The rest of us followed.

"Really?" Marika said.

"George George does love his cassette tapes," I said. "Mix tapes are his favorite calling card."

Elias jerked his head up.

I heard it, too. Police sirens. Fast-moving. Coming, not going.

"Relax," I said, "they're not coming here."

———

"Grave robbing?" Melas said. "Really?" He was in stern, authoritative cop mode, which was a problem. I didn't fancy a trip to jail but I kind of dug the cuffs that were a firm kind of loose around my wrists.

I raised my hands—together, obviously. "Cuffs? Really?" The only thing standing between revenge and me were these handcuffs and a mesh barrier.

"You cannot do this to me," Marika said beside me. Melas had wedged us into the backseat of his police car. "I am pregnant."

Melas's gaze met mine in the mirror. He rolled his eyes. I tried not to smile and mostly succeeded.

I wiggled around inside the cuffs. Melas had cleverly stashed my bag in the footwell, which meant I couldn't get to my lock picks. "How did you know we were there?"

"Someone called in a tip, told us someone was grave robbing up here."

Gus was between us, cuffed and miserable. "I have to get back to my morgue. There are bodies to be processed now that I have room to work."

Elias had scored the shotgun seat and didn't get cuffs because Melas said he was financially obligated to go along with my harebrained schemes, and therefore not nearly as much at fault as the rest of us.

"What were you thinking?" Melas wanted to know.

"It was spy business," Marika said darkly. "If we tell you then we have to kill you."

Jeepers creepers.

"Not you," Melas clarified. "Katerina."

Why was he asking me? Digging up George George's gave wasn't my idea of a good time. But I wasn't about to throw Marika under the bus—not in her condition.

"I love long walks in the rain, piña coladas, and grave digging," I said. "What can I say, I'm romantic."

In the rearview mirror, Melas's lips quirked. My belly flip-flopped. We were barely on talking terms but he still had the power to make me think about scribbling his initials next to mine, maybe carving them on the twisted trunk of an olive tree.

"Maybe a few hours in the lockup will loosen your tongue and you'll tell me what you were up to."

The look he gave me in the mirror suggested that he wouldn't mind me loosening my tongue somewhere between his belt buckle and knees. Talk about confusing. As recently as yesterday the cop would barely smudge my gaze with his.

"You can't do that," I said. "I have to be somewhere."

"Where?"

I said nothing. Melas wasn't family. I didn't want to drag him into this mess.

He tossed something over his shoulder at me. "Do you know what that is?"

In my lap was his police badge. "A sheriff's star?"

"That badge says I can lock you up for at least a few hours."

Beside me, Marika started to cry. "I have never been to jail before."

I patted her hands with mine. "Look on the bright side. A good spy is well rounded. A few hours of jail time will round you out."

"She is already rounded out enough," Elias said from the front seat.

Marika kneed his seat. "I heard that."

"You were meant to," he muttered.

Marika swiveled to look at me. "You are right," she said, drying her eyes with the edge of her hand. "As a spy I might have to pretend I have been to jail. Now I will not have to pretend. Do they have bathrooms in jail? I really need a bathroom."

Bathrooms were a stretch. They had a toilet—a real one, not a Greek squatter—and a hand basin in the cell. "More or less."

"What about a vending machine?"

"I don't think they have those," I said.

"You will not starve," Melas told her. "You get bread and cheese, three times a day. If you behave yourself I will make sure you get extra bread."

"I am eating for two," Marika said. "I have to get a balanced diet or my baby will grow up to be a policeman."

Melas wasn't fazed. He laughed and hit the gas.

———

"I thought you said this place had a bathroom," Marika said. "I do not see a bathroom. I see a toilet, yes, and a sink, but I do not see any privacy."

"I will close my eyes," Gus said.

Marika glowered at him.

Gus gulped. "And I will turn around and cover my ears."

Glare.

"I can sing show tunes while you go, if you like. My mama says I have a voice like an angel."

Greek mothers believe their sons are the second coming of Jesus Christ, so I took his comment with a teeny tiny grain of iodized salt.

The door opened. Melas strolled in, hands in his pockets, looking casual and relaxed. Probably locking people up was like Valium to him.

"You have visitors," he said.

"Already?" Marika said. "But we just got here."

"Visitors." I plopped my butt down on one of the two cots. It was filled with cheap Greek marble and the tears of former detainees. "That sounds ominous. Want to know what I think? I think you mean people who can't spring us loose. You're entirely too cheerful about all of this."

He moseyed on out again, throwing words over his shoulder. "Enjoy your stay."

"It is lucky for him that he has a nice *kolos*," Marika said, "otherwise I would put my foot up it."

"You can put your foot up there whether it's nice or not," I told her.

"I like how you think. Except for the part about robbing graves. That was not your best idea."

"It was your idea!"

"Was it? Pregnancy makes me stupid and forgetful."

In the adjoining cell, Elias snorted.

Marika severed his head with a sharp, dirty look. "We did not even get anything good out of it."

"I wouldn't say that." I wiggled, trying to rearrange the rocks under my butt. "Some of those tapes might be worth a few euros on eBay."

The door opened. Dad strolled in with Grandma on his heels. He was munching on a *koulouri*, a sesame seed covered hoop, not unlike a pretzel.

He grinned at me. "This is a first."

"Not for me." During my first week in Greece Melas had locked me up for disturbing the office peace.

Grandma didn't look happy, but that was her default expression so it was hard to tell what she was thinking. Probably she didn't like having to deal with adversity away from her garden and kitchen. It made me wonder what she did to relieve stress and process information when she wasn't at the compound.

"Are you going to tell me why you were robbing a grave in the middle of the night?" she asked.

"I'm thinking no," I said.

She went on as if I hadn't just sassed her. "What exactly did you think you were going to find?"

"World peace."

Marika sucked in her breath. "You cannot speak to Baboulas that way," she said in a low voice. Then she slapped a hand across her mouth. "Tell me I did not call her Baboulas to her face."

"It's okay," I whispered. "She was looking at me so it wasn't directly at her face."

"That does not make me feel better."

"Marika," Grandma barked. "Explain what you were doing robbing a grave—that particular grave."

"A spy never talks?" Marika said, wincing.

"Wow." I nudged her. "You're good at this."

Wrong. She sucked at it. But Marika was trying, which I appreciated.

Marika beamed. "Thank you."

"No problem." Grandma shrugged. "You will stay here. I told you to keep away from George George and leave the problem solving to me. Here you will be safe. Nikos will make sure of it if he values his life, and I think he does."

Wait—what? No, no, no. With only a few hours left

until George George flipped his lid and brought doom upon my family for failing to pony up Baby Dimitri, jail was the last place I needed to be.

"Dad, are you going to let her leave us here? Seriously?"

He broke off a chunk of *koulouri* and offered to me. I passed it to Marika, who wolfed it down. "Do you remember all those stories I told you when you were a child?"

"About you-know-who?"

Marika perked up. "Voldemort? I love those books."

"Who is this is Voldemort?" Dad asked me in English.

"Bad guy. No nose. Has a hard time finding sunglasses that work."

"Sounds French," Dad said. He winked at me.

"I remember the stories. Why?" I asked him.

"Because my mother will cut off my legs and use them as a scarf if I let you out of here."

Grandma laughed. Someone's English was better than they let on. "Lies. It was Michail's idea to leave you in here."

No way. I looked at his face. Way.

"Dad!"

He grinned. "Call it a time-out."

"I hate you," I told his departing back.

"You have been saying that since you were a little girl, and it is still not true."

They left.

Time was running out.

———

Not easy being behind bars. I thought about carving a shiv to pass the time when really I wanted the clock to stop. I had officially let everyone down: Xander, the family, and poor Laki and his diminishing stash of marbles. Kat Makris, biggest failure to ever mosey into Failuretown. Next I'd be penning a country and western song, that's how sad I was. No—worse. I'd be cobbling together a Rembetika tune. Although, could anyone really apply the word "tune" to that particular strain of Greek folk music?

"Do you have anything I can use to make a shiv?" I asked Marika.

She dug around in her bag, then presented me with a bowie knife. "Will this do?"

"Sure," I said in a faint voice.

Elias glanced over. "*Gamo ton Christos*, who gave this silly woman a knife?"

Bumping uglies with Jesus—there was a whole book about that. *The Da Vinci Code* had sold a few copies, too.

Marika waved the knife at him. "You kiss your mama with that mouth?"

"Not since she died."

"That is a problem," Marika said.

"Does anyone want a prison tattoo?" I asked.

Gus raised his hand.

"That's one customer." I looked at my fellow inmates. "Anyone have a magic marker?"

"I have one of those." Marika pulled an indelible pen out of her bag. Purple. Thin tip. Good enough.

Gus presented his arm. "Draw one of those French girls on me."

All righty then. I stuck my tongue out of the corner of my mouth and got to work.

"What are you doing?" Melas said when he came in to bring snacks. The detective had promised bread and cheese but he had found it in his heart to bring *Tsokofreta* bars, my least favorite Greek candy.

"Police brutality," I said, eyeing the chocolate wafer bars. Nobody could fool me; I knew sawdust sandwiched together with cheap chocolate when I gagged on it.

"Too bad," he said. "*Tsokofretas* are all we have."

Marika made hard eye contact with the candy. "Are you going to eat that?" she asked me.

My mood was lower than dirt and my heart was a hard, heavy rock compressing my lungs, but even in my darkest hour I didn't have it in me to choke down the wafer bars. All I did was hold a flashlight while Elias and Gus dug into an empty grave; I didn't deserve to eat Tsokofretas to pay for my sins, for crying out loud.

"You can have mine."

Marika tore into both packets with the fervor of a wild and starving dog. "I like *Tsokofretas*. They have chocolate. That is good enough for me."

I put the finishing touches on Gus's permanent— according to the marker—tattoo. "Done."

The morgue attendant looked at his arm. "That is a stick figure."

"I only know how to draw stick figures, but she's French. See?" I tapped on the speech bubble, which read "*Oui oui*".

"What is that in her hand?"

"A baguette."

Gus turned it this way and that. "Nice."

Melas leaned against the bars. "How do you do it?"

"Do what?"

"Make the best of every situation."

I shrugged. What did he want me to tell him? When life gives you lemons, you have two choices: make lemonade or hurl those lemons in life's face. Unless it was EPSA lemonade, I wasn't a fan of the sweet and sour juice. So I guess you could say I was a hurler.

"I don't like lemonade that much," I said.

His head tilted. He had no idea what I was talking about. "Your father said to let you all loose in the morning."

Marika was aghast. "What do you mean 'in the morning'? I have children. I am pregnant, you know. I cannot be here. As soon as I get out I am going to call your mama and tell about that thing you did that one time!"

"What thing?" he asked her.

"Anything. I have a secret source who tells me all kinds of perverted things."

Marika's secret source was the peeping Thomasina who lived across the street from Melas. The elderly and widowed neighbor had twitchy curtains and nothing better to do with her days, nights, and late afternoons.

He grimaced.

"It's going to get ugly," I told Melas. "Do you know how often pregnant women need to pee?"

"You can leave," Melas said to Marika. "Nobody around here likes mopping. Katerina has to stay though—Baboulas said so."

Marika sat back, arms folded. "Forget it. We go together or we stay."

Melas grinned. He was enjoying this. "Then you stay. I am just following orders, and you *were* robbing a grave. Did you get anything good, by the way?"

"Cassette tapes from the 1980s."

"Definitely not worth it." He rapped his knuckle on the bar, winked at me, then left.

Were Melas and I good again? I couldn't tell. So many mixed signals, so little time to get back to the compound before George George struck.

I sat on the bunk next to Marika, legs stuck out straight, back against the wall.

"What time is it?" she asked me.

"About five minutes later than it was five minutes ago."

"I was afraid of that."

More time passed. Not much of it.

"What time is it now?"

I turned on my phone. A heavy weight plopped down and used my guts as a sofa. That weight grabbed the remote and switched my emotion to fear. It was almost George George time and I was stuck in here.

"Three minutes after the last time you asked."

"I bet my children have destroyed the apartment by now. Takis will not have put them to bed. Probably they are all playing video games."

I looked up at the ceiling. If I picked the lock, we could stack the beds, punch out the flimsy tiles, and escape that way.

"*Psst.*"

Marika sat up, looked around. "Was that you?"

I was looking around, too. "Not me. Elias? Gus?"

They shrugged.

"Pssst!"

The sound was coming from the barred window that straddled both cells. I went over, stood on tiptoe, but couldn't see anything except night. "Who's there?"

"Yo, yo, yo," Donk said. "Look at you in jail. What is it like?" He sounded much too excited about the situation.

"I tried to make a shiv and I gave Gus a prison tattoo with a Sharpie pen."

"Nice!"

"What are you doing out there?"

The top half of his face appeared in the dark square. He was wearing a white ball cap with PUSY stitched across the front with purple thread. Holy mother of mothering.

"I came to get you out, yo."

"No can do. Melas won't let us go until morning. Apparently orders are orders."

The edges of his eyes wrinkled up so I knew he was grinning. "Yo, yo, not like that. I got man skillz," he said, committing horrific acts upon the English language.

"Mad skills, not man skillz."

"Stay there," he said. The top half of his head vanished.

Outside, an engine revved. I knew that engine. It sounded expensive and belonged to my Ferrari. Holy crap on a cracker, what was Donk up to?

The engine moved closer. Red light leaked into the cell. We crowded around the window, Marika and me in our cell, Gus and Elias in theirs. Elias wasn't a big man but he was the only one with enough height to get a good look. He laughed.

"That boy is *trelos*," he said, not telling me anything I didn't know. Donk was kind of crazy, like every kid with hormones gushing through their systems and a drawer full of sticky socks. "Resourceful, too. Baboulas would be smart to give him a job."

"What is he doing?"

Elias grinned. "You will see."

A moment later there was a loud clank as a chain as thick as my wrist snaked through the window. Donk wrapped it around the bars, and then he vanished again.

"My Virgin Mary, that boy has lost his mind," Marika said. "But I do not disapprove, for once."

The Ferrari roared. Its tires squealed. The bars went nowhere. Greek construction was earthquake proof.

Melas stepped into the room. He was not a happy man. "Am I imagining things or is Baby Dimitri's nephew trying to rip the bars out of my jail?"

"It's just your imagination," I said.

"That is what I thought." He stared at me for a moment, then he left. When he came back a moment later he was carrying keys. "Go, all of you, before the kid makes a mess or destroys that Ferrari."

"What about Grandma?"

"Does it look like I am scared of Baboulas?"

Hard to say. Mostly he looked tasty.

"Get out," he said before I could formulate a witty answer.

Didn't have to tell us twice. We piled into the Ferrari, where Donk was dishing out high-fives. "It worked," he said.

Marika rolled her eyes. "Virgin Mary."

"Let's get out of here." I turned the key, enjoying the sound of freedom. An urge swept over me, a tiny voice inside hinting that hopping on a bus and riding until I reached Zihuatanejo was a fabulous idea. Never mind that Zihuatanejo's beach was a biological hot zone and I didn't have any former jailbird friends building boats down that way.

Donk snapped his fingers as I eased away from the curb. "There was a man and he said to give you a message. That's why I came to find you."

I adjusted the seat some more. Donk's legs were longer than mine. "What man, what message?"

"That crazy old man from the Acropolis. The one who made us ride the bus."

Holy cow. My foot found the brakes. We all lurched forward.

I twisted around to look at Donk. "And the message?"

"He said you have forty-five minutes to get back to the compound or he is going to kill your whole family."

"But we had more time!"

"He said he got bored of waiting and that he has been waiting since the 1980s."

Fear grabbed my throat and gave me a good shake. "When was this?"

"About thirty minutes ago."

I hit the gas.

Chapter 14

DEAD QUIET AT THE COMPOUND. Lights off. Not even a dog around to nuzzle my hand.

My blood froze.

Where was everyone? The guardhouse was empty.

Power outage or sabotage?

The compound had generators to pick up the slack when the power went out, so it had to be foul play.

I drove up to the gate and got out. Everything was dead. No working cameras. I had no eyes in the place. I pressed the red button. The gate didn't move.

I called Grandma. I called Aunt Rita. I called everybody.

Nobody picked up.

What was going on?

The main gate wouldn't budge but there was a second smaller gate behind the guardhouse for foot traffic. I jiggled the handle and was reward with a click. Unlocked.

I went back to my car. "We'll have to go on foot from here."

"Good news," Gus said. "I do not smell blood."

Marika clutched her chest. "My children! Where are my children? If someone has hurt my children I will murder them, then I will drag them back to life and murder them again. And then I will cut off their heads and use them as chamber pots."

"Wait here," I said. I jumped out of the car and went to the back to pop the trunk. The trunk wasn't there, so I walked to the front and helped myself to the crowbar. I handed it through the window to Gus. "This is for you. Marika, do you still have a gun?" Before he locked us up, Melas had confiscated the gun Xander gave me.

"A little one." She reached into her cavernous black bag and pulled out a sawn-off shotgun and a baby machine gun, straight out of one of the Baltic countries or maybe Russia. "Heh. I forgot this one was in here." She handed me the shotgun.

It dangled from my hand. I barely knew guns. Shotguns were beyond me. Did I pump them or squeeze the trigger? Who could say? Not me, that was for sure. "What am I supposed to do with this?"

"Shoot somebody? That is what I will do with it if I have to, and I think I will have to. Takis and my children …" her voice cut out "… I will do whatever has to be done, and so will you."

She was right. I'd pop a cap in someone's butt if they had hurt my family.

Kat Makris. Former couch potato. Temporarily reassigned bill collector. Good daughter and decent friend. I'd never shot anyone to death and now I might have to.

I gave the shotgun a shake. "Can we swap? That one looks easier to use."

"Good idea. Probably you will have to shoot more people anyway."

We exchanged weapons.

Lights trundled up the driveway. Two sets of lights. Hera pulled up to the gate. Her window rolled down and she glared out at me.

"Thought you were busy," I said to her.

"Imagine how disappointed I was when I discovered my mother did not die in a *souvlaki* accident."

"Family issues?"

Hera shrugged a bony shoulder. "I look good in black."

"There is something seriously wrong with you."

Dina puttered to a stop. "Somebody sabotaged my tire."

"Probably the fat one," Hera said.

"Katerina is not fat," Marika said. "She is just not used to Greek sweets, that is all."

The air behind me shifted. Elias was crossing himself hard enough to create a breeze.

A satisfied smirk sprawled across Hera's face. "Do you have a license for that gun?"

"What gun?" I said.

"The one you are holding."

"Are you crazy? I don't see any gun." I nodded to her car. "Got any weapons in that thing?"

"Maybe. Why?"

"The lights are out and there seems to be nobody home. That's not normal."

"Did you call the police?"

"That's kind of a problem right now. We're not the police's favorite people."

Donk stuck his head out of the Ferrari. "I have got-a the skills, man."

Jeepers. Kids these days.

I focused on Hera, which tickled my gag reflex. "I hate to acknowledge that you exist, but we could use backup."

"Ask nicely."

"Please help us."

"With a cherry on top?"

"With anything you want on top."

I had to hand it to Hera, she jumped straight into cop mode. She popped the trunk and grabbed a holster, which she strapped to her waist.

"Is it George George?" she wanted to know.

"Yes."

"I hate it when dead criminals do not stay that way."

That made two of us.

She added to her collection: a beauty queen's sash of ammo and a big gun that looked like it could wipe out a small planet. Hera was stronger and scarier than she looked.

"Did you get that when you battled intergalactic aliens?" I asked her.

Marika cast a rueful glance at her shotgun. "My gun is smaller than hers."

"Now you know how your husband feels," Hera said.

Marika raised the shotgun. I hit the ground. "Watch where you're waving that thing," I yelped. Guns weren't really my thing, mostly on account of how nobody would let me have one, but even I knew that a sawn-off shotgun was as precise as flinging dirt.

Hera laughed and laughed like we were killing her with comedy. "I cannot believe somebody gave the human watermelon a gun."

Boy, she really wanted Marika to shoot her in the face. "Let's just do what has to be done," I said, getting back up on my feet.

"What about the other one?"

Dina was still straddling her moped, working on needlepoint and ignoring the rest of us.

"Kyria Dina, you want to help?"

"That looks like bad news to me, and I do not like bad news."

I showed her my aces. "My father might be in there and he might be in trouble."

Dina dropped the needlepoint like it was lava, arming herself with a heavy looking backpack and a scowl.

"Guns?" I asked her.

She was taking this spying for the KGB seriously if that was the case.

"Knitting needles, crochet hooks, and embroidery needles," she said.

"Really?"

"You would be amazed what you can do with knitting needles and a strong arm. Nobody hurts Michail except me, and then only if he begs, and then only if I can hear him when he is wearing a ball gag.

I grimaced. Where was the brain bleach when I needed it?

My little posse gathered in front of the fountain. Everyone was looking at me like I knew what to do. I didn't. I only knew what I would do if my sunglasses were missing: check my head, check my bag, then scour the place until they showed up. The family wasn't straddling my ponytail or bunched up between an old tissue and an older receipt, so that meant we would have to go room-to-room, hunting for people.

Or what was left of people. My people.

High on adrenalin, my heart kicked its beat up several pounding notches.

"Marika and Dina, you take the east wing."

"Which one is that?" Marika wanted to know.

"The one you live in."

"Good idea." She crossed herself then hoisted the shotgun into position. Somehow a housewife, mother, and amateur spy wielding a weapon was more terrifying than a dozen henchmen with machine guns. Probably because the henchmen knew about things like basic gun safety.

I gave orders like I knew what I was doing, which, for the record, I didn't. "Hera and Elias, take the west wing. That's the other one."

"What about you?" Elias asked.

What about me? Grandma's little secrets: the dungeon and the bunker.

"I'll start with Grandma's house and move on from there."

Donk scuffed the ground with his sneaker. His chin jutted out. He set his ball cap to douche mode, swiveling the bill to the back. "We could get lost in a dark closet by accident."

I suppressed an eye roll "Take my car and go home."

His face fell. "I can't go home."

My heart hurt. Donk was a pain but he was a kid whose uncle was missing and whose mother was … probably someplace worse than Athens during rush hour traffic. "Okay, let me think. Do you know where Kyria and Kyrios Melas live in Makria?"

He nodded. "I know."

"Go there. Tell Kyria Mela I sent you. She'll make sure you get something to eat and a place to rest, okay?"

He didn't look happy, which made two of us. "What if you need me?"

"I do need you. I need you to tell Kyria Mela what's going on."

As Grandma's former torturer, Kyria Mela might be useful. Worst case scenario she'd give Donk a safe place to stay and he'd be able to pass on information to the police if we went down in flames with a mix tape of 80s hits playing as we burned.

I didn't look back to see if he was going to follow my orders, but I heard the car door slam and the motor roar. Giving an unlicensed teenager a Ferrari was madness, but these were not sane times.

Deep breath. Okay. Time to act.

We scattered, moving quickly and quietly. I headed for Grandma's house, watching for the compound's animals along the way. Nothing. No bodies, no blood, which was a good sign. At least I thought it was. But what did I know about this sort of thing? Zip. Nada. None of this was my wheelhouse.

Grandma's yard was empty. I eased into her house, moving from room to room the way I'd watched cops do on television.

Empty.

Oooh, not completely empty. There were fresh *koulourakia* on the counter—or at least the shape of them in the darkness. I bit into one and pocketed two more, for later. If there was a later.

Mmm … scrumptious.

Outhouse? Empty.

I went to the shielded corner of Grandma's yard and pressed the magic button. The pad slowly lowered me into the control room while I nibbled the Greek cookie. They tasted slightly different. Grandma had tinkered with the recipe. Or maybe it was fear tampering with my taste buds.

More darkness, and lots of it, greeted me in the control room.

Again, I did the cop thing, minus their professional bravery. Probably Melas never had skid marks when he went after the bad guys. The underground rooms were vacant, so I moved on to the door between the bunker and dungeon.

I pressed my ear to the door and listened.

"I know someone is there," Monobrow said from the other side of the metal door.

My breath gushed out. I unlocked the door from my side and almost fell through as Makria's only homeless person yanked the door open.

"Katerina?" he said incredulously. "Is that you?" He helped me up.

"What's going on? Where is everyone?"

"Who can say? Nobody tells me anything." He offered me his chair, but I waved it away. Time wasn't a commodity I had in abundance. "I was sitting here reading a good book, when the lights went out. I thought maybe there was a storm."

"If it was a storm, the place has generators."

He chuckled. "Your grandmother prepares for every contingency."

"Does she? If that's true, where is everyone?"

"How would I know? I stay down here like a mush-room, and people feed me the bull's *skata*, and *loukoumia*, when I can get it."

Grandma was the best of the best when it comes to Girl Scouts. So where was everyone, and why had Mono-brow slipped through her careful cracks?

My head was a rock tumbler, and these rocks were crusted with crap.

They had to be somewhere. No blood. No bodies. No animals. How do you make an entire family vanish if your name isn't David Copperfield? Where else could they be?

"The farm," I said.

"Your grandmother," Monobrow repeated slowly, "pre-pares for every contingency."

I gave him a curious look. There wasn't time for ques-tions but I had a metric buttload of them. "You want to come with me?"

"And go out there?" His chin tilted up-down. "No. The outside is not for me."

"Well, just lock up and stay safe. I'll check on your later."

"You are optimistic. I like that about you."

"Not really. I'm just used to there being a tomorrow. It's kind of a given in my Netflix-and-chips world."

He patted my shoulder. "Maybe it will be again, eh? Sooner than you think."

I eased out of his cell and crept along the narrow hall-way, to the door that separated the real dungeon from the window dressing—the door that had a keypad.

Damn it.

No electricity meant no functioning keypad.

The air shifted behind me. "Here," Monobrow said. "I can fix that." He did something to the metal door and it swung open. I gawked at him, mouth open, eyebrows raised.

"Who are you? I mean who are you really?"

"Makria's only homeless person. Now get out of here, eh? And be careful. George George is one sneaky old *malakas*. He convinced the world he was dead for thirty years. Me, I would like to know how he did it, but now is not the time. Go."

He didn't need to tell me a third time. I hurried to the dungeon's other secret exit, wiggling the rock out of place to reveal the tunnel. A minute later, I burst back out into the night. For a moment I stood there, doubled over, taking deep breaths while I collected my jumbled thoughts. Then I set off for the family farm, which was just beyond the trees.

I moved quietly and quickly, crouching down, back to one of the wider trees once the farm was in sight. What options did I have? I had this big gun, which was very nice, but if I hit any bad guys it would be dumb luck and not skill. I had Dad's old slingshot tucked into my back pocket and a front pocket filled with marbles and *koulourakia*, the latter of which were breaking apart with every step I took. I crammed a few crumbs into my mouth because we live in a world where people are starving, and wasting food is just wrong.

Yum. Better than usual, which was really saying something.

I was sort of skillful with the slingshot, but could I take out George George and his men (criminals always bring backup to the party) if I needed to? Doubtful. The sling-shot was more of a one-on-one weapon, and a better tool for distraction than maiming—in my hands anyway.

Seriously, I did not have the life skills for this sort of thing.

My blood was ninety percent adrenalin. There was a chance my heart would flop down and quit working from all the peer pressure.

It was dark at the family farm. Here the animals were still out and about. Occasionally my cow lowed in the stable. Sheep grumbled in their sleep. Goats snored. The outline of the small square table the men used to play *tavli* —backgammon—was visible.

Was I walking into a trap or a Biblical event? Maybe Greeks had their own version of the Millerites, who invented the rapture. I nixed that idea. A Greek rapture wouldn't be a quiet affair. There would be dancing, eating, and serious plate smashing before everyone got sucked up into the sky. Someone would stop to grab the lamb off the spit, and most of the mothers would be hurling wooden spoons and slippers at their wayward children. A Greek rapture would be the ultimate melo-drama. This was silent and no one was hurling footwear.

There was a distinct lack of potty mouths and arm waving.

What else?

No smell of gunpowder.

No signs of a struggle.

Nothing.

I shoveled more *koulouraki* into my mouth and contemplated the state of things. This wasn't Grandma's first massacre; she had patches in good guy stuff and bad guy stuff stitched to her vest and sash.

Know what this smelled like?

A stalemate.

Grandma was—hopefully—hiding, and George George and his goons were lurking out there somewhere, waiting. Nobody was breaking the tie.

Then there was me: the wildcard.

Don't do it, Kat, I told myself. *Call the cops and sit around drinking coffee until they haul George George in. Maybe eat some more yummy* koulouraki *while you wait.* I stuck another shard of hard cookie into my mouth.

The other, less smart part of my brain casually mentioned that Tangina Barrons had told Carole Anne not to go into the light, and that because there was no light here it was completely okay for me to walk out into the middle of the farmyard.

Boy, that part of my brain was a real loudmouth and definitely came from the Greek side of my DNA. But it also had an idea.

I messaged Elias. *Anything?*

Nothing. You?

Nothing.

Where are you?

At the farm, I typed back. *Find Marika and the others and take them somewhere safe.*

At least three quarters terrified, and dangerously close to losing bladder control, I took a deep breath, stuffed my phone back into my bag with shaky hands, and cradled the baby machine gun to my chest. Boy, I really didn't want to have to use it.

Another deep breath, wobbly on the exhale.

I strode out of the trees and into the middle of the farmyard.

"Come on out," I said with bravado I didn't feel. "I can play some Germaine Jackson and then we can go shopping for stonewash denim together, just us girls. What do you say, George George? Do you want me to bring the Aquanet or do you have your own?"

There was the soft snort of someone suppressing laughter behind me in the barn. I recognized that snort.

Grandma.

She stepped out of the shadows, a withered old raisin in a black dress. A withered old raisin who could break a man with a wooden spoon and a dirty look. "You have giant *archidia*, just like mine."

"Is everyone safe?"

"For now."

"And George George?"

"Hiding, like a little boy." She nodded at the tree line. "He is out there, aren't you, George?"

There was a long, pregnant pause, about ten months and counting.

There were soft footsteps on dirt, then George George appeared from between the trees. He wasn't alone; I wasn't that lucky. In his plump hand he was holding one end of a rope, frayed and feathered. The other end was tied to a donkey that could be best described as reluctant. It wasn't the first or the last donkey in history to exercise its stubborn personality with an assortment of snorting, kicking, annoyed braying. This donkey wasn't going anywhere, and it wasn't going anywhere as slowly as it pleased, thank you very much.

George George pulled. Tugged. Worked his way through all the synonyms for pulling. Then he worked his way through several of the stages of grief—the negative ones mostly.

The donkey's head came up. We made eye contact.

"Holy hell, that's my donkey!" I yelped.

George George laughed one of those humorless laughs at which villains excel. I was beginning to suspect one of the local colleges offered courses.

"This donkey?" He pulled back his leg to kick her, but my donkey was smarter. She sensed what he was up to and her hoof shot out, nailing George George in the shin. If he didn't have shin splints before, now he had all of them.

George George squealed. My donkey used to the opportunity to bolt across the farmyard to where I was standing.

"How did you get my donkey?"

"I went into the barn and took it earlier."

That made sense.

"I was going to take the cow because cows are delicious, but I could not get it to move."

"Why take the animals at all?"

"I am a businessman, always looking for something I can sell." Then: "Why did you have to bring up Germaine Jackson again, eh? Why not Michael? Why not DeBarge?"

Lights came on, bright and painful, from a pickup truck with halogens strapped to the roof. The truck was red so I immediately knew it didn't belong to Team Grandma. As old as she was, probably she was Henry Ford's best customer, back in the horseless carriage day.

"What's wrong with Germaine?" I shuffled forward,

shielding my donkey with my body. "He did that one song with Pia Zadora."

"I like that song," Grandma said.

"Me too," I said.

George George waved a gun at us. Somebody wasn't here for the small talk or the 1980s pop music trivia. "Where is Dimitri?"

"Don't know. Haven't seen him." More *koulouraki* crumbs went into my mouth.

Grandma zeroed in on my full mouth. "Are those my *koulourakia*?"

I nodded because it's rude to talk with your mouth full, and my mother was dead but that didn't mean she couldn't or wouldn't come back to scold me.

"My Virgin Mary," she muttered.

A light switched on in my head. "These aren't your pot cookies are they? "

The crumbs weren't green flecked like that one time a bunch of us inadvertently got high on Grandma's baking.

"Not exactly," Grandma said dryly.

"Could you be more specific?"

George George snapped his fingers. "Music. Music. What do I pay you for, eh?"

Someone twiddled a dial. The opening bars to Michael Jackson's *Bad* added gritty glamor to the night. George George's hand slithered into a sequin-spangled glove. He performed the world's worst moonwalk, right into a sloppy pile of cow manure.

A giggle slipped out of my mouth. "I can't believe you managed to hide successfully for thirty years."

Grandma graced me with a frown before sliding it to George George. "I suppose you want to kill us all."

His face lit up. "That would be good, yes."

"And then what?" she asked him.

"And then …" his expression brightened up a few more lumens "… and then I will finish off that *malaka* Dimitri's family. After that I will go back into business, my soul at peace after so many years."

"What business was that?" I asked. All along I'd assumed he was in the Bad Guy business, one way or another. Trafficking. Counterfeiting. Racketeering. Narcotics. Smuggling. That sort of thing.

"I was a shoe salesman," he said.

Well that was unexpected. "A shoe salesman?"

"I owned a little shoe shop down on the waterfront."

Wheels turned. Pennies dropped. "Wait—Baby Dimitri's shoe and souvenir shop used to be yours?"

"His shop? Ha! No. I had a different shop, right next door. A better shop."

I looked at Grandma, who shrugged.

"So what else did you sell?" I went on. "Drugs? Women? Some kind of Greek moonshine?"

"Nothing," George George said. "Just shoes."

Grandma rolled her eyes. "Just shoes, my *kolos*. George specialized in children."

A wave of nausea washed over me. "Please tell me you mean children's footwear."

My last remaining grandparent did the Greek up-down chin tilt. "George sold children on the black market to anyone who wanted them."

More *koulouraki* went into my mouth. Was it just me or were the stars brighter tonight than usual? "Are we talking adoption?"

She made a face, and not a happy one either. "Perhaps some of the buyers had honorable intentions and wanted to start families, but George did not care what they did with the children once they paid their cash."

George George shrugged. "Money is money. And I'm

not that bad a man. I always sent those children away with a new pair of shoes."

Just when I thought criminals couldn't get any lower, along came the George Georges of the world.

"So Grandma killed you and your family because you were selling children who weren't yours to people who maybe wanted to do terrible things to them? That seems fair, now that I think about it."

His shrug was painfully casual. It made me want to tap dance on his chest with a steamroller. "A man has to make money. Do you know how much profit there is in shoes?"

George George was just getting warmed up. He paced back and forth, hands waving. Boy, these old Greek men really enjoyed the sound of their own voices. Confession was good for the soul but annoying for everyone who had to listen to the criminals of the world rant on and on about their master plans, which, if you asked me, were always terrible. Villains never seemed to be blessed with copious amounts of imagination.

"Peanuts. That is how much profit," he said. "I had a big family, too many hungry mouths to feed, and they all looked to me to provide them with what they needed. Then Baby Dimitri came along, my best friend in this part of the world, and he opened his shop next to mine, only he sold shoes *and* souvenirs. And what happened? He puts me out of business because tourists like to buy a little something special to take home with their new shoes. I needed that shop so I could look clean on paper, like a respectable businessman. On Sunday I would go to the church, and people would look at me and say, 'There goes George George who sells fashionable shoes for a very reasonable price.' That *malakas* Dimitri took something important from me, so I took something important from him."

Michael Jackson *shamoned*.

"What did you take?" I asked him. The question was a formality; on some primal, previously subconscious level, I already knew. The answer was just now slowly bubbling up to the surface.

George George grinned a hyena's grin. "The worst thing you can take from a man: his son. The boy was just a baby, but the best money is in babies, unless the customer is looking for a worker in a mine and does not want to have to pay to raise one. Babies cost money, you know. But a baby remembers nothing from before and you can raise them however you like. Or eat them. I don't care. Money is money. Dimitri could not destroy me on his own and take back his son, so he went to your grandmother for help. And help him, she did." He stabbed his own heart with his finger. "She killed my whole family."

"Yeah, yeah," I said. "I got that part. What happened next? Did she give the boy back to Baby Dimitri?"

"No," Grandma said.

Gears spun in my head. Buttons clicked. My brain was creeping toward liftoff. It spat out an answer.

"You're talking about Xander, aren't you? Grandma took Xander and raised him." My brain blipped. How was this even possible? "Xander is Baby Dimitri's son?" My voice reached for a higher octave to express my horror and confusion. "Xander is Baby Dimitri's *son*?"

Shamone.

Grandma spoke up. "Dimitri asked me to take Xander and raise him here, where he would be safer. He feared his enemies would come at him through his son again someday. He also knew my enemies would come at me through my blood first before reaching Xander."

"Like a meat shield?" My gut clenched. The thought of George George selling all those children and Xander into God only knew what kind of life made my stomach want to shed its skin. Penka was right: there were levels. The nausea reminded me I had *koulourakia* in my pocket. I crammed a piece into my mouth, waiting for the queasiness to simmer down, and inspected the gun in my other hand. It would be so easy to empty its contents into George George and rid the planet of another scumbag.

He read my thoughts. "Put the gun down, Katerina."

I gave it a little shake. "But I like it."

Michael Jackson gave a *woohoo*.

"The dead man in my car and the one from the morgue—who were they?"

"I sold the one from your car when he was a child. When I went to hire some men, he recognized me and threatened to expose me, amongst other things. So I killed him and left him for Xander as a little warning gift."

"And the other one?"

"A shoe supplier. He used to sell to me, but when Dimitri opened his shop he gave Dimitri a better price." He hocked a loogie and spat it on the ground. Eww. "Now put down that gun."

"Do as he says, my doll," Grandma told me. "It will be okay. I promise."

George grinned. "For me it will be okay. For the Makris family … not okay." He pinched his fingertips together and kissed them. "When you get to the afterlife, tell my family I miss them.

A click echoed through the night—the ominous sound of a shotgun readying for the kill.

"You can tell them yourself, eh? I like that idea better."

The voice's owner stepped into the light. He was big, round, tall, and he had eyebrows that met in the middle and never let go.

Monobrow had joined the party, and he had a shotgun. George George stumbled backwards. When he regained his footing he slapped on another grin. I didn't like the look of a grin on him; it wasn't a happy curve.

"Look, another dead man has risen from the grave. Where has she been keeping you?"

Grandma answered. "The same place I keep all my treasure: in a vault."

Monobrow chuckled. "That is my girl."

My brain threw up its hands and quit being surprised. "You're Grandma's boyfriend?"

"Katerina," Grandma said, "The last thing I want is another man to clean up after. I am not a woman who enjoys washing a man's underpants."

"So who is he?"

Monobrow shot me with a smile. "Makria's only homeless person."

"That's the world's worst backstory," I told him.

"For you, I will try to come up with a better one, okay?"

I took another lick of *koulouraki* crumbs. I couldn't quit eating them. "Okay … Maybe something funny."

"Funny. I will remember that."

George George stomped his foot. "Enough talking. It is time for you all to line up against the wall and die. You have one gun—"

I waved the gun I'd borrowed from Marika, the one I hadn't put down yet, and swallowed the crumbs. "Two."

George George rolled his eyes. "Two guns. I have more."

I tilted my head. "How many?"

"More."

"Can't you count? They have remedial classes for that, you know."

His face was turning red. "*Skasmos.*"

Monobrow laughed. "I love this girl," he said to Grandma. "She makes me laugh."

George George's voice was as furious as his face. "She will not be so funny when she is dead."

Monobrow wasn't in any hurry to relinquish his weapon. "Where have you been hiding all this time, you fat *malakas?*"

"Turkey. I went there after Baboulas almost killed me. I spent months in the hospital recovering from my injuries, but I did recover. And after I recovered I began working toward my revenge. You do not look so frightening now, old woman."

"Were you cahoots with Kyrios Agapi?" I said, thinking of the dead farmer. "He was the morgue attendant then, wasn't he?"

"When he realized I was alive he stitched me back together using pieces of other bodies. My whole family was in that morgue so it was easy to find donor parts."

"Why did he keep your secret?"

"Because I did business with his father. I sold him his best workers. Children are excellent at picking olives. They are small and nimble, like little monkeys. Agapi was a very grateful man."

Grandma didn't blink. "Why did it take you so long to come back?"

"He always was slow." Monobrow tapped a finger against his temple.

"Do you know how long it takes to rebuild an empire when you cannot reach out to your old contacts? I changed my name, changed my life story." He snapped his fingers. The music jumped from Jackson to Joel's My Life.

"This song is from the 70s," I said to no one in partic- ular and definitely not George George's henchmen, who had us surrounded. One of them looked familiar. The

244

helpful henchman from the Acropolis. "How did you get the tank down?" I called out to him.

"We didn't. We left it there."

"Litterbug."

He made a face. "My mama would beat me with the *pandofla* if she knew."

Amen to that. Greek mothers and grandmothers had serious slipper-throwing skills. We're talking ninja star precision. "I'm downgrading you to five stars," I said.

George George made a rewind motion with his finger. "What was that about the 1970s?"

"This song," I said.

"No. It is from the 1980s."

I made a sound like a buzzer. It echoed in my head. "Wrong."

"You are wrong—again."

"Right."

He whipped out a cell phone, stabbing it with the fingers that weren't shrouded in a sparkly glove. "I will ask the internet."

"You do that."

"I am." Stab, stab. Stabby stab. He threw the phone on the ground and stomped on it. Then he snapped his fingers. "Next song."

"Was I right? I was right, wasn't I?"

"No."

Queen came on. Another one bit the dust.

"1980." George George put on a sinister smirk. "Time to die." He raised his hand and dropped it in a dramatic chopping motion.

A shot punctured the night.

Everybody hit the deck. Okay, just me. I hit the deck. Grandma, Monobrow, and George George held their ground.

"Sorry," Marika called out. "I did not mean to do that." She staggered into the light, hand bracing her lower back. "Pregnancy is making my body do crazy things, like this." She fired again, this time at the tree line.

Given that I was already on the ground, I didn't fall again. I scrambled to my feet, then, while George George's attention was on Marika, slammed my foot into the rainbow colored scorpion climbing up back of his knee.

George George let out a primal howl. "My knee!"

"Scorpion!" I shouted. "It's going for your *kolos*!"

One at a time, his hired henchmen stepped into the light, their guns high and pointed right at us. The old relic's howl turned to laughter. "Here is how this will work," George George said. "First I will kill you, then I will find the rest of your family. And your children? Those I will sell to the highest bidders. A Makris child will fetch good money. Do you know how many enemies you have?"

Grandma made a face. "Not exactly, but I bet it is a very big number."

George George chuckled. "A very big number. Huge. Then I will find that *malakas* Dimitri and shove a boot up his—"

There was a soft *POP*. A big red hole appeared where George George's nose used to be. His expression was one of surprise. For a moment he swayed. Then he fell—*plop*—on his back, a small dust cloud puffing up around him.

His permed mullet fell off.

"Huh," I said. "That was a wig?"

A giggle leaked out of me.

The bad guys lowered their guns and vanished into the darkness.

"Hired guns," Grandma said, eyeing me curiously. "No loyalty except to a paycheck."

The sky was closing in on me. Huh. The stars were pink, not the yellow I'd always imagined them to be or the white my science teachers insisted was more accurate. "Who shot him?"

"Dimitri," Monobrow said. He turned around, waved at the compound's roof, just beyond the trees.

"Dimitri as in Baby Dimitri?" I felt light, floaty. "I thought he left?"

"We put him to work," Monobrow said. "It was security or digging ditches, and your grandmother did not need a ditch."

Was it me or was his monobrow growing? The spiky black hairs were creeping downwards and outwards, headed toward his nose. Yes. Definitely growing. That thing was going to take over his whole face in a few moments. A lock of black hair snaked up his nose.

"Argh!" I bashed him in the face with Marika's gun. "It's alive!"

Monobrow grabbed his nose. He fell to his knees and began howling at the moon, clawing at his shirt buttons with his spare hand. The monobrow spread, overtaking his skin.

"Holy handbag, he's a werewolf! Quick! Do you people have any silver bullets?" I looked around. Grandma was gone. In her place was a unicorn with a sword where the horn was supposed to be.

I panicked. The ground was suddenly lava. I needed a couch and I needed it now. On tiptoe, I ran at the flying carpet that had just appeared on the ground, several feet away, beyond the unicorn.

My face collided with something that wasn't there. Then I was one with the soft, sweet ground. I looked up. An angel with a body hair issue was coming for me. It snuffled my face, heehawed, and then bit me on the shoulder. I pulled myself to my feet and flopped over my savior's waiting back.

"Take me away from all this lava," I mumbled.

Heehaw.

"What is going on?" I heard the werewolf ask in a bewildered voice.

"It is nothing," the unicorn told him. "Katerina ate my special *koulourakia*, that is all."

Chapter 15

I CAME to in Grandma's spare bedroom, the one that had been temporarily mine until a few days ago.

"Here she is," Baby Dimitri said. "The woman who saved an old man's life." He was perched on the edge of the bed, grinning and freshly greased.

My mouth was fuzzier than the back end of a Persian cat. My teeth felt too big for my gums. I scooted up so that I was sitting. The room tilted but at least it wasn't spinning or lava.

"You did the shooting, not me," I said.

"Yes, but you got George George into position so I could take that shot. Without you, I might have died of old age on the rooftop."

"George George is dead, right?"

"Unless he is a zombie he cannot come back this time."

George George was dead and the family was safe. Thanking God was out of the question since Baby Dimitri was the triggerman and God and I were on the outs anyway.

"How do you feel?"

"Like several hours of my life just vanished. There's a big black hole."

"Check the YouTube," he said. "If you go there you will be able to fill in that hole."

That was it. I was going to straight-up murder Takis and toss his corpse into fast-moving traffic.

Something was bothering me—something other than everything. "Why did you come to Grandma, really? So you could be the one to shoot him?"

"You do not know, Katerina? I came to watch out for my son. If George George killed me ... eh ... so what? I have lived a long life, known a lot of women, had more good times than a thousand men. But a son? George George took him once. I would not let him take Xander a second time."

I pictured Xander. Tall. Chiseled. Bronzed. Strong enough to bench-press a bear. Maybe even two cuddling bears. I couldn't reconcile the man who made me hot chocolate and tied my ponytails with this slight and slippery gangster in his sharply pressed pants and white shoes.

"So Xander is really your son? He wasn't adopted, was he?"

The Godfather of Shoes and Sniper Shots crossed himself forehead to chest, shoulder to shoulder. "He looks like his mother. I lost my Vasoula when she died in childbirth."

So Xander never knew his mother at all. There was something in my eye. Dust. Allergies. My finger.

"I'm sorry."

"It was not her childbirth. It was later, after our son was taken. She was in Piraeus helping her sister deliver her baby. When her sister had a contraction, she kicked Vasoula in the head and knocked her into the fireplace."

We exchanged platitudes after that. I was sorry, he was

sorry, we were all sorry. He offered me free shoes for life …
provided I didn't live past the ripe old age of thirty. After
he left, Dad came in to check on me what seemed like
every minute, on the minute. Aunt Rita arrived in a cloud
of perfume and a harmonious melody of colors, carrying
flowers and chocolates. Grandma had hidden the whole
family and the compound's furry menagerie underground
in the armory beneath the farm, my aunt told me. George
George wouldn't have been able to blast his way in with a
nuclear arsenal at his disposal. Grandma did preparation
like normal people did breathing.

Donk showed up holding his cap in front of him and,
for once, not looking like he wanted to pinch my butt.
Kyria Mela had fed him and offered him a permanent bed
if he wanted one. Apparently Elias had swooped in with a
better offer, one that Donk didn't want to talk about yet.

Melas arrived with the rest of his law enforcement
posse. They collected George George and his garish wig
and hauled him off to the city morgue. Thanks to
Grandma, George George didn't have any family to bury
him, so she told Gus to burn him and put the ashes in a
coffee container. Gus seemed okay with that idea.

Law enforcement left.

Melas stayed behind.

He leaned against the doorframe, hands in his jeans
pockets and watched me with dark, serious eyes.

"What now?" he asked me.

"I never eat Grandma's *koulourakia* in the dark again,
that's what."

"Not what I meant."

I knew what he meant. I would deal with Melas, but
not today. Today I wanted to close my eyes and sleep for a
week or until I needed to pee.

"Can I take a rain check on talking about it?"

"Yes, but I do want to talk about it."

"Soon," I said.

Now that I was no longer hunting for George George or being hunted by him, my adrenal gland, determining that there was no threat on the immediate horizon, rolled over and went to sleep.

My hormones could be real dumbasses, but this wasn't one of those times.

I closed my eyes. I slept some more.

———

I eyed the feast on Grandma's kitchen table with suspicion.

"How much of this stuff is spiked with wacky weed or whatever you put in those *koulourakia*?"

"Sit down and eat before I give you the *koutala*."

Grandma had a big wooden spoon and she knew how to use it, inside the kitchen and out.

I didn't need to be told twice. I slid into my usual chair, drooling as I watched Grandma fix me a plate of goodies. *Tiropitas* (cheese pies), *spanakopita* (spinach and feta pie), meatballs, and a thick chunk of crusty bread with a pillowy soft interior. For dessert there was orange cake, *ekemek kataifi* (baklava's hirsute cousin, smothered with cream), and a spiced walnut cake.

"Grandma, are you overcompensating?"

Her eyebrows rose into sharp hooks. "For what? I am perfect and so are my decisions." The edges of her lips turned up. A shadow meandered past her eyes, then vanished.

"What was in those *koulourakia*?"

"Could be it was acid."

Holy cow. I shook my head.

"Why did you ask Gus to burn George George and put him in a coffee tin?"

"How else can you be certain someone is dead?"

"Cutting off their heads works if they're vampires, I think." All that time spent watching *Buffy the Vampire Slayer* and *Angel* hadn't been a total waste. See, I had learned stuff.

Grandma snorted. "Some people would say George George was a vampire of sorts, preying on the innocent. I knew George George and his family were trafficking children, but until that night I did not have permission to go in there and make arrests. It was luck that Dimitri came to me when he did, otherwise my help would have been more limited."

"You mean you wouldn't have been able to get his son back?" I couldn't do it yet, couldn't say Xander's name in conjunction with Baby Dimitri's. The two men sharing blood was 'peanut butter and sauerkraut' weird.

"We might have prevailed and removed the boy safely, but there would have been legal repercussions. Because the mission was government sanctioned, I was able to make it go away when things went wrong. Nobody was supposed to be killed, but in the end everyone perished, except the boy. The raid became a legend instead of a court case, and I believed George George was dead so there was nobody to complain. People do not cry over dead child traffickers. They celebrate."

"You didn't check that he was really dead?"

"I was holding a crying baby in my arms, one with a wet *kolos* and an empty belly. He had been through enough and I wanted to get him out of there before he saw more blood. In hindsight, I should have checked that George George was dead, but that man had more holes in him than one of my colanders. How he survived that I did not know until tonight. The problem with intelligence is that things slip through even the tightest cracks."

I chewed on my lip. I had questions and only enough time to ask a few before the food coma struck. "Does Xander know?"

"Who his real father is? Yes. I have never lied to Xander. He was a good boy and now he is a good man. He deserved the truth."

Something metaphorical slammed me from the side. "Xander. Where is he?"

"That I cannot say," Grandma said. "George George did not kill him, I am certain of that."

"How can you be?"

"George George was evil but he was the chicken's *skata*. He hired men to do his killing. Even in the old days he could not pull a trigger himself. He did not have the stomach for crime."

"He sold children."

"Yes, but once they were out of his hands he forgot about them. He never had to get his hands bloody."

"Maybe he had his hired goons hurt Xander."

"He would have bragged about it if that was true."

Grandma seemed certain. Not me. I trusted Grandma, but I trusted my gut more, and my gut said that Xander was in a terrible, no-good place. My gut and I convened while Grandma bustled around the kitchen, prepping for another one of her baking adventures. She wasn't done spoiling me with food. I, for one, welcomed my gut-stuffing overlord.

"We should get out there and find him," I said.

"Leave it to me. I will find Xander, when he wants to be found."

Xander's absence felt unnatural. Since I'd arrived in Greece he had been an almost constant presence.

In my pocket was that small key, the one we'd found in George George's otherwise empty grave. In the trunk of my car, his cassettes. A burning need came over me, not unlike the desperate desire to pee after a Venti latte from Starbucks. A need for catharsis.

"Where did George George live?" I asked Grandma.

"What does it matter? He is gone now."

"I'm just curious, that's all."

She stared me down, eyes black, shiny, crow-like. Then she did something that surprised me. She grabbed her phone. "I am sending the address to you now."

I grabbed my bag, jammed my sunglasses on my head, then grabbed some sweets for the road.

"Marika will eat those before you reach the end of the driveway," Grandma said. She handed me a plastic container crammed with goodies.

———

Marika dug into the cakes. "Where are we going?"

The Ferrari was nice—very nice—but it wasn't the Beetle. The top was a permanent fixture, and while I was getting the hang of changing gears and working the pedals, I missed the convenience of an automatic transmission.

"George George's house."

"That big place on the edge of Agria?"

I looked at her, surprised. "You know it?"

She licked cream off the spoon Grandma had thoughtfully provided. "Of course. Nobody lives there now because of all the ghosts."

"It's haunted?"

"Who can say? Wait, is that really where we are going? I thought you were joking."

"You can wait in the car if you like."

"Good idea. I will protect the cakes from ghosts."

Except there wasn't any cake left by the time I pulled up outside George George's old house, and there wasn't any house left either. Well, not much anyway. Its bones were wrestling with fire and losing. Long tongues of fire licked the sky. Smoke rose in thick, eye-watering clouds.

"That cannot be good," Marika said. She was looking at the empty container in her hand.

I got out, crouched down on the cracked concrete sidewalk, and picked up the still smoking remains of a do-it-yourself cigarette.

Laki had been here.

Now I had a trunk full of 1980s cassettes and nowhere to perform a ritual burning. Tossing them into the already-burning flames felt less cathartic and more opportunistic.

My phone rang.

"I want those tapes," the caller said in English. Accented. Not Greek. More like Russian. The mysterious probably-not-KGB man who had ordered Dina and Donk to tail me, perhaps.

"Who is this?"

"Call me a fan of 80s pop music."

Wow, his parents must have really hated him to saddle him with a moniker like that. He definitely wasn't German. They had laws protecting children from whimsical, weird parents.

"Okay, A Fan of 80s Pop Music, you can have them. You know where to find me. God only knows you've had enough people following me." I waved to Dina who was parked nearby, pretending to look at the sky. Hera was absent from this party. Maybe the NIS had reinstated her.

I ended the call.

"Let's go," I said to Marika, who was licking the plastic container.

"Where now?"

Good question. I felt lost, in need of guidance or maybe just someone to talk to. So I did what your average Greek did when they wanted to talk to someone without anyone talking back.

I dropped Marika off at the compound.

I went to church.

Ayia Ekaterini was empty. Makria's small church employed Father Harry, a large man who was made from equal parts of warm heart and bear hugs, but Father Harry wasn't here today. Currently he was in the village square, sipping Greek coffee and talking up a storm with a couple of the local widows. Like most Greek churches, *Ayia Ekaterini* had saved a few bucks by skimping on seating. But it had a couple of pews up front for the elderly, the infirm, and for other people who didn't believe in praying on their feet.

I sat in the front pew, dead center.

"This is Katerina Makris," I said. "The younger one, not my grandmother."

Jesus didn't say anything. His eyes were cast upward. "You again," he seemed to be saying with that eye-rolling thing he had going on.

"I know this is a long shot, but Xander is missing. Maybe he's hurt, maybe not. I really hope he isn't. I need to find him because I get the feeling if I was the one missing he would tear the world apart to find me. And I have a boxful of 1980s cassettes in my backseat and a mysterious Russian man wants them." I looked at the small key that unlocked the box of cassettes. "Did I mention this Russian guy might be KGB? That's what he told Dina and Donk, anyway. Could be true. My life is like that lately."

The door separating the church from the back room flew open.

I groaned. "What are you doing here?"

Hera shrugged her slender shoulders. Between last night and today she'd found time to pour herself into skinny jeans and skimpy top, neither of which looked comfortable or practical. Her ears and neck were dripping with gold and sparkly stones that had to be diamonds. "Hanging out with God and waiting on a miracle."

"Melas isn't coming back to you, no matter how long and hard you pray."

"I don't care about Nikos." She flipped her hair. "Okay, I do. But I care more about my career."

"What career?"

She snatched the key out of my hand. "Mine now." Then she bolted out of the church on her stupid kitten heels.

So much for that.

Oh well, A Fan of 80s Pop Music was her problem now. He could wrestle her for the tapes for all I cared.

I looked up at the ceiling, wondering where exactly the microphones were that hooked Grandma into the law enforcement hive mind.

"Hera took the key," I said. "Bummer."

The air shifted. A mountain sat down beside me, with deep blue eyes and fair hair shaved close to the skin. The effect was startling. He was wearing a blue Adidas tracksuit that amplified the color of his eyes to devastating levels.

I was immune, thanks to prolonged exposure to the Nikos Melas and Xanders of the world.

"Can I sit here?"

Wow. Some people really didn't understand the concept of personal space.

Could I inch sideways without seeming rude?

No. Probably not. Greeks were extra touchy about

etiquette and I didn't want to bring shame on House Makris.

"If you have to."

The mountain spoke again. "It sounds to me like you are having a bad day, yes?"

Russian accent. Familiar voice. Yikes. The Russian Alps was A Fan of 80s Pop Music—and here I was without the tapes I'd promised he could have. I wondered if he knew about eBay and all the cool deals they had on old music.

"Shouldn't you be crouching?"

His forehead creased. "What?"

"Russians in Adidas tracksuits always crouch. Why do they—you—do that anyway?"

"We only crouch when there is not a comfortable place to sit nearby. Here there is no comfortable seat but there is this hard wood, so I am sitting here."

Seemed perfectly reasonable to me. "Are you one responsible for Dina and Donk following me?"

"The crazy garden gnome with the fake hair and the sad rapper child? Yes."

He definitely knew them. "Why?"

"I wanted to observe you, to see what you are like as a person."

"Wow, your life must be even more boring than mine."

He tipped back his head and laughed. His whole body shook. It was a lot of body and the pew moved with it. "If you think your life is boring then I would be terrified to see what you consider exciting."

"Netflix and chips," I said.

He smiled. "Netflix and chips. I will remember that."

My eyebrows rose. "Why?"

The smile sprawled out. "I think I would like to take you on a date."

Boy was I confused. "A date?"

"Your grandmother said you were single, and she would like very much for you not to be single. So she called me." He offered me his hand. "Viktor Sokolov."

I took his hand. It was big and warm, like a bear's paw but without the claw issue. "Katerina Makris. With an S."

"What do you think, Katerina, shall we go on our date?"

"Now?"

"How does the saying go … there is no time like right now?"

I looked down at my clothes—my black, mourning clothes—that reeked of smoke. "My family is in mourning. I can't date right now."

"Okay." He chewed on that a moment. "Okay. No problem. Customs I understand. Russians are also Orthodox and we have many, many customs. God is always watching and He carries one of these." A big gun came out of nowhere to rest on his lap. "Oh. My mistake. It is me who carries one of these."

"A gun? Really? Because I won't go on a date with you?"

"Because of the date? No. The gun is so I can get those cassettes."

"George George's cassettes? Haven't you heard of streaming music, MP3s, and CDs? The sound quality is vastly superior."

He put the gun away. "What can I say? I love 80s pop music and I love tapes, and I really want them very much."

I gnawed on my lip a moment, wondering if maybe those tapes weren't really tapes. He was awfully enthusiastic, even for a music fan. The church was wired out the wazoo, so I sure someone's cavalry would be arriving soon. Either the Family, or the police, or someone with a badge that gave them the license to wave a gun around. Stalling seemed like a good idea.

"I don't have them."

"Okay." He shrugged. "Who has them?"

"Well, technically they might be in my car."

"So you do have them?"

"Hera took the key to the box they're stored in. She's probably out there right now, trying to pick my car's lock."

He stood, grabbed my hand and pulled me up alongside him. "Then what are we waiting for?"

Wow, I was really bad at stalling.

My phone rang halfway to Makria's parking lot. Grandma was on the other end, pretending to be a nice old lady who just happened to be casually interested in my dating life like a regular grandmother.

"You have met Viktor?"

"We talked about this," I hissed at her.

"We did? I am old," she said. "Sometimes my memory is not what it used to be."

"As soon as I get back, I'm going to talk and you are going to listen."

"What was that? I cannot hear you. My hearing is not what it used to be either."

She hung up on me.

Viktor glanced down at me. It was a long way down. "I told you your grandmother approves." His head swiveled. We were at the parking lot at the entrance to Makria. Leaning against my car, casual as all get-out, was Hera. She was discretely working the lock.

I whistled. "Wrong door. It's in the trunk."

"Thanks for the tip." Using the butt of a gun, she smashed the driver's side window, reached in and popped the hood.

"Perfect," Viktor said, smiling.

Hera winked at him. "Always."

"Not you," he said. Out came his gun again. He pointed it right at her. "But it is good the way you did the dirty work for me. Give me the tapes."

"Let me think." Hera touched a red-tipped finger to her lips. "No."

Viktor looked down at me. "Okay."

He shrugged. And then he shot her.

Thank you for reading *Good Crime,* the seventh of Kat Makris' adventures!

Want to be notified when my next book is released? Sign up for my mailing list: http://eepurl.com/ZSeuL. Or like my Facebook page at: https://www.facebook.com/alexkingbooks.

All reviews are appreciated. You may help another reader fall in love ... or avoid a terrible mistake.

All my best,
Alex A. King

Also by Alex A. King

Disorganized Crime (Kat Makris #1)

Trueish Crime (Kat Makris #2)

Doing Crime (Kat Makris #3)

In Crime (Kat Makris #4)

Outta Crime (Kat Makris #5)

Night Crime (Kat Makris #6)

Seven Days of Friday (Women of Greece #1)

One and Only Sunday (Women of Greece #2)

Freedom the Impossible (Women of Greece #3)

Light is the Shadow (Women of Greece #4)

No Peace in Crazy (Women of Greece #5)

Summer of the Red Hotel (Women of Greece #6)

Family Ghouls (Greek Ghouls #1)

Royal Ghouls (Greek Ghouls #2)

Pride and All This Prejudice

46364874R00161

Made in the USA
Middletown, DE
27 May 2019